# Derrick was surprised by the raw, unpleasant nip of jealousy.

He quickly acknowledged the overreaction for what it was. It was the private joke that bothered him. He'd been the one to enjoy this type of closeness with Anne once. But now this guy, this complete stranger, Todd, knew her better than Derrick did.

He'd missed her with a pain so sharp he'd feared his heart would never fully heal. Eventually, though, he'd come to terms with his mistake, gotten over her. As crushing as it had been, the email had been helpful in that way. But also difficult to shake. Of course, he'd read it so many times he could recite it nearly verbatim.

To this day, every word was hotly, excruciatingly branded into his brain. "Baseball is who you are. It's all you'll ever be. You're not capable of being more..." He hated how right she'd been, how prophetic the message was turning out to be— an unexpected surge of resentment flooded through him. But no, he was here to get Anne in his corner, not to get lost in the past.

Dear Reader,

I don't know about you, but I can't imagine anything worse for a professional athlete than an injury cutting short their career. Except for maybe a scandal that threatens their family. Newly retired baseball player Derrick Bright is dealing with both. There's nothing he can do about his damaged leg, but his family is all he has left, and he'll do anything to protect them. Even hire his heartbreaking public relations specialist of an ex-girlfriend to help. Working with Anne McGrath is a sacrifice he's willing to make because he knows she's the best person for the job.

Anne disagrees. Vehemently. In fact, she outright refuses Derrick's impassioned plea to save his "innocent" family. (Isn't that what they all say?) But truly, she has good reason to decline.

When Derrick tricks Anne into taking the job, they are finally forced to sort it all out. Facing their feelings turns out to be more complicated, chaotic and fun than either of them imagines. I hope you enjoy Anne and Derrick's story.

Thanks for reading!

*Carol*

# HEARTWARMING

## *His Hometown Yuletide Vow*

—

*Carol Ross*

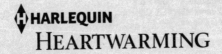

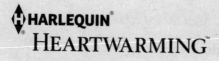

## HARLEQUIN®
# HEARTWARMING™

ISBN-13: 978-1-335-42651-2

His Hometown Yuletide Vow

Please recycle. This product is recyclable.

Recycling programs
for this product may
not exist in your area.

This edition published by arrangement with Harlequin Books S.A.

For questions and comments about the quality of this book,
please contact us at CustomerService@Harlequin.com.

Harlequin Enterprises ULC
22 Adelaide St. West, 40th Floor
Toronto, Ontario M5H 4E3, Canada
www.Harlequin.com

Printed in U.S.A.

**Carol Ross** lives in the Pacific Northwest with her husband and two dogs. She is a graduate of Washington State University. When not writing, or thinking about writing, she enjoys reading, running, hiking, skiing, traveling and making plans for the next adventure to subject her sometimes reluctant but always fun-loving family to. Carol can be contacted at carolrossauthor.com and via Facebook at Facebook.com/carolrossauthor, Twitter, @_carolross, and Instagram, @carolross__.

For Krysty.

My dearest friend, longtime partner in mischief
and all-around favorite human—your loyalty,
love and support are obviously boundless.

PS: I love how we've proved that friendships
can last forever and lunch dates
can *always* be kept.

# CHAPTER ONE

"HERE WE GO," Anne McGrath said before looking down and reciting the tweet in question. "'Just one kernel of my popcorn is smarter than @ginnybell58. Does the scammer truly believe she can scam #DerryPop with the old there's-a-mouse-in-my-food routine? Better get a new scam. She won't be getting any money—or popcorn—anytime soon! #liar #ginnytheninny #nopopcornforyou.'"

Jack Derry, known in the Twitter-sphere as @JackDerryPop, was the owner and CEO of Derry Pop Popcorn, one of McGrath PR's biggest, and arguably most important, clients. He chuckled as his own words were read back to him.

Anne placed her phone on the conference table between them. "Jack, you called her a scammer, a ninny and a liar—all in one tweet."

"Don't forget grifter," he retorted, clearly pleased with his cleverness. "#ginnytheninny was trending there for a bit, which is interesting because I thought #nopopcornforyou would be the one people would—"

"Jack," Anne said firmly. "I think you're purposely missing the point."

"That's because I don't like the point you're making."

She tried not to smile, which wasn't an easy feat because she adored Jack. Not only was he her longest-standing client at McGrath PR, but he was also a good friend. Twelve years ago, when she was a newbie working her first job at Mitchell West Publicity, he'd taken a chance on her when they'd hit it off at a party hosted by her former boss.

Four years after that, when she'd ventured out on her own, he'd come with her. His loyalty had been vital in keeping her head above water as she built her business. Jack sang her praises to anyone who'd listen. As a result, he'd brought her an untold amount of clients in the ensuing years and earned her lifelong devotion.

"We've talked about this, and I thought

we agreed these types of personal criticisms were not going to be a part of your platform."

Folding his arms across his chest, he leaned back in his chair and countered, "Well, she is a liar and a grifter, so would those really be considered *insults*?"

"Let's not get into semantics here. The point is, did you have to tweet about this to your eight-point-three-million followers? She claims she's now being harassed by your fans. She says she's gone into hiding."

"Must not have a very good hiding spot then, if she's still being harassed."

Anne barely managed to stifle a laugh. The man had a point. That was the thing about Jack; nearly all his points were good.

"Anne, come on now! Should I just let people believe this woman opened a bag of my popcorn and found a dead mouse inside? Thirty-two years I've been popping, packaging and selling popcorn without a single legitimate foreign-product complaint. At great expense and against all advice—my late wife, Yvette, being the single exception—I went above and beyond with my safety measures to prevent it from *ever* happening. It's not fair for someone like her to try and harm my reputation with this type of false claim. And the nitwit should know it's impossible with my system. Not to mention this trick has been tried before—a few hundred thousand times."

"She" was Ginny Bellweather, a consumer who'd concocted the mouse-in-my-popcorn claim to try to get money or free popcorn out of Jack's company. But she'd chosen the wrong guy to hustle. Jack was the type of person who would spend every penny he had to right an injustice rather than settle a fraudulent claim. And he had plenty of pennies.

Enough to hire a private investigator, who'd discovered seven similar claims in several states by Ginny spanning the last four years. She was being investigated for insurance fraud in Nevada. Come to think of it, Anne was suddenly grateful he hadn't tweeted about her criminal leanings.

"I agree. She should have done her research before trying this particular angle. Mice, cockroaches, hairballs, severed fingers—very unoriginal. But one tweet from you about this topic was enough. The one we composed denying the accusation, along with providing the link to the excellent article you wrote explaining why it's impossible for a mouse, or any other foreign object, to be packaged inside your popcorn. The proof speaks loud and clear."

Jack frowned. "What if sales take a hit?"

"Have they?"

"Well, no… But she said she's going to sue me to kingdom come. A lawsuit is always bad for business."

"A matter for your legal team, which, you and I both know would, if it comes to that, dispense with the case very quickly and efficiently."

"We would countersue."

"Yet another reason why you should not be tweeting about it."

"Years ago, when I first got on Twitter, you told me to be myself. To tweet the funny things that I think. No matter how random, and not to worry about selling popcorn or even talking about popcorn, remember?"

"Of course, I remember. That's essentially what I'm trying to remind you of right now. I'd like you to stick to your positive vibe."

Jack sighed. "That's hard to do when I'm being falsely accused."

"I know. This woman's scheming is just

that. Calling people insulting names, though, redirects the narrative back at you. It makes *you* look mean. And you are not mean, Jack. Don't give her anything to use against you. You bring a lot of joy to a whole lot of people."

Five years ago, when Anne suggested to Jack that he join Twitter, she knew people would think he was funny. But she could never have predicted the degree of celebrity he'd achieve. People adored him. He had a knack for pointing out the absurd in a funny but harmless way. He'd been compared to a modern-day Will Rogers. Mostly he tweeted his witty and interesting observations about life in quirky Portland, current events and his beloved baseball team, the Northwest Pacific Panthers.

It was their shared devotion to NPU baseball that had first drawn them together. During the party where they'd met, Jack had found her alone in her boss's den watching a Panthers game. Both alumni of NPU, they'd bonded over their mutual love for their alma mater, especially its baseball team.

That she'd been dating Derrick Bright, the university's superstar catcher at the time, hadn't hurt. All these years later, she and Jack were both season-ticket holders and active in the NPU athletics fundraising organization, the Panther Project.

A few years ago, she'd suggested printing his funny observations on his popcorn bags. He'd agreed. Sales had skyrocketed. He'd credited her ingenuity, which had further cemented their friendship.

"This company is my life."

"I know," she answered quietly. "I get that." And she knew he believed her because it was no secret that McGrath PR was her life, too.

"Fine." Jack finally nodded. "I trust you, Annie. I'll lay off. You haven't steered me wrong yet."

"Thank you. You won't be sorry."

"Now, let's talk about this Panther scandal. Haven't tweeted a word about that yet. Can't find the humor or the truth." Jack shook his head. "Poor Coach. Imagine beginning your career with this rotten pile of stink on your plate." The Panthers had a new head coach, Kellan Nichols. Anne hadn't met him, but he and Jack were evidently tight. "Hopefully—"

"What scandal?" Anne interrupted.

"Ah, man," Jack said, wincing slightly.

"You haven't heard from Coach Nichols yet? I gave him your number. He's going to need help with this. It's shaping up to be quite a mess."

"Jack, you know McGrath PR doesn't represent anyone or anything to do with sports," Anne said. But she couldn't resist asking… "What happened?"

"But, Annie, these are our Panthers we're talking about here. Easton Bright is headed for the draft after next season. At least, I'm hoping he is. It's going to break my heart if he's guilty and—"

The name had her tensing with concern. "Easton Bright?"

Easton was her ex-boyfriend Derrick's younger brother, a sophomore second baseman and switch-hitter at NPU who'd just finished a truly astounding season. A few years ago, it was rumored that he was headed down the same rebellious path Derrick had once traveled. But as far as Anne knew, Easton had cleaned up his act. Although she'd believed the best about Derrick once, too, hadn't she? Look how that had turned out for her.

A knock sounded. Keira Chkalov, her best friend and colleague, opened the door and

stuck her head inside. "Anne, you have—"
She cut off her sentence with a bright smile
toward their client. "Oh, hey, Jack!" All of
the staff at McGrath PR loved Jack, too—all
four of them. "Sorry to interrupt. I thought
you were finished."

"We mostly are. Talking baseball now.
What's up?"

"There was an *urgent* call for you. This
person would like you to call back ASAP."

Keira handed her a folded slip of paper.
Anne opened it, saw the name and braced
herself as a combination of curiosity and
apprehension spilled over her. Silently, she
read the entire message: *Kellan Nichols, head
baseball coach, Northwest Pacific University. Please call ASAP.*

DERRICK BRIGHT STEPPED away from the
dining-room wall to survey his handiwork.
Only to immediately realize that it was impossible to appreciate the full effect of a
knickknack shelf when it was bare. Like a
bat without a ball or a stadium with no fans.
Okay, maybe that was a bit dramatic, but it
was important he get this right.

Moving about the room, he gathered his

measuring tape, screwdriver, coffee cup and three candles from the center of the dining table. From the sideboard, he borrowed Grandma's prized geode, which she'd found on one of her rock-hunting excursions, a box of tissues and a crystal dish full of candy. After arranging everything neatly, he backed away again and reevaluated his achievement.

Grandma's friends, "the gamers," would be so impressed when they showed up next week to find her entire pottery collection displayed on a series of handcrafted shelves.

"That's what I'm talking about," he said aloud, even though he was alone in the room.

Spotting his hammer lying on the floor, he reached down and picked it up, then tucked it into place in his new tool belt. His entire life, he'd wanted a tool belt like Grandpa's, and the one now fitted around his hips was as close as he could find. Made from thick, soft leather, it hadn't been cheap, but he'd justified the expense the way he once would have a new pair of cleats or even a mitt. Like an investment in his future.

That was the good thing about retiring young. At thirty-two, he reminded himself every time he started missing baseball that he still had plenty of time left to pursue other hobbies and interests. Like woodworking and…other stuff he was sure he would enjoy once he tried it. So far, he'd been unsuccessful, but he'd get there. He'd find his groove—his other passion that wasn't baseball.

He could even have another career, something he didn't want to think about just yet, even as he couldn't seem to stop thinking about it. Because what did a person do when they'd dedicated their entire life, their body, mind and soul, to one single activity and then suddenly, *bam*, it was gone? After a routine play at home plate, his career had ended. Injuries were always at the back of a ballplayer's mind, and, like most players, he'd suffered his share. But still, he'd always operated under the belief that retirement would come when *he* decided. After he'd had plenty of time to plan his postbaseball life. At least, that had been his strategy once.

He couldn't shake the feeling that his ex-girlfriend Anne had been right all those years ago; maybe he wasn't "capable of being more than a baseball player." Those words, and similar ones repeatedly echoed by his father, kept coming back to him, causing a now familiar and increasingly smothering tightness to knot in his chest.

His nineteen-year-old brother, Easton, sauntered in from the kitchen, steaming mug in hand. Perfect timing, because just his presence reminded Derrick of the other good stuff about retirement. Easton and Grandma May, his family. They were everything to him, and the fact that he would be here to witness Easton's final season at NPU, to help guide him through the decisions he'd have to make as he prepared to go pro, was the best part.

That, and he could now be a consistent presence for Grandma, who, despite an energy level that frequently outpaced his own, wasn't getting any younger. Critical since Easton would be leaving after next season. Finally, he could live full-time in this big old farmhouse he'd bought for them all to share, but where he'd only ever lived temporarily. Giving him time to work on his DIY home-improvement list, hone his carpentry skills and…*not* play baseball.

No more baseball. Ever again.

"Hey! Good morning," Easton cheerfully greeted him. His little brother's grin had al-

ways been contagious, and Derrick smiled
through the chest jabs and took a few seconds to be grateful for the way Easton had
gotten himself back on track.

"You're sure at it early today. Do you
want—?" Stopping midsentence, Easton
glanced at the wall before eyeing Derrick
up and down. "You need a tool belt to hang
a shelf?"

*"Shelves,"* Derrick corrected, pointing
at the stack still to be hung. "I made all of
those."

"Wow. So this is what you've been working on out there?"

"Yep." Derrick had spent the last few days
in the shop sawing, sanding, finishing...*con-
structing* this shelving project. It felt great to
be using Grandpa's tools again, something
he hadn't done since he was a kid. Grandpa
Marty had died when Derrick was twenty-
one, right after he'd been drafted into the
major leagues. But the time they'd spent together had created many of his favorite child-
hood memories. Woodworking alone, he'd
already discovered, was a little different than
puttering around with Grandpa. Derrick definitely had a few things to learn.

"Huh." Easton pursed his lips and tipped his head thoughtfully. "I put together the entire media stand in the family room in like an hour with one little Allen wrench."

"Yeah, well, these didn't come in a package that said 'some assembly required.' Real craftsmanship requires time, patience, skill and a variety of tools."

"I see..." Easton drawled, slowly bobbing his head. "Well, you've got that last one covered for sure. I'm surprised you can walk around with all those gadgets weighing you down," he joked, gesturing at Derrick's tool belt. "I hope you have a supply of water in that thing, too, because if you go down with that bum leg of yours, you're going to be there for a while. You know Grandma's friend Cass? She has this necklace she wears with a button she can press in case of a fall. We could get you one of those to stuff in there, too."

"You're hilarious," Derrick said flatly.

"I know," Easton said, and chuckled. "Seriously, though, it's looking awesome." He angled his chin at the shelf. "Grandma is going to love it."

"Thanks. Have you seen Grandma this morning?"

"Yep, the general is already out in the garden on slug patrol."

"Of course, she is," Derrick said.

Accomplished, strong, resilient and generous, Grandma May had always been the stable force in both his and Easton's lives. From volunteering with the homeless to fostering kittens, she'd do just about anything to help a creature in need. Except for a slug. When that particular enemy invaded her turf, there was no call for mercy.

"We're pickling some veggies later. You want to get in on that?"

Five years ago, after their dad died and Mom relocated to Maryland, Grandma had taken in a young and troubled teenage Easton with open arms. That's when Derrick had purchased the five-bedroom house and farm just outside the city. At the time, there'd been no "farm" left to speak of, just an overgrown field, a plot of weeds, a tangled raspberry patch and the remnants of an ancient chicken coop.

But the house was roomy and charming with an abundance of irresistibly beautiful

details, like thick wood trim, arched door-
ways and leaded glass windows. And while
it had needed some sprucing up, the structure was sound, and the setting both pretty
and private.

Best of all, Grandma May had fallen in
love with it on the spot. That was enough for
Derrick. And he'd agreed with Grandma that
the work fixing up the place would help keep
Easton busy and distract him from the trouble he'd been finding at the time. Grandma
would teach him some "life skills," and the
distance from the city might help, too.

The strategy had worked. With Derrick
happily financing the improvements, Easton
had helped Grandma transform the property
into this sanctuary. In the process, his little
brother had discovered an unexpected passion for farming and "country life."

Derrick hadn't pushed Easton to play at
NPU, but he'd been secretly thrilled when
he'd chosen the local university that was also
his alma mater. Easton had then opted to live
at home on the farm with Grandma. And an
added bonus had recently occurred with the
hiring of Kellan Nichols as the Panthers's

new head coach. Kellan was a close friend and former teammate of Derrick's.

He asked Easton, "Aren't you working out this morning?"

Easton had racked up a truly phenomenal season, but he needed to keep it up. The next one would be critical to determining the rest of his future. Major-league rules allowed college players at four-year schools to be drafted at the completion of their junior year. His stellar performance this season was a double-edged sword. High expectations meant all eyes would be on him for the one to follow.

"Not until later. I went for a run this morning. I'm going to fry a few eggs—you want some? The girls are laying like crazy."

"The girls" being Easton's chickens, nine hens that he doted on.

"Sure, sounds good. How was your date last night?"

Easton had recently started seeing a fellow athlete named Hailey, a talented long-distance runner on the track team. The relationship was new, and Derrick had only met her a couple of times. He silently hoped it wasn't serious, as he knew all too well how difficult it would be for Easton to say goodbye when he signed with a pro team. An experience that had marked the beginning of the end of his relationship with the only woman he'd ever loved.

Easton raked a hand across his jaw but not before Derrick noted the grimace. "Not great. We had an argument."

"I thought you were home kind of early." He'd been surprised to hear Easton come in well before midnight. "What happened?"

Inhaling and then filling his cheeks with air, Easton seemed to consider the question before slowly blowing out the breath. "Long story."

"You can tell me while you help me with the rest of these. I want them up before Grandma hosts the gamers next week."

Grandma had had the same tight-knit group of friends for as long as Derrick could remember. Years ago, they'd started playing board games once a week to "stay sharp." Somewhere along the line, they'd flippantly begun calling themselves "the gamers." The moniker had stuck even as their game playing had evolved to include other activities, such as hiking, canoeing and yoga.

"So… Has Grandma talked to you about that yet?"

"About what?"

"About their most recent, uh, *games*?"

"She told me they've been branching out. I know they're playing something called 'bury the hatchet' next week, which I've never heard of, but she's been wanting some shelves in here for a long time, so I thought I'd surprise her and get them ready before game day. Sharpen my skills at the same time."

"Great idea, although I doubt they'll be playing *that* here in the dining room."

"Well, I'm sure she'll want to show them off, anyway." Derrick lifted another shelf. "Can you hold this for me?"

"Sure." Easton set his coffee on the table and took up one end of the shelf. "Speaking of the gamers, you remember that cardiac episode Grace had last year?"

"Yep." Grandma and Grace had been best friends since elementary school. "But it wasn't serious, right? Grandma said it was just a scare."

"That's right, but—"

"See that mark there?" Derrick asked, pointing to a pencil line on the wall where he wanted Easton to hold the shelf. "You know how I've been trying to decide what to do now that my baseball career is over? I'm thinking I could hire myself out as a handyman."

He was only half-joking. He liked the idea of building things, working with his hands. Maybe he could be a contractor, or craft custom furniture. "Flipping houses" was popular these days, too. He could totally do that. He watched all the shows about it. Home-improvement TV was his not-so-secret indulgence, and the renovation programs were his favorites.

Power drill in hand, he carefully positioned the screw. "Grandma told me I should use shorter screws, but…" Engaging the trigger, he added, "That pottery is heavy, and I—"

*Pop!*

Easton let out a yelp. Derrick flinched, yanking the drill upward. The lights went out. The loaded shelf came down. Glass broke, candy scattered and the geode hit the floor with a heavy thud.

"Holy cats!" Grandma called from the kitchen. Seconds later, she appeared in the doorway wearing her gardening uniform;

rubber clogs, cargo pants and a faded NPU Panthers hoodie that hung almost to her knees. A pink bucket hat was pulled low over her gray curls. "You boys, okay?" she asked, her hands dripping soapy water.

"Did we have an earthquake?" Derrick asked a bit breathlessly, adrenaline shooting through his bloodstream.

"We're fine, Grandma," Easton said, his voice thick with laughter. "And, no, Mr. Handyman, not an earthquake. You might want to put that latest career dream on hold for now. Pretty sure your screw hit a wire and blew a fuse. You knocked the shelf off when you jerked the drill up."

Grandma's expression softened as she took in the scene. "I'm guessing you went ahead and opted for the longer screws?" Nodding, she answered her own question and then observed in a dry tone, "Inherited your grandfather's carpentry skills along with his power tools."

Easton cracked up. Grandma joined in. Derrick chuckled, too, telling himself he had to expect a few setbacks on the path to artisan craftsmanship. They were always running into trouble on those TV shows.

On the table, his phone vibrated with a text. He ignored it to clean up the mess. Another followed. He ignored that one, too, placing the geode on the table. A side benefit of retirement was the luxury of neglecting his phone. It was probably his agent, Trace, texting to remind him about the fundraising benefit he was supposed to attend that evening. He kept insisting Derrick needed to "announce his reentrance into the community." How was he supposed to do that when he had no answers to the inevitable questions? Ones like "What does your future hold without baseball?" and "What are you going to do with yourself now that you're retired?"

Grandma's leg let out a chirp. *She* didn't disregard her phone, though, and instead dug it out of the large side pocket of her pants. As she studied the screen, her features tightened into a worried expression that Derrick recognized all too well. In his wayward youth, he'd brought it on himself more times than he liked to recall.

"Grandma?" Easton asked. "What is it? Is everything okay?"

Easton's phone went off next.

And then Derrick's phone lit up again, too,

this time resounding with the lively notes of "Take Me Out to the Ballgame," his friend Kellan's ring tone. The song, accompanied by Grandma's question and the now-constant chirping from Easton's phone, was officially too much to ignore.

Then Grandma looked up, her gold-brown eyes fraught with alarm as they landed on Easton. "Easton, honey, exactly where were you last night?"

# CHAPTER TWO

"I HAVE A surprise for you," Anne's boyfriend, Todd, told her later that evening, taking her by the hand and leisurely meandering through the dimly lit ballroom of the Sapphire Hotel. The historic structure was considered a true jewel in Portland's cityscape and a fashionable venue for events of all types. Tonight, the place was teeming with dedicated patrons of the Unified Justice Coalition, who'd gathered for their annual fundraiser.

Todd's law firm had cosponsored the dinner and auction, and Todd was chairman of the planning committee. Both the cause, which was dedicated to freeing the wrongly convicted, and the event were near to his heart.

"A surprise?" Anne repeated, forcing a smile. She was most definitely not in the mood for a surprise. But this evening was important to Todd. And to her, for that matter. She'd donated a PR-consultation package and was hoping for her own boost of publicity.

The telephone conversation with Coach Nichols had left her feeling restless and edgy. And yes, a little guilty, although exactly why that was, she didn't know for sure. She had a legitimate reason, reasons even, for turning down his request.

But, just as the coach predicted, NPU athletics were all over social media and the news. Two of the local stations had led with the story on their evening broadcasts.

Anne had watched one segment four times. The lead line was running on a loop in her mind: *A large cache of performance-enhancing drugs, including various illegal substances, was confiscated at the home of one of NPU's star baseball players.*

Not Easton Bright's home, but the home of his friend and teammate, Gavin Turner. Easton had attended the party, however, and the report went on to reveal that numerous student-athletes from other departments had been there, too. Police were currently uncertain about whom the drugs belonged to, or at least they weren't disclosing that information.

Anne didn't want to believe Easton was involved. Didn't believe it, she corrected herself. Innocent until proven guilty. She operated under that assumption. She'd seen way too many clients wrongly accused. Then again, she also knew better than to never say never. Plenty of clients were guilty, too, and/or outright liars. Sure, when she and Derrick had dated, Easton had been an energetic, precocious, adorable child of eight who was incapable of hurting a fly. But boys grew up, even cute ones.

Besides, Easton wasn't a client. Nor would he be.

She'd politely informed Coach Nichols that McGrath PR didn't represent athletes or athletics in any form. And yet, she couldn't help but wonder how much of the story was true? A report on the website of *The Portland Chronicle*, the city's largest newspaper, implied that the police would be questioning all the students who'd attended the party. Surely, Derrick would hire an attorney for Easton if it came to that.

Leading to another question she couldn't shake. Where *was* Derrick? He'd only recently retired from baseball, and Anne didn't know where he'd since settled. She didn't even know if his leg had fully healed from the break he'd suffered after the brutal home-plate collision, which had ultimately led to his retirement.

Todd squeezed her hand and slowed to a stop. She followed his lead, assuming they were approaching the mystery person. Instead, he turned, his expression warm as he focused on her.

"I think I forgot to tell you how beautiful you look tonight. That dress is stunning."

She glanced down at the dark blue lace-and-sequin dress she'd hurriedly pulled from the back of her closet less than an hour ago. A fresh wave of guilt swept through her, and this time she did know the cause. She'd exerted very little effort on her appearance. Running way late after work, and even later due to her ensuing scandal research, she'd gotten ready in exactly twelve minutes and then ordered a ride to save time.

It wasn't until after she'd climbed into the car that she'd remembered why the dress had been relegated to the closet's farthest reaches. The last time she'd worn it, she'd dribbled a blob of chocolate-fudge-brownie ice cream on the front. Her cashmere wrap only barely covered the spot, and she was grateful for the matte lighting from the old hotel's original chandeliers.

"Thank you. You're looking pretty dapper yourself." And he was. Blond hair freshly trimmed, shoes polished, boldly colored tie meticulously knotted, he looked confident and handsome and fit.

Todd avoided gyms, preferring endurance cardio instead. He biked to work most days and peppered in runs a few days a week. A run together on the weekend was one of their favorite ways to catch up after long hours spent at their demanding jobs. Toned and ultratrim, he often appeared too thin in his street clothes but always looked fantastic in his hand-tailored suits.

She reached out and gently tugged his lapel. "This one is my new favorite."

He flashed her an easy, appreciative smile, but his green-brown eyes glowed with intensity as they found hers. "Anne, I've been thinking..."

*Oh, no.* Concern caused her pulse to accelerate. Neither she nor her chocolate-stained dress was up for a conversation about deep emotions and complicated feelings.

Pretending to be distracted, she looked down and replied with a breezy "Hmm?" Then she reached out, brushed an invisible crumb from his lapel and lamely joked, "Saving this for later?"

Disappointment flitted across his face, obscuring the previous brightness. Ugh. She felt bad. But also relieved when the moment seemed to pass. Todd was the best.

A generous, kind, thoughtful man, he was an excellent and undemanding boyfriend. They might not have everything in common, but they always had a good time together, and she cared about him. She just didn't know how big her feelings were yet. Truth was, she didn't even know if she was capable of big feelings anymore.

She certainly wasn't ready for plans that included ring exchanges and talk of the future. Last week, they'd walked by one of those home-goods stores overrun with that currently trendy "farmhouse" decor. Stopping in front of the large window display featuring a simulated front porch complete with wooden rocking chairs and a plush dog, Todd had commented on how he dreamed of having "that" one day. She'd instantly broken out in a cold sweat. Not because it was Todd. Todd was great! But because she didn't want "that" with anyone. She'd lost herself in the rabbit hole of domestic Derrick-centered fantasy once, only to emerge humiliated and brokenhearted.

Reminding her again of Easton and the potential trouble swirling around him and the team. Todd deserved better. He deserved her full attention. She needed to get her head in the game, so to speak. Although, she acknowledged, baseball analogies probably would not help achieve her desired focus.

"Remember how I told you there would be some pretty remarkable celebrities here tonight?" Todd asked with his earlier good cheer.

"Uh, yeah," she said, unimpressed and now slightly depressed that her surprise might include one of them. She worked with way too many "celebrities" to care about their presence at any function she attended. No matter how special they believed themselves to be, or how special the public treated them, at the end of the day, they were just people. Some were good, some were bad. Todd knew her feelings on this topic. It was her job to *find* her own celebrity clients gigs like this one.

"Well, I've arranged for you to meet one."

"Todd—"

"I know," he interrupted sweetly. "I know what you're thinking." He was so adorably smug with confidence that she almost found herself intrigued. Another night, perhaps, when she wasn't wired with nerves about the evening's auction and unduly preoccupied with a potential scandal, which, she kept reminding herself, she wanted nothing to do with. But what if Easton had gotten caught up in something outside of his control?

Todd, she realized, was still talking, "…that there couldn't possibly be anyone here who you *want* to meet. But remember the weather girl?"

She laughed. "I will never forget the weather girl."

Anne had been working with Bailey Reskin, a meteorologist from Channel 4, when she and Todd had started dating. While watching the news one night, Todd had commented how "brilliant" he thought she was. Without revealing Bailey was a client, she'd teased him about having a celebrity crush. He'd had the grace and honesty not to deny it, and Anne had liked him all the more for it.

On a lark, she'd arranged for Todd to stop by her office one day when she knew Bailey would be there. Poor Todd had barely survived the encounter. Bailey had handled the meeting beautifully, harmlessly flirting and leaving him red-cheeked and tongue-tied. He'd also been delighted. It was completely endearing, and she'd never let him forget it.

"This might be your weather-girl equivalent."

"Ha. You wish. You know very well that I don't have celebrity crushes."

"That's good news," he joked. "Because if you were going to have one, I have a feeling this would be it. And I do not think I could compete."

Anne wanted to stop him right there. Was this statement another hint about his true feelings? How long could she avoid this conversation? It wasn't fair to him if he was having thoughts of more and "that."

Determined to avoid it tonight, though, she good-naturedly answered, "Okay. You've got me curious. Let's go meet my weather girl."

"Yes!" Todd said with a triumphant grin.

Intent on his mission, he resumed his previous trek across the room. Anne fell into step beside him, already planning her strategy for the rest of the evening.

After this introduction, she needed to find Keira, who'd texted earlier to report that she was busy circulating, trying to discern who was here from All I Wear, the clothing company whose account Anne had been trying for months to land. Rumor had it they were going to bid on Anne's consultation tonight, and she desperately wanted them to win.

She was scanning the crowd, looking for Keira, when she spotted someone else instead. Her heart nearly stopped as her gaze collided with a pair of intense and all-too-familiar dark brown eyes. No, it couldn't be…

Taking in the rest of him, she discovered a muscle-fit, tall man with dark, wavy brown hair in need of a cut, and a jaw as square as a 1940s film star. He even had the sexy cleft in the stubble-prone chin that made him appear perpetually unshaven.

And just like that, she had the answer to her previous question of where in the world was Derrick Bright? He was here. But why?

She'd seen the RSVP list, and he had not been on it.

A mix of shock and awareness coursed through her body. A part of her wanted to turn around and head the other way. Another side of her, though, felt drawn toward him. Like some sort of rebellious muscle memory had overtaken her body, propelling her onward. But then his lips curled at the corners, and his eyes flickered, and she knew he was inviting her to do just that.

That was enough to sound her internal alarm, restore her good sense and rein in her traitorous limbs. Because she also knew that no matter how sweet the shell, the man inside was nothing but a gooey center of trouble. Oh, sure, he'd lived up to all her romantic expectations for a while. Right up until the moment he'd gotten the contract of his dreams, which, as his PR specialist, she'd helped him secure.

That's when he'd dumped her for the *life* he really wanted. Thinking about her past naiveté was nearly as painful as the heartbreak itself. Which was likely a good sign, right? An indication that her feelings were all in the past, where they belonged.

She looked away, but another compelling thought immediately rushed in; Derrick would have *all* the answers about Easton. None of what had transpired between her and Derrick was Easton's fault. An old familiar pang awoke, jabbing at her heart as the image of the little boy Easton had been materialized before her. That perpetual smile, his sweetness, the boundless curiosity and a sense of humor beyond his years.

When she and Derrick broke up, she'd missed Easton, too. And Grandma May, whom she'd admired and wanted to be when she grew up. Anne still found it strange how people could play such a vital and important role in your life and then, *poof*, not be there at all.

Through the years, she'd proudly kept track of Easton's accomplishments. Watching him play at NPU the last two seasons had been the highlight. Key word: *watching*. No interaction. He'd only been eight years old when she'd known him. He probably didn't even remember her. Yes, Derrick had been a factor in her keeping her distance, but it seemed simpler and safer just to watch and hold her pride in check.

Coach Nichols had asked her to help Easton navigate what was shaping up to be a massive PED scandal. Tell him what to say, how to act, do what she could to keep him above the fray. Similar to what she'd done for Derrick all those years ago.

But Easton's situation was different. Working with Derrick had been more about polishing his image and improving a rough reputation. There'd been no incident to speak of, and she'd had an entire baseball season to accomplish the goal. Easton, on the other hand, was a golden boy suddenly on the cusp of falling from grace. She wasn't sure she could help him even if she wanted to.

As she looked at Derrick again, uncertainty warred with curiosity. Anxiety battled anticipation. She'd known this day would eventually come—when she'd have to face him again. But was she ready for that confrontation now? The answer was definite and immediate. Nope. She was not. And certainly not here tonight.

But then, in a twist she did *not* see coming, the decision was taken from her when Todd slipped a hand around her elbow and led her straight to him.

"DERRICK BRIGHT, I'D like you to meet my—"

"Hey, Anne," Derrick interrupted. He hadn't intended to sound quite so abrupt. But he'd seen Todd holding her hand, watched their intimate exchange. No need to *hear* that they were a couple, too. He hadn't known she was seeing anyone. But then again, how would he?

For a person whose job entailed bolstering the public images of others, Anne kept her private life very private. She had no personal social-media accounts, and her website included only a basic bio.

"Hello, Derrick."

"Wait…" A bemused Todd looked from Anne to Derrick and back again. "You two already know each other?"

"Yes," Derrick answered.

"Not really," Anne said at the same time before tacking on a hasty "We used to."

Todd let out a deliberately dramatic sigh. "Of course, you do." Smiling at Derrick, he said, "Anne knows *all* the cool people. And here I thought I was going to get to introduce her to someone she'd be excited to meet."

While Todd continued to talk, Derrick watched Anne, hoping for a hint of her true feelings about this "introduction." Not surprisingly, he couldn't tell a thing. "A consummate professional"—he still remembered that quote from her boss when they'd first met, and she'd taken him on as a client. Later, after he'd gotten to know her, the notion had occurred to him that the guy had the entire English language at his disposal to describe the sheer abundance of *amazingness* that was Anne McGrath, and he'd gone with "professional."

Not that the description wasn't accurate, it was just that she was all this other stuff, too. It was like she was two people: the PR professional and the person.

Back then, he'd been so lucky to get to know them both. The skilled, efficient, sophisticated businessperson she showed to the world and the interesting, funny, surprisingly down-to-earth woman who'd rather stay in than go out.

Then, in a stroke of incredible good fortune, she'd become his unbelievably awesome girlfriend. He'd learned everything about her; how she hated lipstick, tight sleeves and staying up late. How she loved the scent of vanilla, but perfume gave her a headache. In stark contrast to her stylish work wardrobe, she wore yoga pants on the weekends, usually after running ten miles. She devoured books like candy, a habit they were thrilled to discover they shared.

Then there was her weakness for ice cream and chocolate-chip waffles, both of which she rarely managed to consume without somehow spilling on herself. She was a rather messy eater, a trait he'd found both adorable and amusing. It had become his "job" to look her over for spills, and even now, he found himself squinting at a suspicious smudge on her gorgeous blue dress.

Her only flaw, in his opinion, was that she sometimes took life too seriously. He'd enjoyed bringing out her lighter side, giving her perspective and an appreciation for spontaneity. His absolute favorite thing had been making her laugh until she cried. And her belief in him, that he was an excellent baseball player, but an even better man, had made him feel ten feet tall.

All of that had been a long time ago, though, and if the success of McGrath PR was any indication, along with the fact that she'd declined Kellan's request to work with

Easton, her professional armor had only gotten thicker. He didn't hold out much hope that her answer would change with a request coming directly from him, but he'd agreed with Kellan that Easton needed help. Derrick insisted that it come from someone he could trust. Easton's career was on the line, and, in a manner of speaking, Derrick's own legacy was, too.

He could only think of one way to convince her, and it didn't involve a direct plea. But it was a pretty good plan. If he could only get her to agree.

"Well, it was a long time ago," Anne replied smoothly, echoing his thought. "Nice to see you again, Derrick."

"Yes, it has been a while," he conceded. Although, suddenly, with all the memories and emotions churning inside of him, it didn't seem very long at all. "Good to see you, too, Anne."

"Phew!" Todd jokingly exclaimed. With a congenial smile at Derrick, he added, "Honestly, I was worried that she'd take one look at you, and I'd lose her forever. But since you already know each other, I guess there's not much chance of that."

"Nope," Anne answered a little too quickly for Derrick's liking. "Absolutely none."

"I'm sure," a beaming Todd said, "you know that Anne is a huge baseball fan."

"She was certainly enthusiastic back when I knew her."

Anne's eyes widened ever so slightly before overcorrecting into an assessing squint.

"Never misses a Panthers game. And she has a poster of the Knights on the wall in her bedroom. That's why I thought she'd be excited to meet you."

*Does she now?* A flash of hope sparked inside of him.

"It's a photo, not a poster," she quickly clarified, dashing his optimism. "Of the championship team in 2016. And it was a gift from a client who went to the game." Then she gave Todd a teasing grin. "Nice try, though."

"Dang," Todd muttered through his own verge-of-laughter smile. "So much for my celebrity-meeting payback, huh?"

Anne chuckled. "Absolutely zero chance that I'll start babbling about baseball's equivalent to hoarfrost and graupel." With a wink, she reached out and squeezed his forearm. "I absolutely adore your attempt, though. Well done."

"Good." A laughing Todd slipped an arm around her shoulders and leaned in to plant a friendly kiss on her cheek.

Derrick was surprised by the raw, unpleasant nip of jealousy. He quickly acknowledged the overreaction for what it was. It was the private joke that bothered him. He'd been the one to enjoy this type of closeness with her once. But now this guy, this complete stranger, Todd, knew her better than Derrick did.

For so long, Derrick had played their breakup over and over in his mind, imagining what if he would have done things differently. *What if I hadn't waffled? Why couldn't I have been braver and asked her to go with me? Maybe if we'd never had all those miles between us, then...* The scenarios were endless.

He'd missed her with a pain so sharp he'd feared his heart would never fully heal. Eventually, though, he'd come to terms with his mistake, gotten over her. As crushing as it had been, the email had been helpful in that way. But also difficult to shake. Of course, he'd read it so many times he could recite it nearly verbatim.

To this day, every word was hotly, excruciatingly branded onto his brain. *Baseball is who you are. It's all you'll ever be. You're not capable of being more...* He hated how right she'd been, how prophetic the message was turning out to be—an unexpected surge of resentment flooded through him. But, no, he was here to get Anne in his corner, not to get lost in the past.

Todd pulled him firmly back into the present, as he explained, "When we were first dating, Anne introduced me to this local weather person, and I sort of made a fool of myself. I'm sure you're used to that, right? People probably get silly over you all the time."

"Only occasionally, thank goodness," Derrick said, playing along and forcing a chuckle.

Todd smiled, started to respond, but then glanced away. "Milt is waving at me," he said. "My boss," he added for Derrick's sake. "I need to have a word with him. I'll let you two catch up. It was a thrill to meet you, Derrick. Thanks for being such a good sport, and an extraspecial thank-you for your contribution to our cause."

Derrick returned the sentiment and shook his hand.

"Anne, I'll catch up with you later, okay? The auction starts at eight fifteen, so if I don't find you by then, let's meet at our table?"

She agreed and said goodbye, then Todd moved away, disappearing into the crowd.

Slowly, reluctantly it seemed, she faced Derrick. "Derrick, Coach Nichols already called me, and I—"

"I know he did," he interrupted gently. "And I want you to know that I didn't ask him to. Anne, I promise, I'm not here to try and change your mind."

"You're not?" she returned, a tinge of suspicion creeping into her tone.

"I'm not," he reiterated. *Nope. My plan is for you to do that all on your own.*

# CHAPTER THREE

"Oh," Anne said, surprised by Derrick's admission. Her initial shock at seeing him had given way to the assumption that this meeting wasn't accidental. She'd been prepared to lay out her case.

"Kellan doesn't know about us, our history, I mean. He got your name from a mutual friend, someone named Jack."

"Oh, right," she said, "Jack Derry." And yet, she felt compelled to elaborate. "But it wouldn't change anything, regardless. I didn't say no because of our past. I said no because McGrath PR doesn't represent athletes.

"Besides that, Easton is facing what's commonly called a PR crisis, which is not our specialty. What we do at McGrath PR is more long-term brand building, profile raising, reputation strengthening. We typically employ a slower, methodical approach. More like I did with you."

"What you meant to say was nightmare, right? This is a PR nightmare."

She couldn't disagree. It was a common term, and if Easton was taking, or had taken, illegal performance-enhancing drugs, his life was indeed morphing into a nightmare. "Yes, and there are firms who specialize in that, in crisis management."

"Kellan told me all of this, too, and I understand."

He did? It took her a moment to process his words. She'd convinced herself he was here to ask her to reconsider.

"What are you doing here then?" she blurted.

His knowing smile seemed to suggest he'd anticipated this assumption on her part. "I'm on the auction block tonight, too. Donated some batting lessons."

"I didn't see you in the lineup." Although now that she thought about it, she hadn't seen the final auction-donation inventory, just the guest list. She'd been more concerned with who was attending than who was donating.

"Good one," Derrick said, grinning at her pun, which she only just realized she'd made. "I guess there were a couple of late cancellations. My agent heard about it and suggested it would be a nice way for me to give back to the community and announce my reentrance to Portland society, whatever that last part means. I like the cause, though, so here I am."

"Good call on both counts," she assured him. "The Unified Justice Coalition is a wonderful organization, and the event is getting a ton of publicity."

"I didn't even know you were participating until I saw the program. Before I could find you myself, a friend introduced me to Todd, and Todd asked if I'd be willing to meet you..." Derrick's mouth pulled up on one side like he was trying not to smile. He was all boyish innocence and every bit as appealing as she remembered as he added, "He, uh, he actually asked me if I'd flirt with you a little."

Anne choked out a surprised laugh. "Thank you for sparing us both that awkwardness."

Grinning, he assured her, "It wouldn't be awkward for me." His gaze traveled down and settled on a spot. "You have a little smudge of something on your dress. Let me guess—ice cream?"

She frowned. A combination of embarrassment and discomfort blazed through her.

How dare he draw on their former intimacy like this?

Glancing down, she tugged clumsily on her wrap and thought up a lie. "No, it's, um… oil."

"Oil?" he repeated skeptically.

"Yep." She shrugged and stared him down. "Moonlighting on the oil rig."

He started to smile, to call her out, but then seemed to pick up on her back-off signal. He cleared his throat and composed his features. "How have you been, Anne?"

"For all eleven of the years it's been since I've seen you?" She heard the clear edge in her voice. There was a chance she hadn't gotten over this quite as well as she'd believed. But you know what? What he'd done had been really…hurtful, and perhaps she was still a tad angry. Now that she thought about it, there was no rule stating she had to make this reunion easy on him.

"Well," he retorted, "if you want, you can start with what exactly happened eleven years ago and go forward from there?"

Was he serious? Yes, she realized with a jolt that only an insight of this magnitude could induce. Because, from his perspective, she'd been the one who'd ultimately ended things. And, granted, she hadn't done so in the classiest manner.

She'd sent him an email. Yep, she'd broken up with him behind the comfort of her keyboard. In her defense, she'd been devastated after already being devastated. Derrick had been her first serious boyfriend, her only love story, tragic and clichéd though the ending had been.

They'd been young when they met. Anne was barely out of college and working at her first PR job. Derrick was two years younger and a senior at NPU, as well as a catcher, and mega-hitter for the Panthers. The unqualified star of the team. He was also a good-looking, smooth-talking troublemaker. She'd been assigned the task of improving his image.

The attraction was immediate and mutual, but beyond that, she'd *liked* him. So much. She'd never met anyone who'd gotten her before. Not like Derrick. He'd made her see life differently, to appreciate the little things, the important stuff. He's also had an uncanny ability to get under her skin, but in the best possible way. Or so she'd believed. And then there'd been their mutual love of books.

She fell fast and hard, and soon fancied herself in love. Somehow, thankfully, she'd retained enough sense not to tell him. With his future uncertain, she'd waited for him to say the words first, assuming that after he was drafted, they'd be able to make a plan for *their* future. When the season ended, and Derrick was signed, everyone was thrilled— Derrick, his family, the coach, Anne, her boss.

Hoping for a commitment, she was blind-sided when Derrick instead expressed concern about the wisdom of a long-distance relationship, the seeming incompatibility of their careers. Maybe it would be wise to take a step back, he suggested, and focus on themselves, but remain friends.

Anne wasn't stupid. She knew the words were as good as a breakup. What choice did she have but to agree? Devastated, she somehow managed to play it cool. But, then, almost as quickly, he'd seemed to change his mind. He'd been gone less than twenty-four hours before calling her. The next day, he'd phoned again, and every day after, missing her and hinting he'd made a mistake.

That's when she decided to surprise him

with a visit, naively hoping that their being together again would bring him to his senses. When she'd shown up at his condo, he hadn't been alone. A party was in full swing, and Derrick had been having a *terrific* time. Even now, the image of his arms around another woman sparked the same hurt and humiliation.

Unable to face him, she'd turned around, boarded a plane and flown home, where she'd cried and cried. A friend had brought over a bottle of wine and a tub of ice cream to console her. The next day, alone and hurting and a little hungover, she'd sent the email.

She hadn't mentioned the visit or what she'd seen, opting instead to retain her dignity and build on the foundation he'd already laid. The letter in its entirety escaped her now, or possibly she'd blocked it out, but she knew she'd been kind of harsh.

Undoubtedly, he'd forgotten all about it. Probably, he'd deleted it on the spot. He hadn't answered or ever tried to contact her again, and, after languishing in despair for an embarrassingly long stretch of weeks that turned into months, she'd closed that sappy chapter of her life.

The notion that Derrick would blame her for the breakup had never really occurred to her before. Since they weren't technically together then, she couldn't consider his behavior cheating. Mentioning the incident would have laid all her love cards on the table. Eventually, she'd realized the whole experience was indicative of the life he was embracing as a pro athlete—the life he'd dreamed about forever. One that didn't include her. When he didn't respond, she'd taken it as further validation that she'd done the right thing.

"No, no," she said with a forced chuckle and a breezy wave. "I don't think we need to rehash ancient history. We were young and on different pages with 'incompatible careers.'" Despite her claim, she couldn't resist throwing those long-ago words back at him. "It was for the best, yadda, yadda. So, yeah. I guess I'll just sum up my entire life quickly—I'm great! Eleven years of fabulous."

Inhaling a breath, she tapped into her steely resolve and added, "You can fill me in on you later. Or not," she joked lamely. "I have a good idea of what you've been up to. How is Easton?" She needed this conversation to be over. When could she get out of here?

"Scared," he answered so fast she knew he'd been expecting the question.

"Does he have reason to be?"

"If you're asking if he takes performance-enhancing drugs, the answer is no, and before you tell me how impossible it is for me to know for certain, I want to tell you a few things. Six years ago, our dad died."

"I'm so sorry, Derrick," she offered with genuine sympathy, even though she'd already known.

"Thank you. But the point is that Mom was unable to be there for Easton as a reliable support system. I'm sure you remember how absent she was as a mother, anyway." Anne did remember that. Tabitha Bright had been a busy surgeon obsessed with her career. Their dad, Wesley, had been the one involved in the day-to-day life of raising the boys. His parents, Marty and May, had also been instrumental in their upbringing.

At Anne's nod, he said, "That only got worse as Easton got older. And then, when I moved, I wasn't able to be a consistent physical presence anymore. I did the best I could, but... Anyway, after Dad died, Easton kind of went off the rails for a while. Rebelled, got into some trouble."

"Sounds familiar," she said with a gentle smile.

"Totally," he agreed. "Dad's obsession with baseball and his involvement in our lives was sometimes over-the-top, but he also gave us focus and direction. And he loved us."

Wesley Bright had been a high-school teacher, but he'd lived and breathed baseball...and his boys. A talented player himself, he'd never given Derrick or Easton a choice about whether they'd play, either. Fortunately for him, they both loved the game, too. Depending on who you asked, Wesley was either a devoted baseball dad or a fanatical tyrant.

"Easton had it much worse than I did. I was already grown and gone when Dad died. But even getting into trouble, Easton was still a better kid than me. He never did anything *terrible*. Then, in the midst of his meltdown, Mom accepts what she claims is her 'dream job' and moves to Maryland. There's a lot more I could tell you about that. Long story short, Easton didn't want to go. Grandma

May stepped in, bless her, and she and I formulated a plan to get him back on track.

"Ever since moving in with Grandma, Easton has done everything right. He has his life together, his priorities straight, good grades, healthy hobbies. He wants to go pro after this next season. But now, to have this thing that he did *not* do threaten to ruin everything? I'm not going to lie—it's horrific."

A wave of sympathy welled up from inside of her. Careful not to let it color her objectivity, she asked, "Have the police spoken to Easton yet?"

"No," he said.

"Does he have an attorney?"

"Do you think he needs one?" Derrick looked stricken at the thought. Anne remembered how naive he'd been about the ramifications of his own behavior all those years ago. She immediately reminded herself that he'd since had a professional career where he'd gotten used to the spotlight. Had he really not thought his brother's situation through to this inevitable point?

"He absolutely does if he talks to the police in any capacity whatsoever, Derrick. Even if they reassure him that he's not a suspect or tell him that things will be better for him if he talks. I know people say how retaining an attorney when you're innocent can make you appear guilty, but, in my experience, that's just an initial reaction. Long-term, the advice of a good attorney has saved way more innocent people than it has guilty ones."

"He did not do this, Anne. I know my brother. And *you* know him, too. Granted, you haven't seen him for a long time, but at his core, Easton has not changed. If anything, he's better. He is truly an incredible young man. And I know people always say that in these situations, but in Easton's case, it is true. Truer, even, if that's possible."

Anne didn't know what to say. The thing was, she believed him. No, she *wanted* to believe him. There was a huge difference. Because despite what Derrick claimed, she didn't know Easton anymore. She didn't know Derrick, either, for that matter. She hadn't ever known him as well as she thought she had. That was the problem, wasn't it?

"Derrick—"

"I told you I wasn't here to try and change your mind about taking him on as a client.

But I am going to ask you a favor. No hard feelings if you say no."

She nodded for him to go on.

"Can you come over to the house and meet with him?" Derrick threw up his hands as if anticipating her refusal. "Just to talk. He is panicked, and I'm afraid of what he might do. Or say. If you could just advise him, as a friend, point out how important it is that he not react. Or that he at least reacts calmly."

"At this stage, he shouldn't be reacting at all. He shouldn't fuel any of this gossip in his direction. And whatever he does, tell him to stay off social media. Don't even comment on a post. It would be best if he didn't even access his accounts right now. Someone else should be doing that for him." Like a publicist, she wanted to add.

"See? That's exactly what I'm talking about. Anne, please. I know it's a lot to ask, but I promise if you come over and talk to him, you'll see that this is the same sweet kid you used to know. The one who loves animals and flowers and ice cream, and used to follow us everywhere and… The thing is, like I mentioned, he's exceptional. And I'd like you to see that for yourself."

Anne stared at him, the speech leaving her unsettled and uncertain. And, honestly, a little annoyed. Because despite what he claimed, they both knew he was trying to change her mind. She didn't like how she felt…swayed.

"You know, it's the least you could do. After what you wrote in that email, I think—"

"Are you kidding me?" she interrupted. A hot rush of anger heated her entire body. "I wrote that email because I—" She bit off the rest of the explanation. She could hear her tone betraying old feelings, ones she thought she'd squelched. No, she had squelched them. This was simply a knee-jerk response to the latent bitterness he'd revealed. "Never mind. I thought we agreed we weren't going to go there."

"You're right," he conceded smoothly. "I'm sorry. I'm just frustrated, and I need help."

"You do need help. Easton needs help. I gave Coach Nichols my recommendation. I think Mitchell West would do a good job. Beverly, in particular, would be excellent."

"But—"

"I'm sorry, Derrick. I'm not the right person for this. I need to get going. Tonight is an important evening for Todd. And for me, too, for that matter." She waved at Keira, who'd spotted her and was now eyeballing them curiously, no doubt wondering what was going down in this corner of the ballroom.

"My colleague is waiting. Good luck, Derrick. And, please, give my regards to Easton and to your grandmother."

"So, THAT'S IT, THEN," Keira said after Anne had filled her in on the impromptu meeting with Derrick. "You said no to both Coach Nichols and Derrick Bright." A server came by with a tray of champagne flutes. Keira took two and handed one to Anne.

"I sure did," Anne returned brightly, a sort of giddiness bubbling inside of her as she said the words. It was relief, she decided, that this encounter was finally over. She'd seen Derrick, and she was fine. Better than fine. Even as blindsided as she'd been, she'd handled it very well. From a totally objective PR perspective, it didn't get any better.

"Hmm." Keira took a sip.

"What?"

"Nothing. It's just that... You are absolutely positive you don't want to take this kid on? There is a bevy of badly behaving athletes with big bank balances who could benefit from our… I promise, I did not mean to start this alliterative chain, but now I have to think of a *B* word…" She paused to tap a finger to her chin. "Bountiful abilities, if only we agreed to branch out?"

"Okay, no more champagne for you," Anne joked. "And I am positive."

"Not even for Derrick Bright?"

"*Especially* not for Derrick Bright."

Keira's eyebrows arched high before her green-eyed gaze narrowed in on Anne with a look of blatant speculation.

*Shoot.* Anne silently acknowledged there'd been a little too much emphasis in her response. In addition to an apparent knack for random alliteration, Keira possessed a gift for truth detecting. Her psychology background—specifically, behavioral research—coupled with her natural perceptiveness made her an expert at reading body language. An extraordinarily valuable skill for a PR specialist and one she regularly drew upon to coach their clients. Nearly every interview, news conference, photo shoot, or public appearance included a prep session with Keira.

As her friend, however, Anne felt a switch to turn off this superpower would come in handy.

Keira tucked a length of her silky, shoulder-length blond hair behind one ear. "Remind me again *why* we don't represent athletes, Anne? Now that we're having this discussion, I'm not sure I've ever known the reason. I just accepted it because I don't really care about sports unless I'm the one playing."

Anne made a concerted effort not to do the nervous cheek bite that often gave her away. In her best because-I-said-so tone, she repeated verbatim the answer she'd given Coach Nichols. "Representing athletes or athletic organizations presents a special set of circumstances with unique challenges. We don't have the knowledge or connections to deal adequately with those intricacies."

"Let me get this straight—what you are telling me right now is that *you*, Anne McGrath, baseball *fan*-atic, don't have enough baseball knowledge to represent a baseball player?"

"It's about more than knowing the game, Keira. But, essentially, yes, that is what I'm saying."

"But you used to."

"Not really," she hedged, already realizing the trap she'd laid for herself.

"Not really? What does that mean—yes or no? Did you or did you not work with athletes when you first started?"

"What is this, a deposition? Yes, as you know very well I did, I worked at Mitchell West, where they do represent athletes, so I *had* to, yes. But it was a long time ago, and I learned then how specialized an area it is. Even more so now than a decade ago."

"I'm missing something." Keira tapped a finger to her lip, her expression rife with skepticism. "We will revisit this topic at a later date, but for now, I have to tell you this important bit of potentially life-changing gossip."

"Bring it."

"Pamela Bradshaw is here."

"Pamela Bradshaw, as in Jennifer Katzen's second-in-command?"

"The one and only," Keira confirmed with a grin. "So, word on the proverbial street is that Pamela is going to win both the consult with us and the one with Mitchell West. And *then* Jennifer will decide who to go with on a permanent basis."

Anne felt a surge of adrenaline-charged excitement. For more than two years, she'd been subtly courting Jennifer's business. The founder, owner and CEO of All I Wear, a vegan, sustainably oriented clothing company based in Portland, didn't currently utilize any public-relations firm. But they'd grown so much so quickly that they now needed one in a hurry.

Acquiring All I Wear as a client would be the biggest professional accomplishment to date for McGrath PR. Other companies would follow, boosting their firm to the level of success Anne aspired to. They'd be top tier, right up there with Mitchell West and a small handful of others.

She was completely confident McGrath PR was the best fit for the company. Jennifer's vegan stance bordered on militant and had lately earned her some backlash. Anne had heard that she wanted to polish her edges and find a better way to reach out to her nonvegan customers. If she could get a face-to-face meeting, she knew she could secure the account.

More than that, she would do a better job. Just like Mitchell West would be better for Easton.

"Keira, this could be a game changer for us."

Keira smiled and raised her glass to Anne's in a toast. "It will be a game changer, Anne. I just know it. I have a feeling about this night, and you know how my feelings go."

# CHAPTER FOUR

ANNE LET HER gaze bounce around the room, drinking it in, memorizing as many details as she could. One day, she might look back on this event as one of the pivotal moments in her career, her life. A landmark moment when the long hours, the sacrifice and the hard work all paid off.

Satisfaction settled inside of her because she'd also slain the dragon that was Derrick Bright. The unexpected residual anger and feelings of rejection were already melting away. She was confident that soon they'd be gone for good. She should have faced this down years ago.

Anne made a mental note to congratulate Todd and the event organizers on their choice of a silent auction versus a live one. People were milling around, chatting, laughing, sipping drinks, or nibbling dessert, all while scrolling around the auction app on their phones or via one of the tablets supplied for each table.

"All I Wear has the top bid on your consult," Keira eagerly reported as she slipped into her seat beside Anne at one of the large round tables arranged along the edge of the dancefloor. "A name I don't recognize keeps upping the bidding, so that's fun, too." Bidders could participate with their own names or choose a screen name for temporary anonymity.

"And," she added, "you are currently going for a higher amount than Mitchell West." Anne was relieved to hear that, too. Not that she cared about her consultation going for the most money—it was more the fear that Mitchell West would receive *all* the bids. Okay, so she still had a trace of insecure middle-schooler lurking inside of her. Who didn't?

"Derrick Bright's batting-practice sessions are already up to an outrageous sum. Do you think people are bidding on those for their kids? Or are these like weekend-warrior types who refuse to grow up and are going to end up in the ER with torn rotator cuffs?"

Anne laughed. "That is an excellent question."

"He's going to outshine both the mayor and Christina Belmonte." Christina Belmonte was a talented, up-and-coming singer and actress from Portland. She wasn't in attendance tonight, but she was scheduled to perform in a play here in the fall. She'd generously donated dinner, an acting lesson, a photo shoot and tickets to the production. Anne's niece, Willow, adored her, so Anne had placed a bid but was certain that winning the package would take much more than she could afford.

She wasn't surprised about Derrick's batting lessons. Sure, he'd been one of the best catchers in the league, but he was also a genius with a bat.

"Did you see who Todd was talking to?"

"Who?" She'd barely looked at Todd all evening. Anne felt a stirring of guilt for failing to check in with him. Not that he needed her to, but that was probably something she should do, right? The truth was, she wasn't great at *girlfriend-ing*. At least, she was good at PR.

"Bailey Reskin."

"What?" Anne swiveled in her seat, but, of

course, she didn't see them. "Bailey is here?" Not long after she'd introduced the talented meteorologist to Todd, Bailey had taken a job with the Global Weather Channel and moved to the East Coast.

"Yep."

"Huh. I didn't see her name on the guest list."

"I'm guessing she came with a date? Only a few more minutes left. I am so stoked. Anne, you deserve this."

"*We* deserve this, Keira. You work as hard as I do."

Keira slid her a sly smile. "That's not quite accurate, but thank you. No one works as hard as you, but my innate gifts do make me a valuable asset. I am fantasizing about how business is going to grow…and the vacation we are finally going to take." They often day-dreamed about a girls' trip to one of those all-inclusive tropical resorts, but they'd never felt comfortable being away from the business at the same time. Anne had plans to offer Keira a partnership, too, when the time was right.

She added, "I'm already making plans for when Jennifer brings her business on board with us. She's so savvy. I cannot wait to meet her and work with her and talk about her vision for the future."

At the front of the room, a small crowd had gathered, including Todd, two of his colleagues and the emcee, Maria Diaz. Maria was a popular local television personality who had a regular adventure segment on the morning news called "Checking it Out with Maria."

Well-spoken, witty and engaging, she'd done a fabulous job of providing entertainment while keeping the event moving along. Before dinner, she'd given an overview of the charity's purpose and briefly described every offering, all while good-naturedly fostering a competitive spirit that had continued to resonate throughout the evening. Anne knew Maria and adored her. She was a celebrity worth knowing.

Behind her, the giant monitor screen came alive with the final countdown.

"Reminds me of a rock concert," Anne joked as screens lit up all over the room while a last-minute frenzy of bidding ensued. Keira lifted her phone and swayed like a groupie.

They were still laughing when a breathy Todd joined them at the table. "Hey!" he said, eyes sparkling, smile electric. "What a night! Can you believe this? We've already broken the fundraising record set last year. Like majorly crushed it."

"Congratulations!" Anne said, reaching for his hand. She was thrilled for Todd. He'd put so much time into this endeavor, along with the sixty- or seventy-hour weeks he already worked. That was one of the best things about their relationship, how they both understood the importance of each other's jobs and the demands it placed on their time.

She glanced at a giddy-looking Todd. How long had it been since she'd felt giddy? Was it time to reevaluate their priorities? Maybe they needed to spend *more* time together and actively move toward "that."

"Thanks, Anne." He squeezed her hand, then let go to pick up a tablet.

"How's Bailey?"

Todd's brow drew up as if he was surprised by the question. Then he grinned and tapped on the screen. "She's great. She asked about you, of course. Said she'd try and find you after the auction. She wants to—"

Three loud chimes sounded as the bidding

closed. The app went black, and so did the room for a few long seconds.

"Nice!" Keira called approvingly to Todd when the lights came back on. The room erupted with applause. "I can literally feel the suspense."

Maria gave a short speech, thanked everyone for their participation, told a funny joke about attorneys and then got right to it. She began announcing each auction's high bid. Behind her, the winner's name flashed on the big screen.

Todd was beaming, and she couldn't blame him. People had been generous. The Portland Speedtrack racing school brought in a substantial sum, as did the glassblowing lessons by a well-known artist. The build-a-canoe packages were popular. Lunch with the mayor brought an exorbitant sum, but, in the end, didn't quite edge out Christina Belmonte. A collective gasp went through the room at the final price of Derrick's batting lessons.

As more and more high bids were revealed, Anne could see why Todd was on top of the world. And soon, if luck was on her side, she'd be joining him there.

"Next up, we have the consultation and PR plan with Anne McGrath of McGrath PR. Hi, Anne." Maria waved and pointed in her direction. "Love that girl."

Anne returned the gesture.

"I gotta tell you, this item went wild there at the end as we had a couple of bidders duking it out, so to speak."

"How cool!" Todd said, grinning at her.

But Anne was no longer smiling because, across the room, a certain pair of brown eyes had just met hers. No, they were latched on to hers, and something in Derrick's expression put her on alert. No, he wouldn't, would he? Not after their conversation, after she'd given him an unequivocal *no*. Except, she knew very well that when Derrick wanted something, he could be both single-minded and relentless in his pursuit.

Anne squeezed her eyes shut as Maria confirmed this terrible truth. "And the winner of the consultation and PR plan with Anne McGrath of McGrath PR is Derrick Bright!"

THE FOLLOWING MORNING Derrick was flat on his back atop the fireplace hearth, shining a flashlight up the massive chimney, when

Easton leaned in and yelled, "I don't think he's coming."

Between the structure itself—hearth and mantel—and the surrounding stone, the old fireplace took up a good share of one wall in the living room. Since the very first time Derrick had seen the old farmhouse, he'd fallen in love with the behemoth and dreamed of one day filling it with a cozy fire.

A vision he now acknowledged might prove somewhat more challenging than he'd initially anticipated. The previous owners had not only capped the chimney, but they'd also "sealed it."

"What? Who?" he asked, shifting so he could see Easton. He'd heard "he," but had Anne called to cancel?

"Santa Claus," Easton answered glibly. "You are months early, bro. Plus, I'm not sure he can even get down this chimney. It's capped."

Derrick chuckled, turned off the flashlight and inched out of the space. "Nice to see you still have a sense of humor."

"Well, Anne *is* coming to save me, right?"

"Easton, that's not what I said. I—"

"She'll help me, Derrick. I know she will."

His voice was firm and confident, with a trace of juvenile bravado that made Derrick want to hug him.

Emotion coiled tightly in his chest. Easton was putting too much stock in this, in Anne. His fault, he knew, because he'd told Easton he'd find a way to get Anne to meet with him. He'd certainly accomplished that much, hadn't he?

Winning her consultation hadn't been part of the evening's plan. But there it'd been right there on the app—Public Relations Package with Anne McGrath of McGrath PR. Everything he was asking for, she was just giving away to someone else. And across the room, she was laughing and smiling like all was right in the world. At the same time, he'd been stewing in disappointment and desperation. So, yes, perhaps there'd been a bit of his old rebellion and some email payback mixed into his decision. Whatever it was, at that moment, he'd identified a solution. And he'd taken it.

Anne had not been pleased. He could see the shock in her expression followed by anger flickering hotly in her blue eyes. Impressive how she'd managed to remain all smiles when he'd found her at the end of the evening and arranged this morning's breakfast meeting. Although what choice did she have with a crowd of people around?

He knew that "forcing" her to meet with them might not have been the wisest course of action. Which was why he'd also called Sally Cabot, an acquaintance at *The Portland Chronicle*, and anonymously leaked some information. Sally had texted to say her story would go live at noon. If things went according to plan, Anne would already have made her mind up. If not, this would be the added push she needed.

Easton said, "Grandma is making a quiche, but I'm doing chocolate-chip waffles, too. Remember how much Anne loved those? I hope she still likes them. Maybe she only pretended to like them because of me."

As mature as Easton could be in many areas of his life, in other ways, he was still a kid. Derrick had often wondered if Easton was making a mistake by forgoing his senior year of college for the draft. Derrick had opted to wait until after he'd finished college, and he'd never regretted the decision. That final season at NPU, he'd had the time of his life, on and off the field. Of course, he'd been dating Anne for most of that year, too. The relationship had kept him grounded, motivated, happy.

"No, she didn't. She genuinely liked them," Derrick assured him. "But you know, Easton—"

"Don't say it, Derrick," Easton interrupted, waving a hand like a stop sign. "I know. I know she might not agree to help, but like you said, just talking to her will make me feel better. Since last night, when you told me she was coming over this morning, it's the first sliver of hope I've had. It might sound weird, but I want to hold on to it for as long as I can."

"No, I get it," Derrick said. And he did. Not only had Easton inherited Grandma May's sunny optimism, but he'd also adopted her philosophy of living in the moment. It was a skill that would serve him well in the future. Savoring the highs and leaning into the lows would help him navigate the severe ups and downs of a professional baseball career.

"Seriously, though, what are you doing down there?"

"I'm going to fix the fireplace."

Easton's eyes widened, a trace of alarm showing on his face. "Really?"

"Yes. We're going to have a fire this winter." He could almost smell the cedar kindling, hear the crackle, feel the heat. He could see all three of them gathered around drinking hot chocolate. At Christmastime, their stockings would hang from the stone mantel and be backlit by the flames.

"Okay, um, yeah, that sounds cool." Easton tried for enthusiasm, but his face crimped with concern. "Do you know how to do that, though?"

"Of course," he said with slightly more optimism than he felt. He'd read about it, watched a couple of YouTube videos, and the process didn't seem overly complicated. He just needed to take some measurements and figure out a few details first.

"Morning, boys!" Grandma May called out as she hustled into the room, all smiles in her dirt-smudged overalls. "What's up? What time is Anne getting here?"

"Ten thirty," Derrick answered.

"Good morning, Grandma," Easton said. "Fresh eggs in the basket."

"How many?"

"Five."

"Fantastic! That gives us more than enough for quiche and waffles. Those girls are on task."

Grandma peered down at Derrick as if just noticing his prone position. "What are you doing down there on the floor? Your leg okay?"

"Leg is fine," Derrick answered and then held out a hand for Easton to help him up. After three surgeries and countless hours of physical therapy, her concern was legitimate. It wasn't yet back to a hundred percent. But it likely wouldn't ever be. Arthritis was already creeping in, but the doctors assured him that staying active was the key to long-term mobility.

"Derrick is going to build us a fire," Easton explained, taking Derrick's outstretched hand and helping him to his feet.

"He...what?" Grandma looked startled. She pointed at the fireplace. "Not in there, I hope? The chimney's been capped."

"Hey," Derrick said with a palms-up shrug. "Can you two give me a little credit here? I know the chimney is capped, *and* I know what I'm doing."

"Can it wait until after breakfast, at least?" Grandma asked. "I don't want you burning down the house while we have company."

Easton choked out a laugh.

"I appreciate your confidence in me, Grandma," Derrick replied dryly.

"Derrick, honey, it's not that I don't have confidence in you, it's just that…" She trailed off. "You know what? Never mind. Your entire lives, I've never coddled you boys, and I'm not about to start now. That is the reason I'm not confident where your home-improvement skills are concerned. Not that I don't think you *can* do it—it's just, like your late grandfather, rest his soul, you have a tendency to plow ahead with a plan before you fully think it through."

# CHAPTER FIVE

KEIRA RAISED ONE eyebrow so she could attempt a proper glare at Anne. The way it distorted one side of her face into a snarl was even more effective than her friend's usual full-on grimace. Anne told her so.

To which Keira responded, "You know, sometimes I wish we didn't live in the same apartment building."

On weekend mornings, Keira liked to sleep in. Anne knew this, so on the way back from her run, she'd detoured to the Grumpy Crumpet and picked up her friend's favorite, a large Earl Grey, before rousting her at the "ungodly hour" of 8:00 a.m. Never mind that Keira rose at five thirty no matter what other day of the week it was. Saturdays for Keira were sacrosanct.

Considering they'd been out late the night before because of the auction, Anne knew she might have to resort to bribery here. So, bribe she would; she could not do this alone.

"I know you don't really mean that," she said, her voice dripping with sweetness. "Who else is going to corral the spiders in your shower?"

"This is true." Keira's mouth twisted to one side as she tried not to smile. One of Anne's duties as a "bestie neighbor" was trapping wayward spiders. *Trapping* being the key word here, because Keira did not want the arachnids "euthanized." So every time she spotted one, she called upon Anne, who had to bring down her "spider transport module"—a cottage-cheese container with holes poked in the lid. After securing the spider, Anne had to cart it downstairs and release the critter into the building's courtyard. Not on the balcony, because "Really, Anne? Do you know what's worse than a spider? An angry spider who's been evicted from her house."

Now Anne pointed in the general direction of the balcony, where she knew the sun was already bright in a strikingly blue sky. In the morning light, on a clear day like this one, a snow-capped Mt. Hood dazzled. A glorious sight they often enjoyed gawking at together.

"Do you want to sit outside and drink these?" She hefted the cups, fully aware of the enticement she held.

"Might as well," Keira answered, now slightly less irritable than moments earlier. "I'm up now."

"I'll scoot ahead and meet you out there," Anne chirped and fled the scene.

Keira called after her, "Noted how you are taking my tea so that I won't double back to bed."

Tossing an evil laugh over her shoulder, Anne hustled into the other room and then unlatched the French doors leading to Keira's veranda. The charming space looked like a snapshot from an outdoor Paris café, with its tiny table adorned with a checked cloth and a vase of fresh flowers in the center. Four stylish bistro chairs were tucked around the table. Potted plants dotted the space.

Anne took a seat and waited. Moments later, Keira shuffled out and joined her. After sighing at the view, she adjusted the sunglasses on her nose, picked up her tea and took a substantial guzzle.

"I'm so sorry about the auction last night. What if we call Pamela Bradshaw and offer Jennifer a free consult?"

Anne shook her head. "I'm not here to talk about last night's debacle. Well, not that part of the debacle, anyway."

"Oh?"

"Will you come with me to the meeting with the Bright family this morning?"

Keira lifted her glasses to squint at Anne. "Do I have to?" The point hadn't sunk in yet that this request wasn't work-related. "Can't Oliver do it? He works most Saturdays, anyway."

"No, you don't *have* to," Anne said before sipping her Irish breakfast blend. "I'd just like to have someone along."

"Why don't you ask Todd? And why is it so early?"

"Todd is sailing." Sailing was Todd's passion, an activity Anne had tried hard to enjoy but found to be a convoluted, stress-filled chore.

It included excessive amounts of water, wind, rope and fabric, and a vocabulary that she could not comprehend but that Todd insisted on shouting at her in what she swore held a trace of "pirate" accent. "Starboard! Aft! Port! Anne, make way!" What misguided sailor had first decided it was a good idea to complicate simple directions like right and left, anyway?

"And it's early because I'm going to the beach this afternoon, remember?"

Anne spent two weekends a month in Pacific Cove at her brother Rhys's house. After their older brother, Evan, and his wife, Vanessa, had died, Rhys had retained custody of their daughter, Willow. Anne had promised to help, vowed that she'd always be a part of her niece's life. Even though Rhys had since married Camile, and Willow was now a teenager, it made no difference whatsoever in her mind.

"Sailing," Keira repeated blandly. She shared Anne's opinion of the activity. "Of course, he is. What better way to celebrate his triumph?"

"I know. He deserves it, right? The only good thing about this breakfast meeting is that it won't be taking place on a sailboat."

"You realize that I know next to nothing about baseball. Less than I know about sailing."

"Doesn't matter." Anne breezily brushed

a hand through the air. "It's going to be a lovely drive. We can stop at that fruit stand you like, the one where they sell the jams and homemade pies."

When Keira didn't say no, Anne looked out at the view before layering on more enticement. "Can you believe this weather? The beach is going to be stunning. Wait, I have another idea! Why don't you pack a bag and come to Pacific Cove with me? We can leave from the Brights' house."

Keira paused before answering, her gaze assessing and curious. "Why, Anne McGrath, it sounds like you're trying to bribe me."

"Caught me," Anne confessed with a grin. "I am absolutely attempting a bribe, which we'll get back to in a sec. I am also asking you, as my best friend, to please come with me."

"Why is this so important to you?"

"I'd like you there to help me maintain my professional distance."

*"Pfft,"* Keira scoffed. "Professional distance. When have you ever needed help with that? Besides, you already know this guy, right? You talked to him last night."

"Okay," Anne said and inhaled a deep

breath. "Here's the thing—you were right. What I said about athletes requiring an extra level of knowledge and a certain amount of specialization is all true. But the real reason I made that rule is called Derrick Bright."

Keira settled into her seat, waiting for her to expound.

"We used to date, and then he broke my heart, making me biased against all athletes. Irrational? Yes, but it made sense to me at the time."

"I knew it! I knew there was something." Keira looked up thoughtfully for a split second before snapping her fingers. "The Bright Rule, can we call it that?"

"No," she said with a chuckle. "We cannot." Just confessing this to Keira lightened her spirits. "Listen, I need to be both the Tin Man and the Lion today, and I don't think I can do that alone. I need you, oh great Wizard, to help me. Plus, I'd like your objective opinion on Easton. I haven't been around him since he was a kid. He was the cutest little guy, and I adored him. Meaning, I don't know if I can be objective. So, in addition to pie and an all-expenses-paid night at my brother's beach house, I'll throw in a day at Nebula." Nebula was their favorite day spa.

"Well, then." Keira grinned and flipped her glasses back into place on her nose. "Since you're finally calling me by my proper title, then, yes, I will go. Two conditions." She held up her thumb and index finger and ticked them off. "You come with me to the spa, *and* you tell me everything about you and Bright. No, three conditions." She added a finger. "I want two pies because I can never decide between apple and peach."

"Deal. Now get dressed. I'll be down to get you in an hour, and I'll give you the whole unfortunate history on the way."

"You know I was faking that ditzy, sleepy, reluctant bit so you'd come clean, right?"

"Keira!"

"Hey, I saw you with him last night. And the fact that you're knocking on my door at eight o'clock in the morning and asking me to come with you shouts romantic intrigue."

"No, no," she denied. "There is no romantic intrigue here. This is me helping out an ex-boyfriend. No, it's not even that. It's me helping the younger brother of an ex-boyfriend."

"ANNE!" EASTON CRIED later that morning, throwing his arms around her and holding on tight. When he stepped back, his smile was as cheerful as she remembered, but his eyes were shimmering with emotion. "Wow! It's been way, *way* too long. I am so happy to see you. I wish it weren't under these crazy circumstances. But thank you for coming."

Well. So much for the notion that Easton wouldn't remember her. Anne couldn't bring herself to point out how his brother had bid an exorbitant sum for this meeting, so she'd essentially had no choice.

All the way here in the car, she'd relayed the whole pathetic story to Keira, answered questions about her and Derrick's relationship, including memories of his family, especially Easton. At the same time, she'd warned herself about getting emotional at the sight of him. He was no longer a kid. He'd had a lot of years to change and to get into all kinds of trouble. Some of which, despite how Derrick claimed to be tapped in to Easton's life, his older brother might be unaware of. Did Derrick even know who Easton's girlfriend was?

But if this greeting wasn't sincere, Easton was one of the finest actors she'd ever met.

And she'd met a lot of those, professional and amateur alike, and considered herself very good at discerning sincerity. The problem was she couldn't trust herself in this case. Hence, Keira. If anyone could ferret out the truth of Easton's core, it was her.

Over his shoulder, she glanced at her friend, who'd gone wide-eyed. *Wow*, she mouthed.

"Easton," Anne said, "I'm really happy to see you, too. It has been a long time." She meant every word. This initial greeting didn't require any acting on her part.

She'd seen Easton on the ball field, of course, but this was different. She took a moment to note all the changes. He'd always resembled his brother. Similar smile and the same wide, expressive brown eyes, although Easton's were lighter and shot through with gold flecks. His hair was almost as dark as Derrick's, but his curls were reminiscent of Grandma May's. The shape of his face was where the brothers differed the most. Easton had a rounder, softer jawline in contrast to Derrick's square dimpled chin.

All in all, standing before her with his hands shoved into his pockets, a crooked smile on his face, he seemed like a taller, muscled version of that eight-year-old kid she'd adored. And just that fast, Anne felt her heart begin to soften inside her chest. But not, she told herself, her resolve.

Keira stepped forward, and Anne introduced them. "This is my friend and colleague, Keira Chkalov. Keira, Easton Bright."

The two shook hands. Keira joked about how Anne had forgotten the code to the gate, which Derrick had texted her the previous evening. "And the numbers are her birthday."

"Out of order!" Anne cried in her defense. "And I only looked at them once." Truthfully, she'd been flustered with nerves, although now that they were here, the butterflies were calming slightly.

Easton laughed. While they were all chatting, Grandma May had emerged from the house and now descended the broad porch steps. Anne was thrilled to note how she looked the same. No, she looked better. Fit and spry with even more of a twinkle in her eyes, if that was possible.

Anne ventured forward to greet her, and May pulled her in for a quick, tight embrace. "It's been a while, Annie," she said, releasing her and stepping back. "It's so *good* to see you again. Beautiful as ever. I hope you've been well."

"Thank you, May. I have. It's wonderful to see you, too. You look incredible!"

"Don't I?" she agreed enthusiastically. "Doing my best to stay fit and keep sharp." Lifting one hand, she tapped a finger to her temple and turned toward the house. Anne followed her lead, and May draped an arm around her shoulders. "The quiche just went into the oven. There's a pot of coffee percolating, and Easton made fresh-pressed apple juice."

"Fresh-pressed apple juice?" Keira repeated. "Apples are my favorite. Anne has promised me an apple pie from that farm stand down the road. Do you know the one I mean?"

"Oh, we know it very well," Grandma said. "It's wonderful. Easton sells his eggs and honey there."

"I'm sorry," Keira fired back quickly, "he does what with his eggs and whatty?"

May chuckled and explained, "Easton keeps chickens and bees. He sells or trades his surplus at the market."

They were almost to the porch when a deep voice sounded loudly from above. "Hey!"

They all looked up. A startled Keira jumped. "Oh, my goodness! Why is there a man on your roof?"

"THAT'S MY BROTHER, DERRICK," a grinning Easton explained to Keira.

"I see," she replied, one hand pressed to her chest.

"Hey, Derrick?" Easton called out in a wry tone. "This is Anne's friend, Keira. She wants to know why there's a man on our roof. Would you like to answer that, or should I?"

Derrick knew how ridiculous he looked, but at this point, it seemed futile to try and spin his way out of this embarrassing predicament. Best to embrace it.

"Hey, Keira!" He offered a friendly wave. "Nice to meet you. Hi, Anne."

"Hello, Derrick," Anne answered. Her amused, curious smile reminded him of old times, of the teasing, quick-to-laugh Anne. Stranding himself on the roof might be worth the humiliation if it alleviated some of her anger. He didn't relish the private conversation he expected they'd soon be having. And yet, he'd managed to get her here to the farm, hadn't he? He'd also taken steps to ensure she stayed. That part he wouldn't tell her about, though. Ever.

"Ladder tipped over," he explained with a sheepish shrug. "You want to help me out, Easton?"

"Sure!" Easton shouted and held out his arms. "On three. Ready? One... Two..."

The crowd burst into laughter.

Derrick chuckled, too. What else could he do?

"I told you not to use that ladder," Easton said. To his audience, he clarified, "The ladder is wobbly because one of its feet is broken. Derrick climbed up on the roof using a broken ladder because I secretly think he wants to break his other leg."

When Grandma and Easton had gone to the store for some last-minute items, Derrick decided he had just enough time to examine the chimney situation from above. He'd put a brick under the broken stabilizing foot. What he hadn't realized was how soft the ground beneath it was until too late. He'd seen Grandma and Easton come home, but at that point, he hadn't even realized the ladder had tipped over. Only when they were back inside the house, and he'd decided to come down, had he discovered his predicament.

The house was two stories with an attic, so alerting them proved tricky. He'd tried stomping, yelling and even tapping on the gutter. That had given him the idea to scale down the pipe. A worthy notion, except the roof was not only tall, but also steep, and in the end, he didn't trust the gutter to hold his weight. He'd been puzzling over the best way out of his dilemma when he'd seen Anne's car coming up the driveway. Of course, she was early, and for a moment, he'd panicked at the notion of looking like a fool.

But, then he'd gotten a bird's-eye view of Easton and Anne's reunion. She'd been much happier to see his brother than him. If she'd been questioning Easton's innocence before, his genuine, heartfelt greeting would surely help his cause. For a few seconds, Derrick wondered if he'd made the right decision by contacting Sally.

Grandma's earlier comment about his impulsiveness sprang to mind, contributing to his unease. But, even accounting for Anne's initial reaction to Easton, he couldn't predict what she would decide. Besides, it was too late. Things were already in motion.

"You're in trouble now," Easton said. "Grandma specifically asked you to wait until after breakfast to burn the house down."

Keira erupted with a delighted laugh.

Anne looked at Grandma May. "Do *you* know why he's up there?"

"Because he's a numbskull."

"Thanks, Grammy!" Derrick shouted. "Love you, too."

Grandma May sighed and shook her head. "I have half a mind to leave you up there." She and Easton exchanged considering looks.

Easton quickly explained to Anne and Keira about Derrick's plans to fix the chimney. And then, cupping his hands around his mouth, he yelled, "Which he should *not* be doing by himself. I told you I would help."

"I was just checking it out. Making a list of what we need from the hardware store."

Muttering, Grandma shook her head and resumed her trek to the porch, with Anne still tucked into her side.

"Grandma!" Derrick called. "Come on! Cut me a break here, will you? And Easton…"

Derrick hitched a thumb toward the back of the house. "Get me that ladder."

WHILE KEIRA HAD gotten ready that morning, Anne had scoured the news and social-media sites, compiling as many of the hard facts as she could find. There still had been no arrests, and the police were remaining tight-lipped about what the press was now calling the "NPU steroid scandal," even though the drugs confiscated weren't all technically steroids.

Using social-media posts, she'd compiled a timeline for the party, but she needed the details of Easton's attendance. How long had he been there? Whom had he spoken to? Her search had also uncovered a photo of Easton at the party.

He hadn't been the intended subject, but she'd spotted him in the background. Next to him was a girl whom Anne believed to be Easton's current love interest. If that individual was whom Anne suspected, then rumors were going to escalate. She was surprised they hadn't already.

During their drive, Keira had continued checking social media for any breaking news.

People were talking about it and speculating. Rumors were flying. Jack, bless him, had tweeted an eloquent statement of Panther support encouraging people to withhold judgment until all the facts were in, and #PantherPride had trended for a while.

Keira read comments aloud and declared that public opinion was pretty evenly split. A promising sign at this point because the mob mentality online could be powerful indeed. If they started calling for coaches to resign and kids to be suspended and kicked off the teams, things could get ugly in a hurry.

"So," Derrick said, joining them inside the house. "How about a quick tour before breakfast?"

Anne agreed. She needed to have a conversation with Derrick, but this would allow her to gather her thoughts while Keira got a read on Easton.

# CHAPTER SIX

As Easton led the way through the spacious farmhouse, Anne took in the details, analyzing, assessing. She could see Keira doing the same. The furniture consisted of beautifully made, well-loved antiques in a style Anne thought was primarily country French. Mixed as it was with an eclectic assortment of knickknacks, the decor felt sophisticated yet comfortable and pleasing to the eye.

Stepping outside was an absolute delight. The variety of sights and sounds and smells caught Anne off guard and temporarily delayed all thoughts of her earlier intent to have it out with Derrick.

Beside her, Keira whispered, "What in the world is this magical place?"

Anne's own gaze was sweeping here and there, as she tried to absorb the sheer beauty before her. "It's like a park or a garden or..."

"Paradise," Keira suggested with a tone of finality.

Derrick, Easton and Grandma May stood quietly nearby as if used to this kind of reaction.

Derrick said, "Grandma and Easton have done all of this."

"Derrick helped, too," Easton said.

"When he's home and not stuck on the roof," Grandma joked.

Crossing the patio, Easton proudly pointed off to their left. "Grandma's dahlias." Many of the deep green stalks stood as tall as six feet with vibrant, colorful blossoms gracing their tops. The blooms came in every shape and size imaginable, some as big as dinner plates.

The group set off across the thick green lawn. The sound of buzzing seemed inordinately loud, and Anne looked down to discover the stems interspersed with clover and tiny purple flowers she didn't recognize. Bees were mobbing the blossoms.

"Easton's bees," Derrick explained.

Keira looked at Easton. "You're an actual beekeeper?"

"Oh. Uh, yeah," he answered with a shy,

half shrug. "Back there." He pointed toward a large patch of fruit trees beyond the grass. "In the middle of the orchard are my hives. You can just see them between the apple and pear trees..."

Anne had no idea where he was pointing, but she could see where the grass gave way to a couple of dozen neatly pruned fruit trees. The scent of apples drifted pleasantly on the rapidly warming breeze.

Derrick said, "The orchard produces a steady supply of fruit all summer long—cherries, pears, plums, apples. Grandma and Easton freeze and can and dry the fruit. They make jams and pies and pickled stuff. Easton bakes. He's pretty much perfected this pastry-pie thing called a galette. I can't tell you the ingredients because I don't want to know them. Mostly because, aside from apples, I'm sure that none of them are on my trainer-approved list of foods for him. What I can tell you is that the crust is light and flaky, and when I was on the road, I would sometimes dream about it."

They all chuckled. Easton said, "The secret is cold butter and fresh apples."

"Uh-huh," Keira agreed with a touch of

sarcasm in her tone. "I'm sure that's all there is to it."

Derrick had been slowly moving forward and now stopped and turned to face them. "In addition to beekeeper, he's a gardener, farmer and chef." He made a dramatic show of sweeping both arms to one side. "Vegetables here." Lush greenery and vines overflowed into a series of raised garden beds. "Berry patch there." He pointed to the other side. "Blueberries, raspberries, marionberries and strawberries."

"Grandma and I do it together," Easton clarified.

Beyond the yard, near the fence line in a spacious pen, chickens strolled around, clucking quietly, and occasionally pecking the ground.

"Chickens!" Keira exclaimed. "How cute."

"Affectionately referred to as 'the girls.' Easton built the state-of-the-art chicken mansion, too. Five years ago, when we bought this place, it was a wreck. The trees had gone unpruned for years. This was a weed patch." Derrick indicated the ground beneath his feet. "He and Grandma put in the lawn, made the garden beds. They do the maintenance, the gardening and—" he paused to bring both arms up and out "—everything else."

Keira was staring at Easton with open admiration. Anne thought he might be blushing.

"Can I meet them?" Keira asked.

"The girls?" Easton exclaimed excitedly. "For sure. Come on."

"What do you think?" Keira said to Anne. "You want to say thank you to these ladies for providing the raw materials for the quiche we're about to consume?"

Anne chuckled. "You two go ahead. We'll catch up. I'm just going to have a quick word with Derrick."

Chatting like old friends, Easton and Keira took off toward the chicken yard. Grandma excused herself to check on breakfast.

As soon as they were out of earshot, Anne said, "Impressive."

"I know," Derrick replied. His gaze captured hers and held on tight. "This is what I was trying to tell you last night. Why I wanted you to meet with him, what I wanted you to see. *This* is Easton's life. This place says everything about him."

"He only 'eats clean,'" he said, adding air quotes. "A lot of organic. Ideally, what he and Grandma grow or buy locally. He trades honey and berries for grass-fed beef and venison. He's been a model student at NPU and maintains a three-point-eight GPA. He volunteers, hangs out with Grandma and her friends, meditates and reads, and plays chess. He's about way more than baseball.

"There's even more I could tell you, but bottom line, the kid does not, has never, *would* never, use steroids or performance-enhancing drugs of any type. I can—"

"Derrick, stop. You didn't let me finish. As impressed as I am about all of this, I know what you're doing, and I don't appreciate how you're trying to manipulate me."

"I'M SORRY," DERRICK blurted on a renewed sense of desperation. There was no point in denying the obvious.

It didn't surprise him that Anne had seen through his ruse to get her here. The surprise was that it hadn't worked better. He'd genuinely believed if she saw Easton, got a glimpse of him here in his element, heard about his life and accomplishments, she'd waver. Then, once Sally released the information from her anonymous source, the choice would seem, if not easy, then certainly not as difficult.

That was some severely roundabout logic he silently acknowledged. Possibly, he'd miscalculated. Raking a hand through his hair, he snuck a glance her way and attempted to gauge her level of irritation. Was it his imagination, or did he detect a trace of sympathy there? Likely the apology had helped. Honesty, he realized, or at least as much of it as he could spare, might be the most effective tool of persuasion of all.

Burying his hands in his pockets, he looked her in the eye. "I am sorry, Anne. Truly, I am. I should not have gone to these lengths to get you here. Just so you know, I didn't go to the auction planning to win your consultation. I was anxious and frustrated. And when you wouldn't listen, I thought—"

"Derrick, I did listen!" she interrupted. "And I get it. What I forgot is how single-minded you can be."

"What does that mean?"

"It means that when you want something, you'll do whatever it takes to get it. You're impatient, and you don't always think about the consequences before you act."

Those words were all too much of an echo of his own earlier misgivings, not to mention Grandma's proclamation, variations of which he'd heard from her a million times. But how else did he get what he wanted if he didn't go for it? And he'd be a fool not to use *all* the tools at his disposal, right?

"I prefer to think of it as problem-solving. I needed your time and attention. I saw an opportunity, and I took it. It's like getting a hit in baseball. You can't *plan* to get a hit, but you do have to swing at the right pitch when it comes along. It's a split-second decision. As for being impatient, yes! Time is of the essence here, Anne. I needed you to hear me, to believe me, and I knew the best route to doing that was to get you here."

Lifting both hands, she tossed them up as if throwing around her own frustration. "I believe you are sincere in your intentions. I can see you are certain about Easton's innocence. But you cannot force me to—" She halted abruptly, then inhaled a deep breath and held it for a few seconds before slowly exhaling and starting over. "I understand your concern and your urgency. Both are valid. I've learned some rather concerning details myself, which we'll discuss in a moment. I even understand the Hail Mary you performed to get me here. As irritated as I was, *am* still, I get it. You want someone you can trust, and you think that person is me.

"Seeing this place, hearing about Easton's life, breakfast with Grandma May? Excellent strategy. You learned very well from your own experience with me. This will all be good for Easton, for his image, if not his innocence. And whichever PR firm you hire will surely use it. His attorney, too, if it comes to that. None of this alters the following points that a, I'm not going to represent him, and b, he's got a crisis on his hands that a dozen fresh eggs and a pot of honey are not going to fix."

Harsh words. But impressive, too. It wasn't that Derrick had forgotten what a brilliant mind she had or how articulate she was, but seeing her in action reminded him of how much he'd respected her abilities and her opinion. The notion assuaged his guilt and boosted his determination. He needed her to agree to help his brother. For Easton's sake.

"Anne, I am asking you to do this for him, for Easton. I'll pay whatever you ask. The auction last night was my easy out of getting you here. I don't intend for it to cover your fee."

"Don't insult me on top of everything else. This isn't a negotiation. It's not about the money, Derrick, although you likely cost me a huge account with your impulsive bid. But that's beside the point. I already told you, just like I told Coach Nichols, McGrath PR doesn't represent athletes."

He should have known better than to go with the money incentive. "Why would you even have such a policy?"

She explained, but her speech sounded contrived and rehearsed, and he quickly countered, "You have plenty of baseball knowledge. And connections. Kellan told me you represent Jack Derry, a friend of his and one of the Panthers' biggest supporters. Plus, you own the company. Can't you make an exception?"

"Jack isn't an athlete. Unless you consider ax throwing a sport. But, yes, I do own the company, which means I make the rules, and I don't have to explain them to you. Final word—" she paused and looked deeply into his eyes as if to make sure he was listening

"—I am not going to represent Easton, but I will follow through with this consultation.

"I will talk to him. Give him some advice. Keira will coach him on a few points, too. She's an expert with image and social-media response. The package you won includes a few other items, and I'll make sure it's worthwhile.

"Upon Easton's agreement, I will call Beverly Frankel at Mitchell West and personally ask her to represent Easton. She works with several pro athletes and has proven incredibly successful. In the meantime, I hope you called your attorney."

"What? Why?" How had she turned this conversation around on him so quickly?

"As I mentioned, I did some research of my own, and Easton is in this much deeper than you've revealed. There are details that you either don't know or haven't yet told me."

"Now you're scaring me. What are you talking about?"

She took out her phone and pulled up the photo she'd found from the party. "Do you recognize this young lady?"

As Derrick studied the image, she explained, "I found it scrolling through one of the partygoers' albums on Facebook."

The image was of five smiling students, arms around one another, red plastic cups in hands, mugging for the photographer. One guy was eating a taco. "Who am I looking at?"

"The couple in the background. Enlarge it."

He did. The pair were standing close together. She had her arms crossed. He was scowling, hands tucked into his back pockets—definitely Easton.

"I think that's Hailey."

"What is her relationship with Easton?"

"Not sure," Derrick said with a light shrug. "They just started dating. I've only met her briefly a couple of times. He hasn't talked about her much. I know she runs on the track team. He did mention they argued that night. I figured if they were arguing already, they aren't going to last long."

"You don't know who she is, do you?"

"Both the nature and tone of your question tells me that I do not," he answered smoothly, even as dread inexplicably pooled in his gut.

"Her name is Hailey Greenwich-Legion."

"Should I know that name?"

"She's Celia Greenwich's daughter."

"Celia Greenwich? You mean...?" Derrick trailed off, not even wanting to say the words aloud.

"President of the university, yes," Anne confirmed, the information suddenly making her demeanor clear. And the problem so much worse.

"No, I didn't know."

"That's not all," she said, sending Derrick's already rocketing blood pressure to new heights. "Have you called your attorney?"

"Not yet. I was hoping this—"

"You need to call him. I'm assuming you didn't know Hailey was accused of blood doping last year, along with some of her track teammates."

"No."

"She lawyered up. Two teammates were arrested and suspended. They swore she did it, too. She denied it. In the end, they couldn't prove anything. It appears Celia used her influence to keep it quiet."

"What does this have to do with Easton?" he asked, even though he knew it couldn't be good.

"Maybe nothing. Maybe…a lot? Either way, you need to be prepared."

KEIRA AND EASTON had gone inside while Anne and Derrick were talking.

"We better get in there," Derrick said. "Grandma is old-school about being late to the table."

Anne agreed, and they started for the house. To break the awkward silence, she said, "So you're finally going to get your fireplace, huh?"

They walked in silence for a few steps before Derrick said, "You actually remember that?"

"Of course, I remember. You used to talk about how you wanted to sign with Colorado or Minnesota, someplace with cold winters so you could cuddle by the fire. Christmas stockings hanging from the mantel, hot chocolate and your family gathered around."

*And me*, she added silently. *You also implied you wanted me to be there, too, remember?* Embarrassing how much she'd loved those little hints that he'd wanted a future with her. How once she'd wanted "that," too. With him.

His chuckle was almost scofflike. "That part of my life did not go as planned, either."

What was that supposed to mean? What part of his life? With the possible exception of an earlier-than-anticipated retirement, the rest had gone exactly as he'd wanted. She should know; he'd told her his plans many times.

"Yeah, must have been a hardship lounging on the beach in Florida instead," she joked.

They'd just walked inside when Anne's phone chirped with a text from Keira:

Initial assessment, this kid is both innocent and a grand-slam home run of a human being. (See what I did there? Baseball is my new favorite sport.) I'd bet my spa day and one pie on it. Just kidding, I'd bet both pies. Are you POSITIVE we can't help him?

Ugh. She'd been counting on Keira to help her stay strong.

Anne tapped out a response:

Bev at MW will help him!

Not like we can. There's a reason you left that place, remember?

There was, and it was simple. A degree of wayward behavior went with the territory in the public-relations business, but there was a line Anne wouldn't cross. She didn't tolerate lying or reprehensible conduct from clients.

She tucked her phone into her pocket and continued into the dining room, where she took the empty seat across from Derrick. Fruit salad, biscuits and sausages were already on the table, along with some smaller dishes of what looked like butter, jams and honey. Grandma May came in with the quiche and set it in the middle of the table. The smells of bacon and butter and cheese wafted deliciously from the steaming casserole.

"Back in a jiffy," she said and dashed into the kitchen.

Easton emerged next with a large platter laden with an unmistakable sight.

"Are those waffles?" Anne asked, her insides now officially turned to mush.

"Chocolate-chip," he confirmed proudly,

his smile a little shy. "I hope you still like them."

Keira snorted out a laugh. "Like them? She eats the toaster kind almost every morning." After a beat, she added, "And sometimes for dinner, too."

Anne felt an unexpected sting of tears. The good kind, though. The type that suggested she'd made an impact on him, too. "Easton, thank you so much. I don't think I've had the homemade kind since we made them together. I can't believe you remembered."

Beaming, he set the platter on the table and then placed a small dish of syrup in front of her. "I also remember how you like to dip yours in real maple syrup."

"Oh no…" Keira whispered, looking down at her phone.

"What is it?" Anne asked, alarmed by her tone.

"I was just running one more check before we dug in to our breakfast here. *The Portland Chronicle* just published a new story on their site."

"About Hailey?"

"Nope, although the first post about her and Easton also went up on Facebook a few minutes ago. It mentions the blood doping, too."

"Blood doping? And what about Hailey and me?" Easton asked, sounding confused. Was it possible he didn't know about her past allegations?

"No," Keira answered Anne. "The article is about us. Well, you, mostly." To Easton, she said, "We'll get to Hailey in a minute."

Then she read from her phone. "'Amid the continually evolving NPU athletics performance-enhancing-drug scandal, an anonymous source has revealed that MVP baseball player Easton Bright has consulted with McGrath PR and will be retaining their services. The same source has revealed public-relations hotshot Anne McGrath, owner of McGrath PR, was responsible for polishing the image of Bright's older brother, Derrick Bright, recently retired catcher and mega-hitter for the Florida Knights. In a story published eleven years ago, Bright even credited McGrath with helping him land the contract of his dreams.'"

Keira looked up. "It goes on to cite a lovely quote from Derrick about how instrumental you were in his last year at NPU."

Anne felt the anxiety tighten like a cinch around her chest. How was she going to extricate herself from this? Derrick was right; her excuse about not representing athletes sounded completely lame in light of a story about their previous working relationship, not to mention her involvement in the Panther Project. Plus, anyone who knew her even remotely was aware of how much she loved baseball. She needed to get out now.

In the kitchen, Grandma May could be heard asking someone for their name. Anne hoped it was a spam call and not a request for comment. She hadn't yet instructed her not to talk to anyone and hoped that Derrick had.

Anne said, "We'll have to issue a statement explaining about the auction, saying I agreed to an initial consult as an old friend. Tomorrow, or the day after, we'll quietly pass it off to Mitchell West."

"Pass what off?" Easton asked. Before her, the giant stack of waffles teetered like a tower of shame. "Anne, are you talking about me? You're not going to help?" He looked not only stricken by the thought, but also sad, and Anne felt like the biggest jerk in the universe.

"Old *friend* is going to be tricky to sell," Keira said with a deliberate look at Anne.

Anne felt herself scowling. "What do you mean? Why?"

"There's a photo of you two—" she pointed between her and Derrick "—kissing. Along with a paragraph about your past relationship and how close you were. This anonymous source, 'close to the Bright family,' is quoted here again. 'Anne is an old friend. I know Anne. Her integrity is above reproach. If she isn't working with Easton, then you can be certain she believes he's guilty.'"

Like a blow, the statement stole her breath. "Who would say that?" she wheezed.

As if the situation couldn't get worse, Grandma May hurried in from the kitchen holding her phone. "There are a bunch of reporters at the gate."

"What?" Derrick and Easton said at the same time.

"Who?" Anne and Keira asked.

"The one who buzzed in said her name was Sally Cabot from *The Portland Chronicle*. She's asking to speak to Easton and Derrick."

"Sally Cabot," Anne repeated, groaning inwardly. The animosity between her and Sally went back years. She needed to get ahead of this. Despite her rules and her anger toward Derrick, she knew she couldn't abandon Easton now.

She looked at Derrick. "Will you please make that phone call we were discussing?"

"Yes," he said, standing, already tapping on his phone.

She turned toward Grandma May. "May, can you go around and lower all the blinds and try to stay out of sight? I know they're camped at the end of the driveway and can't get through the gate, but there are phenomenal camera lenses out there these days. And I do not trust Sally Cabot."

"On it," May said, springing from her seat.

"Keira, what do you think about conferring with Easton and writing a short statement? We'll figure out how to deliver it later."

"Definitely," she agreed, her smile as bright as the sun because these instructions were all Keira needed to know what Anne had decided.

"What sort of statement?" Easton asked.

"Don't worry," Keira said, patting his shoulder. "It will be one of those, 'I want you all to know I am anxious to answer your questions. I have important things to say, and I plan to say them soon, et cetera.' But because of your crack PR team—" she paused to wink at him "—you really won't be saying anything at all. But you will have *said something*, and that's the key."

"Precisely," Anne agreed, making it clear to them all that she and Keira were now that team.

Easton got the message, and the mix of relief and gratitude on his face told Anne she'd made the right decision.

Derrick came in from the kitchen, where he'd been talking on the phone, presumably to his attorney.

Once May reappeared and resumed her seat at the head of the table, Derrick asked, "What now?"

"Now," Anne declared, "let's dig in to this breakfast before it gets any colder. We have a lot to discuss and a strategy to plan."

# CHAPTER SEVEN

EASTON DRIZZLED A large scoop of honey into his tea. Of course, he was a tea drinker, as if he needed another way to win over Keira.

Anne had just finished asking him about Hailey.

He said, "I knew Hailey's mom was president of the university, but I don't know anything about this blood-doping thing. We're just getting to know each other. We've only gone out a few times."

Anne swirled another delicious bite of waffle in the thick maple syrup. "Derrick mentioned you two had an argument the night of the party?"

"Yeah. I didn't want to go to the party at all."

"Why is that?"

"I don't know how much Derrick told you about my, uh, teenaged rebellion, I guess you could call it?"

"He mentioned it, but I'd like to hear the details from you. Don't leave anything out."

"Okay." Easton slowly stirred his tea, the spoon clinking rhythmically against the mug as if he was trying to decide where to begin. "After our dad died, during my freshman and sophomore years of high school, I was sad. And angry, although I couldn't see that until later. Terrible grades, getting into trouble at school, suspended for skipping class…"

He went on. Anne listened and was reminded about the deaths of her brother and sister-in-law, which had occurred in relatively quick succession, a stroke and a car accident, respectively. Her compassion for grief-ridden behavior was infinite. As a grieving adult, she'd done some odd things herself. So had her brother, Rhys. She couldn't begin to imagine how a child dealt with the death of a parent, especially when the remaining parent was emotionally absent and, presumably, trying to cope, too.

Easton was thorough, outlining a laundry list of infractions. They ranged from relatively harmless pranks like sneaking into the school at night and "relocating" every item in the hated English teacher's classroom to the gymnasium, to increasingly more serious transgressions like stealing hood ornaments and tagging alley walls.

"Sophomore year, I got busted at a party and charged with being a minor in possession of alcohol. It was stupid. But kind of rock bottom, too. Right after that, Mom took the job in Maryland, and I moved in here with Grandma. Derrick flew home and had this long talk with me, pointed out all the ways I was messing up my future. He found me a therapist, which helped a ton. I started going to yoga with Grandma, and to church. Meanwhile, we started working on this place. I got the chickens and bees, and all of these things gave me a new perspective.

"There was suddenly all this meaning to my life that helped me to get my act together. Knowing how much Derrick and Grandma cared about me and believed in me, I didn't want to let them down. I didn't want to let myself down anymore.

"So now, as a rule, I don't go to parties or anywhere where there might be alcohol or drugs. I don't drink, or smoke weed, or even use CBD or anything like it. I'm constantly aware that after my past behavior, even being seen at a party could make me guilty by association or whatever. Besides, it's just not an atmosphere I'm comfortable with anymore. I'd rather be productive with my time—you know what I mean? There's always something to do around here, and it's an awesome feeling to be needed."

Anne assured him she did know even as she silently vowed to cut back on her Netflix binging. Derrick was absolutely spot-on about the effect Easton had on people. The Bright Effect. *That* they could use. Or even The Bright Side? She made a mental note to call a reporter she did trust, one who might want to do a human-interest story on Easton.

Easton buttered another waffle and went on. "But this party was at my buddy Gavin's, at his parents' house. Gavin is on the baseball team, too, plays third base. We've been playing ball together, or against each other, since we were like six years old. He still lives with his parents, and their place isn't all that far from here. It's on my way to school, so we commute together a lot. Anyway, it wasn't supposed to be a party, per se, so much as a gathering of NPU athletes. From all the different sports. But I didn't trust it would stay that way—you know what I mean?"

At Anne's nod, he continued. "Hailey really wanted to go. I didn't. We argued about it because she wanted me to go with her because I was the one who knew Gavin. Finally, I told her I'd drop her off, but I wasn't staying. Once we got there, I asked Gavin to watch out for her, but it turned out there were a bunch of people she knew—other kids from the track and swim teams. Tons of people I knew, too. So I made sure she had a ride home, said hi to a few friends along the way and left. Seriously, I was there for like ten or fifteen minutes tops.

"Later, Gavin texted to tell me the cops had shown up, but I didn't see the message until the next morning."

"When was this?"

"He texted at about one in the morning. Gavin and Hailey both messaged me at about that time. When I got up at five thirty, I read their messages but didn't respond because I knew they'd both still be crashed. I always turn my phone off at night." He paused to wince a bit as if they'd judge him harshly for this possible transgression. "I need my sleep. It's way underrated as far as staying healthy goes.

"Anyway, I felt bad for Gavin, but honestly, I remember thinking how happy I was that I hadn't been there. But then Grandma's friend Grace sent her a screenshot of an Instagram post, a photo taken at the party. I was tagged in it. Exactly why I didn't want to go." Easton lifted his arms in a palms-up shrug of frustration. "People should have to ask permission to take your photo."

"A nineteen-year-old who turns his phone off at night," Keira chimed in. "How refreshing."

Easton managed a small smile. "I have to take care of the girls before I leave in the morning. I like to have tea with Grandma, or work in the garden or do some baking. Sometimes, I'll go for a run."

"What did Gavin say?" Anne asked, steering him back on course.

"I called him after Grandma showed me the Instagram post. He said the party wasn't wild at all, which Hailey confirmed. I believe them because there were athletes from a lot of different sports there. And, like me, a lot of athletes don't drink alcohol or do drugs, but some of them will still go to parties to hang out and stuff. Anyway, Gavin said the cops showed up because they got a tip drugs were being used."

"Is that true?"

"Gavin said not that he knows about. Hailey didn't see anybody using. As far as I know, besides the PEDs, the police didn't find anything other than a minimal amount of marijuana, which was all legal. Or, at least, it was legally purchased. Might have been some underage smoking, but no one was arrested for it. Gavin said all the weed smoking was done outside, like way, *way* outside, behind the pool house. And I can confirm that this was likely the case. Gavin doesn't smoke, but his older brother, Gray, does. Their mom despises the stuff. They're always joking about how she is like a drug-sniffing dog who can smell it in trace amounts. Gray thinks the neighbor got a whiff of that going on behind the fence and made assumptions. He's complained about Gray's smoking back there before."

The story sounded plausible to Anne, with just enough detail thrown in to be convincing.

"Gavin was talking to the cops on the

porch. Said everything was fine, and they were about ready to leave, but then some underage girls walked around the side of the house. Gavin didn't know who they were, but they were obviously drunk. Police talked to them, and they admitted they'd been drinking—said they got the alcohol inside the house from some 'college guys.' That's what prompted the cops to search, and they found the PEDs."

"Do you know what it was?"

"All Gavin said was illegal stuff, packaged to sell, inside two duffel bags he'd never seen before. No one fessed up or ratted anyone out."

Anne knew that PEDs, or performance-enhancing drugs, were a problem in nearly every sport. Testing for them was a regular part of athletics now, at both the collegiate and professional levels. But different substances were synthesized in the body at different rates. They didn't stay in the system forever, and some could only be detected for a very short time. Not to mention, the types of drugs and methods of consumption were constantly evolving. It was a challenge for authorities, and law enforcement, to stay ahead of the technology. Not to mention the logistics and expense of consistently testing so many athletes.

"Do the police think the PEDs were Gavin's?"

"I don't know." Easton shook his head. "They didn't arrest him."

"You don't believe they were his?"

"Nope. No way. He doesn't do drugs, either. He drinks a little, but we've talked about the risks a lot. He's hoping to get drafted after his senior year and wouldn't do anything to jeopardize his chances."

Anne wondered why the police hadn't arrested Gavin. There was obviously more to this story than Easton knew, or he wasn't saying. She desperately hoped it wasn't the second possibility.

May got up, retrieved the tablet from where she'd placed it on the buffet, resumed sitting and rechecked the cameras.

Keira, who'd risen to refill her mug, moved to stand behind her. "Still there?"

"Yep." May sighed and lifted the screen so Keira could see. "More of them now."

"How long do you think they're going to be here?" Easton asked.

"Until you give them something," Keira answered. "You or Derrick."

"You mean like go out there and talk to them?" Easton's expression reflected terror at the thought. "You want me to give some statement, right? I'll do it! I'll just say I'm innocent because that's the truth. Aren't you always supposed to tell the truth in these situations? The truth will out, right?"

"Not necessarily. They would love it, of course," Keira said. "But you don't have to give the statement yourself. People make that mistake a lot, so we don't usually recommend it. They'll ask questions. It can be difficult not to answer. And at this point, you can't trust anyone not to twist your words around. Plus, the police will be watching."

"What if I leave?"

"They would love that even more. Filming you in your car pulling out of here would make the news. The problem is if you leave without saying anything, they will make you look guilty."

Easton shook his head. "I can't believe this."

Anne decided it was time to make him fully understand what he was facing. She didn't want him to say anything to anyone, not even harmless communication with friends, or Hailey. Especially not Hailey, who was destined to be chased by reporters, too. Virtually anything could be used against him if it landed in the wrong hands.

She explained, "I know, Easton. Unfortunately, you don't have to have done anything. They won't *say* you're guilty. They'll just talk about how you left your house without saying a word, how you refused to comment, they'll mention your friendship with Gavin, your relationship with Hailey. And how your brother is Derrick Bright. Then they'll recite your batting record and the phenomenal season you had this year. Questions will be posed to *experts*, like 'Could the nineteen-year-old have had some *help* with all those home runs?' Then they'll make sure to mention that you have a high-powered attorney retained by your superstar brother, and does that imply guilt?"

"So I'm trapped?" Easton reached around with one hand and gripped the back of his neck. "What about Grandma? This isn't fair to her." He looked at May. "Grandma, I'm sorry. I should never have shown my face at that party."

Anne exchanged a look with Keira, whose expression once again asked if this kid was for real.

May reached over and patted Easton's hand. "Stop that. I'm just fine. You know me, I'm ninja-tough. And so are you. I know you didn't have anything to do with this. I can handle anything except for you putting poison into your body."

"Speaking of poison," Anne said. "I think we should get you drug tested. That way, if the police do question you, your attorney can plop the results down in front of them and possibly head this whole thing off."

"Yes! Absolutely," Easton agreed. "Test me for everything."

There were a few clinics with in-house labs, where they occasionally sent clients for various types of testing. Public relations could be a peculiar business. They'd had clients tested for everything from cholesterol levels to drugs to pregnancy and toxins. Once, she'd discovered a client was being slowly poisoned by his wife. After a decline in his health and mental faculties, Anne had recommended a routine physical. The wife had been so resistant to getting the lab work done that Anne had had to sneak him out of his own house to get the test.

That's when she was struck with a stroke of brilliance, the kind of "inspired thinking," as Mitchell used to call it, that made her so very good at her job. She fired off a text to Jack and hoped he wasn't out rowing on the lake, where he always turned off his phone.

"Don't be too hard on yourself, Easton," Keira said. "The party was at your teammate and best friend's house, several other team-mates were there, as well as the young lady you've been dating. Between Hailey's mom being the university president, the blood-doping accusations against her, Derrick's fame, the incredible season you had and the draft talk, there'd be speculation about you eventually."

Easton groaned with frustration. "You're probably right." He dropped his head into his hands. "Man, Derrick, I don't know how you handle all of this."

Derrick said firmly, "Hey, listen, kiddo, you are not alone here." Easton lifted his head. "You know that one-day-at-a-time thing? Sometimes it's necessary to go smaller—one hour or even a few minutes at a time. We'll get you through this, Easton. That's what we do for each other, right? And I promise I will do whatever it takes to help you."

Anne couldn't help but admire Derrick's ferocity. She knew his loyalty to his family unit was genuine. He'd always loved them, cared for them, with this same steadfast devotion. Clearly, that had not changed. What would her life have been like if she would have been invited into this fold? If only he could have loved her like this, too?

Derrick softened her up further when he said, "Now we have Anne and Keira, too. You can take it from me. There is no one better for this job." He cast a grateful smile between her and her colleague.

Easton nodded.

May chimed in, "He's right. No one messes with my boys and gets away with it."

At that moment, Anne's gaze connected with Derrick's, and for a few seconds, they did that thing they used to do, the one where they communicated without speaking. She assured Derrick that she, too, would do whatever she could to get Easton through this mess. Her heart remembered how it was done, too, and responded with a series of familiar fluttery beats.

*Okay, Anne. Enough.* This was precisely what she'd feared, wasn't it? These unscheduled trips to Regretville and What-if Land. For about the hundredth time, she was grateful Keira was here to keep her grounded and focused.

Her phone vibrated with a text from Jack. A mix of affection and gratitude rushed through her as she read his response:

Heck yeah, I'll do it. I'd be honored. Text me the address and write my speech. #Panther-Pride

Looking around the table at the Bright family, she asked, "Is there another way out of here, by any chance? Besides the main driveway?"

"Yes," Easton and May answered at the same time.

Easton elaborated, "There's an old dirt-and-gravel logging road behind the orchard. It was built years ago by the previous landowner, who divided the property and sold half to our neighbor, Skip Miller, and half to Derrick. It crosses Skip's place and comes out at Hillshire Road. There's a gate, but it's not locked. I run back there all the time, and Skip gave me permission to ride my four-wheeler."

"So you can drive on it?"

"Sure. I mean, it's kind of overgrown and grassy this time of year, and there are some ruts. No problem for a pickup or SUV or a vehicle with high clearance."

"Perfect," Anne said, even better than the hike she'd anticipated. Then she told them her plan.

# CHAPTER EIGHT

JACK SHOWED UP less than an hour later. Anne had asked him to arrive looking as inconspicuous as possible, and he'd obliged. She felt certain no one in the press would immediately recognize him in the aviator shades and bucket hat he'd pulled low over his close-cropped brown hair. Blue jeans and a dark blue, short-sleeved button-down completed the ensemble. He looked handsome and fit and a good decade younger than his seventy-odd years.

By the time the press figured out who he was, he'd already be acting in his new capacity as the Bright family spokesperson and issuing the statement she and Keira had written.

Anne hugged him. "Jack, thank you so much," she said and then made introductions.

Turned out, he and Easton had met before, courtesy of Coach Nichols. "Hey, Mr. Derry,"

Easton said, shaking his hand. "Good to see you again, sir. I don't know how to thank you for this."

"It's my pleasure, son. I'm always game for a little intrigue, and there's nothing that pleases me more than thwarting the press. I've suffered the snowball effect of salacious storytelling myself a time or two. Thanks to Annie, I haven't gotten crushed by an avalanche yet."

"Jack Derry," May said, stepping forward. "I am thrilled to meet you. Big fan. I was so happy to see you take that Ginny the ninny to task. I'm getting tired of a world where there are no consequences for lies and bad behavior."

Jack granted her a roguish grin. "Why, thank you, Ms. Bright. It's a pleasure to meet you, as well."

"No popcorn for you!" she spouted gruffly.

Jack cracked up laughing and looked at Anne. "See? I told you that one would resonate with a certain crowd."

Anne gave him a good-natured eye roll but couldn't contain her smile. It was impossible not to feel good around Jack. He was just so...ebullient. Kind of like May, she realized, as she watched the two of them chatting in that way you do with a new friend you feel you've known forever. Sort of like she and Derrick when they'd first met. Surprisingly, it had been a book and not baseball that they'd bonded over.

The first day they'd met in her office at Mitchell West, he'd spotted the spy thriller she'd been reading on her desk and pulled the very same book from his bag. They'd both adored the characters, delighted in the plot twist, and after speculating about the ending, the conversation had turned to their favorite authors, several of which they'd shared. Anne still had her copy.

Anne and Keira huddled together and tweaked the final statement. Then she and Keira went over every word with Jack.

"You can take a few questions if you want," Anne said when they finished. "But don't answer them."

Jack belted out a laugh. "I know how to do that. I'll give them the old let-me-check-on-that-and-get-back-to-you spiel."

"Perfect," Anne said.

Then she looked at Derrick, Easton and May. "Road-trip time. You guys pack your bags while I alert the press that your family spokesperson will soon be saying a few words on your behalf. When Jack heads out to the gate, we'll slip out the back. May, is there a friend or neighbor you trust who could take care of the chickens and the garden while you're gone?"

"I'm staying," May declared. "I was thinking I could go out there with Jack? Stand beside him while he talks. We could present a united front. I can *not* answer a few questions, too, if that will help."

"That would be extraordinarily helpful," Anne said.

Easton appeared stressed by this revelation. "Grandma, are you sure?"

"Positive. I'd rather not leave this place abandoned. I'd like to get a jump on canning our green beans. Besides, once Jack announces that you guys aren't here, they'll leave, right?"

"That's what we're aiming for," Anne said. "Hopefully, the police will make an arrest soon, or something new will break and divert the attention elsewhere. In the meantime, we'll get Easton's drug test and prepare for whatever might happen next."

DERRICK HADN'T ANTICIPATED the guilt. Their "escape" had gone off without a hitch. The road was easily accessible and had come out right where Easton described. He kept telling himself he couldn't have known how Sally would expound on his anonymous tip. He certainly hadn't asked her to dredge up the stuff about his and Anne's past. The look on Anne's face when she realized she was… trapped was haunting him. What if she found out what he'd done?

He glanced over at Easton, who'd weathered the detour to the medical clinic with a tense yet stoic determination. And now, with every mile that passed, he seemed to relax more and more, which alleviated Derrick's own angst to a significant degree. The bottom line was that it had worked. That was the point, right? Yes, he'd gotten what he wanted, and he'd done it for Easton. So why couldn't he smooth this scratchy conscience?

His gaze traveled to the front seat, where Anne was driving, skillfully navigating her SUV along the quiet back roads, spiriting them away from the chaos. She was explaining how her brother, Rhys, his wife, Camile, and their niece, Willow, lived in a gorgeous, gated compound overlooking the ocean.

"Complete privacy and total peace," she assured Easton, glancing in the rearview mirror. "I promise you won't get bored."

Conversation flowed easily, and soon the Pacific Ocean began to appear in picturesque snippets between stretches of thick green forest. Derrick had been to Pacific Cove a few times over the years, but he hadn't known that Rhys lived there now. Back when he and Anne had dated, her parents and oldest brother, Evan, had resided in Portland. He'd spent time with them all, even baby Willow. But Rhys had been in the navy, so he'd only met him once.

"Remember the time you guys took me clam digging?" Easton asked.

"You mean when you cried because you learned we were going to eat the clams?" Derrick teased. "So we ended up *freeing* them in a weird little ceremony of your invention."

"So nice how you remember all the details," Easton returned dryly.

"It was three limits of clams," Derrick said. "Did I mention you shouted before each one?

'Free clammy!' I think you called before tossing them one by one back into the ocean."

A laughing Anne said, "And then, after you finally freed the last one, you announced you were starving and suggested we go out for cheeseburgers."

"At that point," Derrick said, "I so badly wanted to raise the issue of where ground beef comes from."

"Seriously, can't believe you didn't," Easton said. "What got in to you?"

Derrick shrugged a shoulder. "Well, I'm a thoughtful and conscientious big brother, that's all."

"Tell the truth!" Anne cried. "I begged you not to! I pleaded with him, Easton."

"Thank you, Anne," Easton said. "For allowing me to have my moment. I haven't been to the ocean in ages. Do you think it will be safe for me to go on the beach?"

Nice, how Easton was all in where Anne's strategy was concerned. And, Derrick silently admitted, his reaction to Anne's suggestion of a drug test had been a bit of a relief. Not that he didn't trust Easton, but it felt like one more brick in the defensive wall Anne was building. And one more reason not

to feel guilty about the way he'd comman-
deered Anne.

"Of course," she said. "Put on a hat—not
a Panther one, though, please. Now that I
think about it, let's all forgo our Panther and
NPU gear and baseball trappings in general.
Put on a pair of sunglasses and do your best
to ignore anyone who looks like they might
know you. We'll avoid the popular spots."

Keira peered at Anne. "Do you even own
a sweatshirt that doesn't have a Panther or
some other baseball-related thing on it?"

"Keira," Anne said in a comically prim
tone, "don't be silly. Of course, I do." She
paused. "I think I have two."

"Are either of them packed in your bag?"

"No," she confessed, "I'll have to borrow
something from Camile or Willow."

Everyone laughed. Derrick was pleased
how Anne's love for baseball hadn't faded
over time. If only her love for him had followed the same course. How many games
had he looked into the stands and experienced a spike of longing to see her there?
This was a consequence he hadn't fully considered, how spending time with her would
rekindle such vivid memories and feelings.

Her phone rang.

"It's Jack," she said, reminding him once again what had brought them back together and why. He needed to be careful about this reminiscing. He couldn't let his gratitude and respect for her turn into something more.

"TALK TO ME, JACK," Anne said, pulling off the road into a viewing area to answer the call. "How did it go?"

"Fantastic. No problems whatsoever. We recorded the whole thing like you suggested. May is emailing it to you right now."

"Perfect. Thank you."

"What did you do to that Sally Cabot, any-way? She seems to have it in for you."

"Sally and I go way back, and not in a good way. Remind me to tell you later when I have more time."

"Something personal, is it?"

"Unfortunately."

"You still on the road?"

"We are. I pulled over into an ocean over-look so I could take your call."

"Okay, I'll let you go. We'll talk later. I'm going to stick around here for a bit, can some beans, make sure none of those jackals double back to harass May."

"That is superthoughtful, Jack. I appreciate that so much, and I know Derrick and Easton will, too."

"And May, too, I hope," Jack said and then quickly added, "Not that she couldn't take care of herself."

"Very true," Anne agreed.

"She's, uh, quite a lady, isn't she?"

*Hmm.* "One of the best I've ever known."

"Good to know."

"Have fun. And thanks again, Jack."

"HEY!" EASTON SHOUTED A couple of hours later. "You can't just blast all my star shiners and leave me with nothing."

"You've got one left," Willow countered with a wicked grin. "Use your furnace jet…"

Anne had no idea about the meaning of the video-game lingo, but she was pleased with how Willow had so seamlessly made Easton feel at home. It buoyed her spirits to see him comfortable and stress-free.

"Thank you for taking us all in on such short notice," Anne said to her sister-in-law, Camile, who also had a knack for hosting.

After arriving, Rhys had proudly given the new guests a tour. It was fun for Anne to see Derrick and Easton's admiration for the incredible custom home Rhys had built with his own two hands. The property was unique, too, situated on a bluff high above the ocean, along with an old, historic lighthouse and cottage, both of which Rhys had painstakingly restored and meticulously maintained. There was even a World War II bunker located in the woods near the edge of the cliff.

Keira had been keeping up on the social-media buzz surrounding NPU athletics, and so far, the reaction to Jack and May's statement was highly favorable. Anne had watched the recording and was pleased to see the pair had pulled off a convincing simulation of closeness and camaraderie shared by old friends. She knew better than to believe it was over, but maybe the fallout would harmlessly brush by Easton after all.

Anne took a seat on a stool at the bar that separated the kitchen from the dining area. The open floor plan allowed her to see across the spacious great room to the TV, where Easton and Willow were camped. Derrick and Keira were outside on the deck with

Rhys, who was firing up the grill. Camile was in the kitchen prepping salmon fillets with some type of buttery herb sauce that already smelled delicious.

"Are you kidding?" she said, brushing the glaze onto the fish. "We're thrilled to have you—all of you."

Anne knew she meant it. Camile was one of the kindest people she'd ever known. Her sister-in-law co-owned a dance studio in Pacific Cove with her friend Harper. She'd fallen for Rhys when he'd hired her to teach him to dance for Willow's cotillion. The only thing Rhys was worse at than dancing was socializing. That Camile had managed to both teach him to waltz and charm him through dance was evidence of her sheer amazingness.

"Quick question, though," Camile said, stepping over to the counter. Leaning her elbows on the surface, she whispered, "You've never brought clients here before. What's going on? Rhys told me you and Derrick used to date? And how did I not know you once had a boyfriend who was a major-league-baseball player?" She tipped her head, gesturing toward the crowd outside. "Derrick

Bright is outside on our deck right now. My dad would… I don't even know what he will say when I tell him he stayed at our house."

Anne chuckled. "It was ages and ages ago," she said, waving it off as if it was nothing. "We were kids. He was still playing for NPU when we dated. That's how long ago it was."

"Huh."

Anne followed Camile's gaze to where Derrick was now leaning against the rail, chatting with Keira. Rhys had his cell phone pressed to his ear.

"Seems like a nice guy, though, huh?" she commented. "For such a superstar athlete, he seems so grounded and…normal."

"He is, he does," Anne agreed and realized how true it was. Watching Derrick with Easton and Grandma May had reminded her of so many of his good qualities—kindness, loyalty and generosity. She appreciated how he knew when to draw on his sense of humor to help Easton through this difficult challenge. Most impressive, though, was his unwavering belief and dedication to Easton. And to Grandma May.

He'd be such an incredible father. She wondered if, now that he was no longer married to baseball, he'd opt to have a family. A wife. She almost winced at the bite of jealousy that notion produced.

And Derrick seemed genuinely content to be here at Rhys and Camile's. Charming and courteous, he expressed his gratitude and appreciation at all the right moments. Both he and Easton were enthralled with the property, hanging on to every word Rhys relayed about the house, the construction process and the furniture he'd crafted to fill it. Easton couldn't get enough of the landscaping, noting how Rhys had used primarily native bushes, trees and flowers.

Derrick was a good guy. Both her latent bitterness from the past and her current auction irritation were dissipating, which was a relief. What was it her mom often said? "Untended anger, no matter how small, will forever fester in your heart." Possibly it was time to let it all go.

The problem, however, was that for true forgiveness to occur, they would have to talk a few things out. Talking would mean admitting to those long-ago feelings, confessing to just how badly he'd hurt her. Did she want to go there? What would be the point? Maybe she could just let part of it go and call it good.

Now that she thought about it, her dad was no slouch in the area of wise adages himself. One of his favorites was the old "let sleeping dogs lie." That could work. Ignore the past, complete this job for Easton and be done. Because once everything was resolved, she would go back to her life, Derrick would go back to his and it would likely be years before she saw him again, anyway. If ever.

Besides, she reassured herself, this weekend, they'd all be in pretty close quarters. How would she even find the time or place to broach such a personal topic? Not to mention, they needed to stay focused on Easton.

"Cute, too," Camile added, sliding her a brow-raised grin.

"He is," she agreed, because he was.

"Hmm," Camile drawled with a dreamy look on her face. "Any chance you two…"

"Nope. No," Anne said. "Don't even think about it, Camile."

"Got it," she said, but managed to look a little disappointed at the same time. "Which reminds me, are you still dating Todd?"

Todd! Oh, jeez, she hadn't thought about

him all day. He knew she was going to the beach, so it was likely he wouldn't have expected to hear from her. He was sailing. None of this was particularly unusual for them as they often went a day or two without conversing. Not generally on the weekends, however.

"Yes. Still dating Todd." She removed her phone from her pocket and fired off a quick checking-in text.

Keira came inside looking content and fashionably windswept. Rhys and Derrick followed, after which Rhys promptly announced, "Willow! Great news! Harper just called. We're on for tomorrow."

"Yes! Yay!" Willow shrieked excitedly. "We're going for a jet-boat ride tomorrow."

Rhys asked, "Anyone else want to join us?"

"I adore jet boats!" Keira repeated eagerly.

"Is this one of those rides where you feel like you're going to smash into rocks or crash at any second?" Easton asked.

"That's it!" Rhys said. "Tons of fun. We're hiking up to Ritter Falls after, too,"

"Supposed to be a gorgeous day," Camile said.

"That sounds awesome! I'd like to go,"

Easton said. "I mean, if there's room on the boat."

"Room for everybody," Rhys assured them all. "Our friend Harper is a photographer, and she's chartered the boat."

"I am so in!" Keira said.

*Jet-boat ride.* Anne couldn't help the laughter that came bubbling up and out. One look at Derrick, and she could almost see his stomach churning. His gaze collided with hers, and she placed a hand over her mouth to stifle her laughter, but it was way too late. Everyone was looking at her.

From across the room, Derrick delivered her a playful scowl. "It's nice how all these years later, you still get a kick out of that fiasco."

"Well, Derrick," she said in a voice thick with laughter, "in my defense, I've never seen anyone get sick on flat water."

"I think *flat* is a bit of an exaggeration," he countered, strolling in her direction.

"It is not! Even the captain of the boat thought you were joking, remember?"

Smiling eagerly, Easton asked, "What happened? Derrick, you got sick?"

"Your brother and I went for a jet-boat

ride once. It was not a positive experience for Derrick."

"He gets sick on amusement-park rides, too."

"It's an inner-ear problem," Derrick said, lifting a finger to point at one. "It's real." He looked at Rhys. "Once was enough for me, thank you, Rhys. I appreciate the invitation, but I'm going to pass. With my leg still wonky, I'm supposed to stay off the uneven ground, too, so a hike probably wouldn't be wise either."

"That's a bummer. But I understand. What about you, Anne?"

"Unfortunately, no. Client call in the morning. He's in London, and it's important. I really can't reschedule."

Derrick stood beside her now. Angling closer, he said quietly, "Looks like it's just you and me tomorrow." That made Anne's stomach churn, too, but in a decidedly different way. One that she both liked and didn't at the same time.

# CHAPTER NINE

THE ADVENTURE CREW was up before dawn.
Anne was both an early riser and a light
sleeper, and she enjoyed waking to sounds
of their hushed but excited chatter, going
over the schedule and lists of supplies. This
outing was just the thing Easton needed to
keep his mind off the chaos. She wondered if
Rhys had made this happen for just that purpose. Her brother was extremely considerate
in many ways. Once the house was silent and
she knew they'd departed, she climbed out of
bed to prepare for her client call.

Since she planned to take a run on the
beach later, she donned her running gear,
pulled back her hair and reviewed her notes.
Her client rang right on schedule and had
very few questions and concerns about the
documents Anne had sent. They ended the
call way ahead of schedule, leaving her with

virtually no follow-up tasks and the rest of the day at her disposal.

Coveted circumstances if it hadn't been for the other houseguest who'd remained behind. Nervous energy bundled inside of her as she contemplated an entire day alone with Derrick.

The truth was when they'd been a couple, there hadn't been many bad times. Virtually none that she could recall. Aside from the end, her memories were sweet. Because she'd spent so many years trying not to think about them, now they somehow felt fresh, too. She couldn't seem to stop the replay in her mind.

Staying busy would be key. That shouldn't be difficult as there were always tasks that needed attention. She began by making a list in her head. She'd been pondering a call to David Beyer, who wrote for *Just Say Sports*, one of the largest online sports news outlets in the country, to pitch that human-interest story about Easton. He lived in Seattle, which was an easy drive to Portland. Since it was a promo piece, it could run whenever, but it would be nice if Easton could be photographed at the farm. And soon, while the flowers were still in bloom and fruit was on the trees.

She could call Jack and see if anyone had contacted him, brainstorm some tweets and find out what gossip he'd heard from his connections at NPU. And she wanted to check in with May to see if the media crowd had thinned at the farm.

Enough stalling. She pulled open the bedroom door only to be met with a shockingly quiet house. Almost eerily silent. She wondered if Derrick was still sleeping. Checking the time, she found it was still early by most standards.

That's when it occurred to her. If she was lucky, and careful, she could sneak out of the house without seeing him at all. Yes! This was the answer to her dilemma. She'd drive into town, go for a run on the beach and then prowl around Pacific Cove for an hour or two. She could even call her friend Mia, a veterinarian in town, and maybe drop in for a visit.

Was it rude to leave Derrick here on his own? Without a car to drive, he'd be stuck. She took a few seconds to consider this. At the moment, escaping felt more important.

He was a big boy—she'd only be gone for a few hours, and it wasn't like she needed to entertain him. Besides, Easton was her client, not Derrick. With Easton safely under Keira's watch for the day, she had nothing to feel guilty about.

All excellent points, she assured herself. She'd leave Derrick a note, and if something important came up, he could call or text. She would even pick up some lunch on her way home as a sort of peace offering.

Encouraged by this impromptu plan, she slipped back inside the bedroom, put on her shoes, stuffed a bag with anything she might possibly need and then padded softly out into the hall. Pausing, she held her breath only to be met with… Blessed and absolute silence. She continued in stealth mode until, near the end of the hall, the floor creaked loudly beneath her feet. She froze, waiting and listening and feeling like a cat burglar.

After a few seconds of nothing, she continued into the great room. A quick sweeping look of the space revealed no sign of Derrick. Kitchen was still dark. No lights on anywhere. Also absent were the smell of fresh coffee, and sounds of running water, or footsteps. Confident now, she glided across the room and grabbed her keys from the side table.

She was reaching for the door handle when...

"Good morning!"

"Crikey!" she shrieked, jumping and turning in time to see Derrick pop up from where he'd been lying on the sofa. Dressed for the day in worn blue jeans and a T-shirt, he was holding a book in one hand, and he set it on the coffee table.

"Going somewhere?" he asked in a tone that suggested he knew her intentions.

A giant blast of heat burned through her. Like she'd been caught in the act of an actual burglary. How embarrassing.

"Whew!" she puffed, readjusting the bag on her shoulder. "You scared me."

"Sneaking out so I wouldn't see you?" His gaze skimmed over her. With her shoes on, bag stuffed and keys in hand, she couldn't exactly deny it.

"I was trying not to wake you," she said and knew how comical she sounded.

"How considerate," he gushed in a way that told her she'd been caught out. "But not necessary. I got up with the herd this morning. Camile left us coffee in the carafe. And your brother made muffins. How nice is that? This place is like a bed-and-breakfast."

"I, uh…" She was trying to work up a reason why she needed to leave, anyway, when Derrick spoke again.

"Rhys left you a note asking if you could let in a delivery guy in a couple of hours."

Accepting that her plan was now good and truly foiled, Anne trudged to the kitchen to fetch herself a cup of coffee.

"Don't think it's because you're some hotshot ballplayer that you're getting this consideration," she teased as she filled a cup. "They treat everyone this way."

"Don't worry about that," he said wryly. "I have no misconceptions about being special, especially where your brother is concerned. That guy's got *genuine* skills. Truly phenomenal, this place, this house, the yard…" He gestured toward the dining room. "That table." A few years ago, Rhys had crafted the dining table from a large maple tree that had fallen over on the property.

"Ah," Anne said with a nod. "Did he show you his workshop, too?" Her brother was an extremely talented craftsman. "Yeah, pretty sure there isn't anything Rhys couldn't make." He worked as an engineer designing prosthetic limbs, and in his spare time, he crafted all sorts of things out of wood, metal, glass, or whatever he pleased. His people skills, however, were not so refined. Camile was so very good for him in that regard.

"Yeah. Don't even get me started on the work he does for wounded veterans."

Rhys was also a former Navy SEAL and had started a charitable foundation called the Other Front Line, benefiting wounded veterans.

"I know. My brother is exceptional in many ways. Kind of like your brother."

"Right?" Derrick agreed. "This is where Easton is headed, isn't he? He's going to be this type of interesting and accomplished Renaissance man. I have no idea what I've been doing with my time."

"I know what you mean," Anne said and then chuckled. She joined him in the living room, taking a seat on the sofa next to Willow's cat, Alistair. "But I imagine baseball has taken up a fair amount of your days."

"That's pretty much it, though. That's all I can do, and now I can't even do that anymore. You were right about that much. Without baseball, I am nothing."

Ugh. So he did remember the email. Maybe it would be better to just get this over with, clear the air once and for all. Then she could truly move on.

"Derrick—"

"I know," he interrupted with a small smile. "I agreed that we weren't going to do this. But now that I can't play baseball anymore, I'm realizing how prophetic your words were all those years ago."

"Look, I don't remember everything I wrote in that email, but I do know I was harsh. I am sorry about that, about some of the things I wrote. But to be fair, I was very, very upset." She stretched one arm over her head. "Like over-the-top upset." There, she hadn't mentioned the *L* word, but that ought to get her point across.

He let out a snort of disbelief. "Not as *upset* as me, I'd wager."

"You're going to make me say it, aren't you?"

"What?"

"Derrick, you *broke my heart*. You act like you're completely innocent in what happened. Let's clear that up right now. I was devastated. You ruined everything."

"I didn't mean to, though! For me, that email came out of the blue. I thought we were getting back together. As far as I was concerned, we hadn't ever really broken up. I mean, I know I said some stuff about taking a break or whatever, but I didn't really want to. I was just...overwhelmed trying to figure out how we were going to juggle everything. My contract took me clear across the country. Your career was taking off. Dad was hounding me about staying focused. And it seemed like too much to ask for you to stick with me. I wanted us both to be sure, and when you didn't try and talk me out of it, I thought that's what you wanted, too."

Anne thought about this, and before she could respond, Derrick went on. "After I left, I regretted it. I told you that, and I—"

"Derrick," she interrupted because none of this changed the most crucial element. "You don't have to do this." But apparently, she did. She had no choice but to wake the grumpy, sleepy dog after all. "I saw you with *her*."

"Saw me with who? What her? What are you talking about?"

Anne placed her coffee on the end table, drew in a breath of courage and said, "The day before I wrote that email, I was in Florida. I came to see you."

"You were in Florida? When? Never mind. I got the email on February twenty-seventh, so it would have been the day before that, on the twenty-sixth."

He knew the exact date? Anne fidgeted in her seat. So much for the notion that he didn't remember all the details. But again, this was not her fault!

"Yep, I flew to Tampa to surprise you. I rented a car and drove to your house. When I got there, I saw you with another woman."

He scoffed, his denial now loud and clear. "Anne, that is not possible. I didn't even look at another woman when you were in my life—or after. I didn't date for more than a year after I got your email. Closer to two years, if I'm being honest. And even then, I didn't... Never mind. The point is, I was *not* with another woman."

Why was he doing this? His denial was making it worse. Frustration welled inside of her, giving undue force to her reply. "It was you, Derrick!" She paused to gather her patience. "You were kissing another woman. Maybe you don't remember. Possibly, you'd been drinking?"

"No. Nope. No way. I've never had more than one beer when I was in training. You knew that, and it never changed."

Anne wasn't sure what to say. She'd been prepared for anything but this blatant denial. Embarrassment, apologies, excuse-making, yes. She'd always imagined, if confronted, he'd opt for the she-didn't-mean-anything-to-me line. After the incident and the months went by, she'd taken it as proof when the curvy brunette was no longer around.

But he had, in fact, kissed her. The woman was unforgettable, and that had only made it worse.

"ANNE, WHY WOULD I lie about it now?" Derrick asked her, thinking back to that night.

The house he'd lived in then was a rental on the beach that he'd shared with two teammates, Buck Thane and Kevin "Goody" Osgood. He remembered the night well because it was Goody's birthday. He hadn't been in the mood for a party, but Goody's girlfriend, Zale, had gone to a lot of trouble planning the event. She was a sweetheart, and he hadn't wanted to be a killjoy.

He specifically remembered watching Goody and Zale with envy. They were so in love. Pining for Anne, he'd gone to his room and called her. When she didn't answer, he'd texted and then remained there, alternately checking his phone and reading a book while hoping for a response.

Eventually, he'd gotten hungry, and with the windows open, the scent of barbecue proved irresistible. Buck was a master with the grill, and he'd made chicken and ribs with his homemade sauce. Zale, with help from Goody's family, had provided potato salad, mac and cheese, baked beans, salads, cake— the works. Derrick had emerged to devour a plate of chicken, his favorite, and visit long enough so as not to appear rude.

Who else had been there? In addition to Goody's family, there were other guys from the team, their girlfriends, friends. He remembered Goody's sister remarking on how much Derrick and Goody looked alike. People commented on that often, especially back then, before Goody had started losing his hair. A few years later, he'd shaved his head and kept it that way. But back then, he and Derrick heard it frequently.

This one time, when Zale was at the house, she'd come up behind Derrick and slipped her arms around him, thinking he was Goody. She'd been embarrassed, but Goody had gotten a kick out of it. She hadn't done it the night of the party, but...

"What was I wearing? What did this woman look like? What was she wearing?"

"What?" Anne asked in a prickly tone. "I don't know."

"Yes, you do. Please, Anne, try and remember," he urged. Because if she did—if he was right—it would explain so much. "Tell me everything you remember. Start from the beginning."

"Fine." She shrugged, as if this was a pointless endeavor. "As I said, I flew into Tampa, where I rented a car, and then drove to your house. When I got there, there were a bunch of cars parked around. I got out, and I could hear a party going on in the backyard. I walked around the side of the house. I didn't see you at first, so I headed over to the grill to ask the guy cooking if he knew where you were."

"Okay, and then…" He prompted her with a rolling, impatient motion of one hand.

"There was a woman with long, pretty brown hair. She was wearing a red-checked halter top and short denim shorts—you know the frayed-off kind? I remember because she also had on high heels, and I thought to myself that I could never pull off that look. Anyway, the guy, the cook, handed her a plate piled high with ribs. He pointed to a table, and I specifically remember him saying, 'Take this to Derrick.'

"Naturally, I followed. The woman walked over to a table where you were sitting. You were kind of sideways to me, but you were wearing a black cowboy hat. She reached around and set the plate in front of you, and whispered in your ear. You grabbed her and pulled her onto your lap. She was giggling, and then you kissed—"

"The birthday hat," he stated flatly, even as his pulse began to pound fast and hard.

"The what?"

"One second." He picked up his phone, and as he texted his friend, he silently pleaded, *Please, see this, Goody, and please still have that pic on your phone.* "That was Goody's birthday hat. It wasn't me you saw. That was my roommate, my teammate, Kevin Osgood. Everyone calls him Goody. And the blonde was Zale, his girlfriend—now his wife. And she was wearing that outfit as a gift, a joke. Goody said he wanted a visit from Daisy Duke for his birthday. Zale showed up dressed as Daisy, gave him the hat and told him if she was going to be Daisy, then he had to be her cowboy."

"No." She was shaking her head. "I would have known if it wasn't you."

"Anne, think about it. You know I don't like ribs."

"Yeah, I did know that, but I thought *they* must not know... Wait, Derrick, so, that wasn't you?"

His phone chirped with a response from Goody:

Here you go. If you post this ANYWHERE Zale will TAKE YOU OUT (that's a quote from her.) Also, she sends her love. And so do I. We miss you, buddy.

And there it was, the photo of Goody and Zale from that very night. Of course, Goody had it right at his fingertips; it was one of his most prized possessions. Derrick held up his phone for Anne to see.

She studied the image. Derrick watched her as the truth slowly sank in.

"It wasn't you," she finally whispered.

Shocked, Derrick took a moment while his thoughts and memories scattered and then re-formed. All these years later, everything made sense. If Anne had thought she'd seen him kissing someone else, then that email had come from her own place of hurt and anger. Considering the circumstances, she'd been nicer than he would have deserved had he indeed done that. But he hadn't. The only thing he'd been guilty of was missing Anne and being antisocial on his friend's birthday.

The greater point here was that if she'd traveled all the way to Florida to surprise him, then that meant…

He looked at her then, right into her eyes, and before she could avert them, before she could shutter her feelings from him, he saw it. And the truth pierced his heart like an arrow. She'd been in love with him, too.

This changed everything.

# CHAPTER TEN

*THIS DOESN'T CHANGE ANYTHING.*

Anne sprang to her feet. Derrick did the same. She had no idea why she'd stood or where she intended to go, but shock seemed to be keeping her there. Or maybe Derrick was, with his overwhelming presence now so close to her. She couldn't be sure of anything, because suddenly she felt…different.

Okay, so maybe it changed things a little. Derrick hadn't been kissing that woman. The relief, the joy, the release from so many negative feelings gave her a rush and left her light-headed.

"Anne," he whispered. She could feel his gaze, sincere and intense, as it searched her face. "I never would have cheated on you."

All at once, she wanted to laugh and cry and apologize and, and…travel back in time.

"Not in a million years." He shifted closer.

"The only woman I ever wanted to kiss was you."

Her face went warm while her pulse began to pound fast and hard. She brought one hand up to cover her mouth, but all that did was remind her of how he used to kiss her and how much she wanted to kiss him now.

Removing her hand, she whispered, "Derrick, I'm so sorry." And then, to prevent herself from following through with that impulsive desire, she hugged him instead. Also a mistake, she immediately realized as his muscled arms gathered her close. Inhaling deeply, she was overwhelmed both by the comfort and familiar scent of him and the memories rushing through her at warp speed. Holding him felt so good, so right. And she felt…so much. Too much.

Positioning his mouth so that it barely grazed her temple, he whispered, "Me, too." Then he pulled away just enough to look at her. "I'm sorry, too. I'm sorry I wasn't strong enough back then to tell you how I felt and ask you to come with me."

She wanted to pull him back into her arms. Instead, she dipped her head because she couldn't look at him. This was all her fault.

All these years, she'd blamed him. She'd agonized over how badly she'd misjudged him, beat herself up for being so naive. The experience had dictated so much of her life and all of her relationships.

"Anne?"

Wincing, she opened one eye. "Ugh. That email." She opened the other. "It was unforgivable."

"No, it wasn't." His expression was tender with a hint of sadness. "Not under the circumstances. You thought I was kissing someone else. I wouldn't have been nearly as nice as you were if I'd seen what you thought you saw. I probably would have punched the guy and ended up in jail." His grin was adorable, and she couldn't believe how well he was taking this.

"Wow," she said, still dazed. Thinking, she let her gaze travel around the room. "I can't believe this. I don't know what to do or how to make this right."

"I do."

She looked at him again. "How?"

"For starters, you can let me kiss you again," he said, lowering his head as if to do just that. "Like I should have done that night, and every night since."

Heat flooded her bloodstream. Now she remembered how romantic he could be, too. Irresistibly so.

At that moment, she would have let him kiss her. She *wanted* him to. She looked up. He dipped his head but halted just shy of contact, and with his mouth almost brushing hers, he said, "But then you'd be doing to Todd what you thought I did to you. And I don't think you could forgive yourself for that."

Todd! Another shock went through her, immediately followed by a proper douse of shame. What in the world was wrong with her? Derrick was right; she was the worst kind of person.

"Um, right, yes. Todd and I are… You know what? I think we both need time to process all of this and—"

"I don't," he stated firmly. "I don't need time, Anne. All I need is for you to break up with Todd. Call him right now, or maybe it would be better to do it in person. Whatever works for you." Grinning, he added, "I don't, however, recommend an email."

"What? Derrick, no! I'm... You cannot be serious."

"I am completely serious. I've never cared about anyone the way I did about you. Our breakup was a misunderstanding. We should still be together."

"So you think we can just pick up where we left off *eleven years* ago?"

"Yes. As soon as you end things with Todd, then absolutely we can explore what this is between us. Anne, I still have feelings for you. I always have. And I bet you still feel something for me."

"What if I'm in love?"

Derrick's eyebrows drifted upward while a teasing glint flittered in his eyes. "That would be ideal, as far as I'm concerned. But you should take some time to be sure."

Her stomach cartwheeled. "You know very well I meant with Todd!"

"You're not," he stated confidently.

"How in the world could you possibly know that?"

"*Are* you in love with Todd?"

"Well, it's not..." She'd walked right into that trap, hadn't she? "It's complicated."

Shaking his head, he let out a chuckle.

"No, it's not. You either are, or you aren't. And you two don't act like a couple in love."

"How would you know?"

"Because I was in love with you! The entire night of the auction, I saw you and Todd together for a total of about seven minutes, which was the time it took for him to introduce you to me. Then he took off. You wandered away. You didn't spend the evening together. And Todd was…" His sentence trailed off, but Anne didn't care because she needed a moment.

Derrick had been in love with her? A fresh pang cramped her heart. Maybe if he'd told her that all those years ago, she would have been more confident; she would have questioned what she'd seen and marched right up to "him" at the party… What was the point in speculating about this? Just as she feared, it was only causing more pain. Granted, not in the manner she'd expected, but a different reality was here just the same, in the present, where she and Todd were a couple. Todd was a decent man, a good guy, and he deserved her loyalty.

"Todd was what?" she demanded, now feeling fidgety and a little irritable because what did Derrick know about her and Todd's relationship?

"He just seemed awfully..." He paused, searching for a word. "I'll go with *busy*. I didn't see you hanging out together at all, not until the auction. And then, you didn't even leave together."

"Of course, he was busy! He was chairman of the auction committee. And that's how our relationship is," she said, disliking her defensive tone. "He does his thing. I do mine." Realizing how that sounded, she quickly added, "And we do plenty of stuff together. It works."

"Sure, it does," he agreed with a shrug. "If you're not in love. Do you remember how when we were together, we couldn't stand to be apart? Even when we were at a party or an event, we gravitated toward each other. Most of the time, we couldn't wait until we could leave and be alone."

Anne's heart knocked against her rib cage and then began beating a wild rhythm in her chest. All of this was true. Sometimes, they'd set a time limit for how long they needed to stay and not appear inconsiderate or unsocial. When they were at an official function, and she was acting as his publicist, she'd forbid him from staying by her side the whole time.

Derrick always broke her rules.

Everything else he claimed was true, too. But despite what he apparently believed, they could not go back in time. They were different people now. What they'd had was incredible, yes. But that was part of the problem. She'd poured everything into their relationship, and when it ended, she hadn't gotten all of it back. It was about more than her heart; she couldn't risk losing herself like that again. She'd spent so many years building a life—a good life, where she was in control.

"Derrick," she said, "I understand what you're saying. And I get romanticizing our relationship—I've done that, too. But it really was a long time ago. We were young. Our lives went in different directions. We've had completely different experiences. I doubt your memory of me would live up to the reality of who I am now."

"Anne," he returned flatly. "Come on."

"Derrick," she replied, mimicking his tone. "I am obsessed with my career. I am set in my ways. I don't have time for...fluff."

"Fluff?"

"Yes, you know, love and stuff."

"Fluff and love and stuff," he repeated, his expression blank and unreadable. He waited a beat, then asked, "Are you finished?"

"Yes."

"We weren't that young, Anne, and people don't change that much. How long do you think I need to see that you are the same person at heart? As much time as it took you to figure that out about Easton?"

Anne didn't know what to say. It was pretty apparent Derrick hadn't changed much, either. Still the same stubborn, brash, opinionated, wildly appealing man she'd been head-over-heels in love with and who *hadn't* been kissing another woman. But still, she couldn't just...

She winced. "More than two days, that's for sure."

"How many days?" he demanded.

"Derrick!"

"I'm serious. How long will you give me to prove to you that we belong together?"

"I'm not sure what you mean?" she answered, stalling. She knew what he meant.

"It's simple. Get ready, Anne, because I'm going to try and win you back."

"Win me…what? You can't just… What about Todd?" she asked, even as the idea of Derrick wooing her made her a little light-headed and happily woozy. Because if there was one thing she knew for certain, it was that if Derrick wanted to win something badly enough, he would.

Eyebrows lifting, mouth twitching with a smile, he said, "Well, Todd will just have to step up to the plate, won't he?"

PACIFIC COVE WAS a quaint little hamlet situated on the edge of the Pacific Ocean. The wide sandy beach and the interesting rock formations made it popular with tourists, and the town itself offered a variety of charming shops and delicious seafood. There was also a strong sense of community among the locals, most of whom felt privileged to call "the Cove" home. It felt like a happy place with a peaceful vibe, or maybe that was just how Derrick was feeling at the moment.

The main thoroughfare was Mission Street, which intersected the coastal highway and ended at a large cul-de-sac, where a generous-sized gazebo was perched above the beach below. A long wooden boardwalk stretched from either end, paralleling the ocean and providing stunning views. It was a popular walking and jogging path.

Anne parked in a public lot not far from the center of town. Mission Street consisted of several blocks lined with shops selling typical beach necessities and every possible type of souvenir. Everything from beach toys, clothing, towels, candy and antiques, to gourmet dog treats, recycled footwear, spirit crystals and "hand-fired" lava lamps—whatever that meant. If someone was in need, or want, or didn't even know *what* they wanted, they could find it here.

Boogie boards and surfboards were available to rent, along with scooters and bicycles. Ocean cruises, fishing charters and whale-watching tours could also be secured.

Derrick liked how there was an entire shop dedicated to kites. Outside Kassie's Kites, a kaleidoscope of options fluttered in the wind. One glance in the direction of the beach, where specks of brightly colored nylon dotted the horizon, suggested they were doing a booming business.

Even more, he liked how Anne had agreed to bring him here. "This town is so great,"

Derrick commented, stopping before Wishing Well Candy and Fudge Shoppe to watch the saltwater-taffy pull work its magic. "I haven't been here in years."

"Isn't it?" Anne grinned at him. "I love it."

"You know what's even better?" he asked, turning to face her.

"The weather?" she guessed. "This is such a perfect blue-sky breezy beach day."

"I like that, too, but I was going to say our first 'date' in eleven years."

"This is *not* a date," she said in a tone that wasn't quite scolding.

"You're right," he said, but couldn't contain his grin. "I want our next first date to end with a kiss like our *first* first date did. And this one can't, so I'll concede that it's not."

"Derrick, you can't just—"

"I can," he interrupted, "but I'll drop it for today. I promise."

"Don't make promises you can't keep—we both know what you're capable of when you want something."

That comment managed to knock down his good mood a few pegs. If only he could go back in time and *not* talk to Sally, then everything would be so much easier. At that moment, he'd never dreamed he and Anne getting back together was a possibility. Not that it made what he'd done right, but he wouldn't be feeling guilty and nervous that she was going to find out. Of course, then he wouldn't have done it because he wouldn't have needed to.

Still, how could he not dedicate himself to winning her back? She'd admitted he was right that they should never have broken up. How could she not want to try this again? And no matter what she said about Todd, he knew two things; she didn't love him like she should. And for a man who loved her, he'd been awfully cozy with another woman at the auction.

"Ha!" Derrick made a triumphant fist. "So you're admitting that you *do* still know me?"

Anne rolled her eyes. "You are relentless," she said and then continued their stroll down the sidewalk toward the beach.

"That I am," he called out to her.

To himself, he said, *You haven't seen anything yet.*

SIDE BY SIDE, they descended the concrete steps, both lost in thought and awed at the stunning sight before them. No matter how often she visited, Anne was always impressed with the magnificence of the ocean.

She exhaled a happy sigh. Happiness that didn't have anything to do with being here with Derrick, she assured herself. They both needed to process what had happened all those years ago. His attention and flirting was harmless. She understood his longing for what they'd had. If she didn't have Todd, she might long for it, too.

"I love the smell of the beach," she said. "This place just recharges my batteries. I almost moved here last year."

"Really?"

"Yeah, when our sister-in-law, Vanessa, died, Rhys got custody of Willow. I had promised Evan that I would always be a part of her life. Rhys wanted my help, so I was going to move here. Or, you know, have my base be here."

"What happened?"

"Rhys met Camile. Willow already had friends in Portland, and she liked having that connection. So we decided I'd stay there and visit every other weekend. Or she'd come and stay with me. It's worked out great. It's nice for her to spend some time in the city and get a bit of the atmosphere, so to speak. We do *all* the sites, too, not like a lot of people who live somewhere but never take advantage of the local options, you know what I mean?"

"I do. I lived in Florida for all those years and never once went to that big amusement park people are always raving about."

"Your stomach thanks you," Anne teased. "Willow and I make a point of it. We go to museums, plays, concerts, take tours, learn the history, eat at interesting places. She enjoys doing fun runs with me, and I think I'd be hard-pressed to find anything that we haven't done. Plus, my parents live a half hour outside the city, and they are a huge part of her life, too."

"She's lucky to have you."

"Thank you, but I feel lucky to have her. I worry she won't want to spend as much time with me when she gets farther into her teenage years. But at least she'll have the memories and the knowledge, and hopefully the assurance that she can always come to me for anything."

"I understand. Teenagers can be challenging. I wouldn't give her a choice," Derrick said.

"What do you mean?"

"Easton tried that too-cool-for-us-oldies thing for a while, too. At Grandma's advice, we just ignored it. No matter what kind of attitude he tried to cop, we pressed on. When it was time to play Scrabble, and he complained? We let him. A trip to the farmers' market had him sneering? We gave him a bigger shopping list. He didn't want to go hiking? We hiked farther. Of course, the gamers helped, too, because they are legitimately cool, even by Easton's standards."

Anne grinned. "Your grandmother is amazing. Does she ever date?"

"Date? No! Grandma isn't interested in dating. She's happy with her hobbies and taking care of the farm, and hanging out with her friends. And Easton and me. I was worried thinking about Easton leaving next year, but now that I'm back, I can take care of her."

"Take care of her? Is anything wrong with her health?"

"No. She's in great health, thank goodness."

Anne stopped on the top of the stairs. "Then why would she need you to take care of her?"

"I don't mean like be her caregiver—I just meant I'll be able to be her family now. Full-time."

"I see." Anne hoped Derrick didn't have an issue if and when May ever decided to date. Then again, maybe she was wrong about the romantic vibe she'd picked up on between Jack and May. She'd love to see Jack find someone, especially a woman like May.

A sign on the edge of the beach caught her eye, indicating the house beyond currently under construction. "Hey, I know this guy."

"Who, the contractor?"

"Yep. Camile and Rhys have this great group of friends who have become my friends, too. Jay is a building contractor. He's married to Mia, who is a veterinarian here in town. Easton mentioned you were interested in maybe doing some building or renovation. You want to go take a look?"

Anne watched his expression tighten. He glanced toward the ocean. "Yeah, I was, but I don't know…"

"Don't know what?"

"What I'm going to do with the rest of my life." He smiled at her, but there was a touch of melancholy to it. "I, uh, wasn't joking when I said how your email was right about some things, like how baseball is all I'm good at."

A cold stone of guilt and regret settled in her gut. "Derrick, no." Surely, he hadn't hung on to those words all these years? "I didn't mean it. I admit, on one level, I wanted to hurt you. And I'm so sorry if you spent any time thinking those words were true."

"No, it's okay." His smile was gentle and sweet, and she wanted to wrap her arms around him and beg his forgiveness. "My dad used to say similar things, too. He would tell me how it was my one chance at greatness. How baseball is what defined me, and I couldn't waste my gift."

"Derrick, I'm sure he was trying to motivate you."

"He was. But still, I thought about it on and off over the years. Most of the time, it was fine because I was playing baseball. I was living the dream. I didn't have to worry… It's just been since my retirement that the words have really started to hit home. Like what else is there for me?"

It dawned on her then how difficult this forced retirement must be for him. What would she do if someone suddenly took her business away? Where would she find her self-worth? How could she make this better for him?

In a perfect case of terrible timing, John Fogerty's "Centerfield" began blasting from inside her bag. "That's Jack," she said, scrambling to retrieve her phone. "But this is not over. We're revisiting this conversation ASAP."

She answered the call. "Hey, Jack, what's up?"

"Anne, did you get my texts?"

"No, I've been—"

"Doesn't matter. It's about Easton. I'll hold while you take a look."

"I'll put you on speaker. Derrick is with me."

"Wait," Jack said quickly.

"I'm here," she said, keeping the phone pressed to her ear.

"Is Easton there?"

"No, he's not. He's gone on an outing with my family."

"Okay, good, because you might need a

strategy to deal with this before you talk to him."

"Understood."

A nervous knot began to form in the pit of her stomach as she loaded the image he'd sent. After the morning's revelation, Anne would have bet that a bigger shock couldn't be possible. This photo proved her wrong. Adrenaline surged through her body, shaking her to the core.

"What is it?" Derrick asked.

"Jack? Who has seen this? Putting you on speaker now and Derrick is with me." She turned on the speaker and positioned the phone so that Derrick could see the photo of his brother. Easton was sitting in a chair, the sleeve of one shirt pushed up onto his shoulder. A woman was standing with her back to the camera, syringe in hand, injecting Easton with the needle.

"Everyone, Anne. It's all over Twitter. I'm surprised Keira hasn't seen it by now."

"Keira is gone, too. She's with Easton."

Anne had encouraged Easton to leave his phone behind to avoid the temptation of responding to messages and calls. He'd agreed.

"Derrick, do you know anything about this?"

"No," he said.

Anne could tell by his expression that he was just as shocked as she was, maybe more.

# CHAPTER ELEVEN

CLAUSTROPHOBIC, THAT'S HOW Derrick felt as a crushing weight seemed to settle on his chest. As soon as Anne ended the call with Jack, he asked her to forward the photo to his phone. The background was blurry, making it difficult to discern the detail, but the person in the chair was definitely Easton.

"I can't believe this…" Derrick whispered, struggling to accept what was before his eyes. "And he just had to be wearing a Panther shirt, too didn't he?"

"Do you recognize the young woman?" Anne asked him.

*Young* was the operative word. She appeared to be a teenager, too. "No, but Grandma might."

"Jack said she's on a canoe trip and not picking up."

"That's right. She was going paddling with

the gamers today. They have a no-phone rule."

"How do we even know it's real?" he asked. "It looks kind of fuzzy. Maybe it's been photoshopped."

"I sent it to one of my employees. Oliver is an expert with this type of stuff. He'll be able to tell us a lot more. Any idea where this was taken?"

"None," Derrick answered, peering at the image. "Nowhere I recognize. Looks like someone's home."

In the photo, Easton was sitting on a stool in what looked like someone's kitchen. Stainless-steel appliances dotted the background. Objects were hanging on the walls, but they were too blurry to distinguish much detail. The young woman was sidewise to the camera, obscuring her features, but she was wearing blue jeans and a pink knit shirt. Her hair was up in a bun.

Derrick was afraid of what Anne was thinking. Truthfully, he was afraid of what *he* was thinking. *Was* Easton using PEDs? Could it be possible he was a con artist, or worse? Wouldn't he know if his own brother was some sort of sociopath? He thought about those hapless family members you watched on TV who were "shocked" when they learned their brother, sister, uncle, or cousin was a bank robber or a serial killer. Derrick always believed they couldn't possibly be so clueless to have missed the signs. Surely, Grandma would have suspected.

A throbbing began in his temple. After the lengths he'd gone to in order to get Anne to help, if Easton had done this, Derrick would ship him to Pluto. No, shipping him anywhere would be too kind. Not to mention, Derrick's credibility and reputation would also suffer by association. For the first time, he was almost grateful he was no longer playing ball.

Awareness slowly dawned that Anne was perfectly still, watching him.

"Are you okay?" she asked.

"No, Anne, I'm not."

"You think he's guilty, don't you?"

"Don't you?"

"Not necessarily."

"Come on, Anne, you can tell me the truth."

"I am. Things aren't always how they appear, Derrick. Look what happened to us when I made assumptions."

"This is different. This isn't a case of mistaken identity. That is a picture of Easton with a needle in his arm."

Anne's phone chimed. "That's Oliver," she said, picking it up and reading the message. "He's one-hundred-percent sure the photo is genuine." Fingers flying, she tapped out a response.

Derrick's body began to tremble as a flood of anger and despair rushed through him. Dipping his head, he slid his hands behind his neck and linked his fingers. Easton would almost certainly be arrested now. What would this mean for the draft? His career could be over before it even began.

"Oliver will work his magic and let me know when he has more details."

"What more could there be?" he asked, forcing himself to look at her again.

"Like when the photo was taken, where it was originally posted, where it originated, the location where it was taken. Stuff like that."

"Can he do that?"

"Heck, yeah. You'd be amazed by what you—someone like Oliver, I mean—can glean from a photo posted online. He is a genius. He also does computer-forensics consulting work for the police."

Derrick doubted any of that would make a difference. Things had gone too far. "What do we do in the meantime? This is proof, right? How can he possibly deny it? The police are going to be calling for sure. I should call my attorney and warn him. He's agreed to represent Easton, so he'll likely be getting calls from the press. And Grandma!" Derrick groaned. She was going to be distraught.

"Derrick," Anne said. "You need to calm down. There might be a logical explanation for this."

"Yeah, you're right," he answered, his tone rife with sarcasm. "Maybe he's getting a flu shot."

"Sure, why not?" She shrugged a shoulder.

"Anne, he's clearly not at a doctor's office or a pharmacy. That girl looks like a teenager, she's in street clothes, and he's getting a shot of something in his arm in someone's kitchen!"

"Let's go to Rhys and Camile's and wait for them to get back. I want to look at the image on a bigger screen."

Derrick didn't want to wait. He wanted to

track down Easton right now, hear him admit the truth and then execute damage control. "I think we need to go find them and get ahead of this. Make another statement or something."

"Derrick, listen, I know this is difficult, but you have to let me do my job. Once they return, we will talk to Easton. We'll get the details about the photo from Oliver. Then, Keira and I will plan our next steps."

"DON'T BE CONFRONTATIONAL," Anne advised a few hours later, back at Rhys and Camile's, as they waited for the troupe to arrive. Keira had texted to say they were on their way. As expected, she'd seen the photo and immediately texted Anne. She hadn't mentioned anything to Easton.

Now that the moment was almost here, Anne was nervous. Before this unfortunate surprise, she would have bet a lot of money on Easton's innocence. How could her radar be so off? The funny thing was her gut was still telling her that Easton was as good as he seemed. Innocent, even. Was this proof that she shouldn't have taken him on in the first place?

Despite her encouraging words to Derrick, she was stressed. She had no idea how she was going to deal with the photo. The one thing she would not do was lie for him. She had a strict policy of not lying for clients when they'd behaved either illegally or unethically. Spinning a story was one thing, but there were certain lines she would not cross.

For example, if a client was caught on camera kicking a puppy, she wasn't going to pretend he'd been defending himself against a wolf. If they were doing drugs, they would pay the price. Even if the drugs were of the performance-enhancing variety. Illegal was illegal. But until they knew for sure, she would do her job.

"I'm surprised the police aren't here yet," Derrick said grimly.

Anne huffed out a sigh. "Will you stop? This wasn't armed robbery. Even if he is guilty, they're not going to send a SWAT team out to get him."

An alert from the security system told them Rhys's SUV had driven through the gate. She and Keira had agreed that the best way to proceed would be to calmly show

Easton the photo while she, Keira and Derrick watched his reaction.

Soon the sounds of joy-filled chatter and laughter reached them. Slamming car doors followed.

"Here we go. Let's intercept him on the porch."

Derrick agreed, and they headed outside. Everyone was smiling. Funny stories followed about jet-boat induced screams and who got the most drenched by the icy cold water. Easton and Willow were laughing so hard they could barely speak when Camile told the story of Rhys losing his sunglasses. A chuckling Rhys excused himself to make a phone call. After another few minutes, Camile and Willow gathered up their gear to head inside.

Easton was beaming as he reached into the trunk and removed his pack. Anne hesitated, hating to steal his joy.

Derrick, however, had no qualms. "Easton, can you hold up here for a minute? We need to talk to you."

"Sure."

Anne handed Easton her tablet with the incriminating photo on the screen. His face twisted with what looked like confusion, and for a few seconds, Anne thought he was going to deny it was him.

After a moment, he looked up at them and said, "Where did you get this?"

"Easton!" Derrick barked. "Does it matter?"

Easton seemed taken aback by Derrick's insistent demeanor. "Uh, yeah. To me, it does. I don't remember a camera being there."

"Well, clearly it was! If you are injecting PEDs, or have used them at any time in the past, then we need—"

"Derrick," Anne interrupted, raising her arms, palms out and down in the international gesture of "please, be rational." "Let's let Easton finish."

Easton glared at Derrick. "Wait, you think that's a photo of me injecting *steroids*?" He spat out the word as if it was the filthiest of profanities.

Derrick's answer was an exaggerated blink and a helpless shrug.

"You are unbelievable!" Easton cried. "You said you believed me one hundred percent. You see one old photo, and suddenly you think I'm guilty?"

"One photo is enough. How old is it? Old enough not to show up on a drug test—is that why you were so gung-ho about taking one?"

"Look at it, Derrick." He shoved the tablet at him. "Where does it say 'performance-enhancing drug" on that syringe or anywhere else in the photo?"

It was a good question, Anne thought, and one for which she did not have an answer. And one his attorney would take note of, too, if it came to that.

"You're sitting in someone's home, getting a shot by a fellow teenager from the look of it. What else could it be? Unless it's street drugs—heroin or something."

Easton's mouth opened and then closed again. He was clearly at a loss for words. Save one. "Heroin?" he whispered incredulously.

"Derrick, okay," Anne interjected, then looked pointedly at Easton. "Easton, if this isn't you, then we'll prove it. There won't be any need to convince anyone. But to be fair, strictly from a PR perspective, this doesn't look great. Surely, you can see that?"

"It's me." He threw another glare at Derrick. "Remember a couple of years ago when I tried being vegan?"

"Yes," Derrick answered with an impatient shake of his head.

"Well, I got anemic and then low in B-12. So my doctor recommended injections."

"B-12 injections," Anne repeated, letting the relief sink in. Now to prove it.

Easton went on, "Soon after, I started eating meat again and haven't had a problem since." He waited a beat and then added, "No factory-farmed meat, though. Only animal proteins, where I know the origin, and that they were treated humanely."

"Of course," Keira agreed without a trace of condescension. She had the same aspirations, although she didn't always manage to live up to this lofty ideal. Anne suspected she'd make a new vow to do better.

Derrick said, "I remember that now."

"So it's a prescription?" Anne asked hopefully, because that would be so easy to prove.

"Yes. You can call Dr. Lenox's office. She's one of Mom's old partners and my doctor. She gave me the prescription."

"Easton can get a copy of the order from the pharmacy," Keira offered.

"Where was this? Who's giving you the injection?" Anne asked.

"That's Dr. Lenox's house. That's my friend Brita giving me the injection. She's studying to be a nurse and asked if she could try giving me a shot for a project she was working on. I asked Dr. Lenox if it would be okay, and she agreed to teach Brita. She's there, too. You just can't see her in the photo."

Anne and Keira exchanged relieved smiles.

Derrick exhaled a sigh that sounded like part relief, part frustration. "Easton, I am so sorry. I am the biggest jerk ever."

"It's okay, Derrick. I get it. Anne is right. It doesn't look good." He turned toward her. "But, Anne, how is anyone else going to believe me when my own brother thought I was guilty?"

"If it makes you feel any better," Derrick said, "Anne didn't believe you were guilty."

Easton managed a small smile. "It does a little."

Anne didn't point out that it was her experience with this job that prevented her from jumping to conclusions. The photo was still a nightmare, although a copy of the prescription and confirmation from this Dr. Lenox and his friend Brita would knock it cold. But it was clear they had a larger issue.

"Easton," Keira said, addressing Anne's concern, "can you think of anyone who would do this to you? Make you look guilty?"

Easton frowned and shook his head. "Absolutely not. I go out of my way to be kind to people."

Anne suspected this might be a part of the problem. There were people out there who took pleasure in bringing good people down.

ONCE INSIDE THE HOUSE, Anne asked Easton to check his phone for a call from the police. While they waited, Derrick tried to find the words to form another apology. Why hadn't he just listened to Anne and let Easton explain?

"Nothing from the police," Easton announced.

"Great," Anne said. "So far, so good."

"There's a ton of other junk on here, though. Messages from reporters and friends and supporters and wacky comments from people hating on me."

"Don't answer anyone," Keira insisted.

"I won't. I feel like throwing it away. Can I just get a new number?"

"You can," Anne said. "That would be a great idea. Although, we need you to hold onto that one for now in case the police ask for it."

He shrugged. "The police can have it. I don't care."

"We'll get you a new phone tomorrow," Derrick said, realizing he'd do about anything to make this up to Easton.

"In the meantime, can you tell me who called and texted you?" Keira asked. "I want to make a list. If we're going to figure out who has it in for you, that would be a good place to start."

Easton handed her the phone. "You can look yourself. The code is two-four-nine-three."

"Willie Mays, Ted Williams, Babe Ruth," Anne said.

"Who, I assume, are famous baseball players?" Keira inquired in a playful tone.

"Willie Mays was number twenty-four, Ted Williams number nine and Babe Ruth wore number three," Anne informed her while everyone chuckled.

"Right." Keira said wryly, "That was my next guess."

Anne said to Easton, "You should probably pick something less obvious for your new one. Anyone who knows you would know that these guys are your favorite ballplayers."

"I will," he assured her. "When are we heading back to the city?"

"Tonight," Anne said.

"Ugh," he said. "I wish we didn't have to go back already."

"Late, though, under cover of darkness. We'll go in through the back, same way we left."

Keira tried to ease his mind. "Easton, you are going to call the pharmacy and get a copy of your prescription. First thing tomorrow, we'll release it to the press with a strong statement about your innocence. They'll move on, especially now that Hailey is in the news, too."

The details had broken about Easton's girlfriend, including her mother's identity and the previous blood-doping accusation. Other athletes were being singled out, as well, although none with the fervor currently directed at Easton.

"Speaking of Hailey," Easton said. "She sent me like a hundred messages. Can I call her yet?"

"No!" Anne and Keira cried at the same time.

"I know it's difficult," Keira said. "But anything you say right now can be twisted and used against you."

"We're not suggesting Hailey would do that," Anne explained. "Not on purpose, anyway."

"I understand," he said.

"Hey, sorry to interrupt, but I have an idea," Camile said, entering the dining room from the kitchen. "Easton, you can stay here if you'd like. Anne, I don't know how all this PR stuff works, like if you need him closer. But we're taking Willow to your parents' house on Tuesday. Assuming things have settled down, we can drop him off then."

"That would be amazing," Easton said and then followed up immediately, and asked, "Are you sure, though? I don't want to put you out."

"Positive," Camile assured him with a smile. "We wouldn't offer if you weren't welcome."

"Anne, would that be okay?" he asked eagerly. "Can I stay? I'll have to call Grandma and see if she can take care of the chickens and stuff."

"Yes," Anne said. "It would be preferable if we didn't have to worry about the press, or anyone else, finding you."

Camile smiled and clasped her hands. "It's settled then. If anyone knows how to keep you hidden and safe, it's my husband."

ANNE, KEIRA AND Derrick departed just after dark. May had called to say the reporters were back at the farm. They decided to drop off Derrick on Hillshire Road with a flashlight, so he could venture home on foot via their original escape route.

Anne and Keira discussed the next steps they needed to implement along the way. They speculated about who could be targeting Easton. Oliver had discovered the photo was first uploaded from a "fake" social-media account, meaning the person it was registered to didn't exist. According to him, that said a lot in itself. Someone with at least a certain level of knowledge was involved, and they didn't want their identity known.

He took this as a personal challenge and felt confident he could dig up even more information.

They were nearing the turnoff for the farm when Derrick leaned forward and said, "Bad news. Grandma texted to say a reporter is now parked on Hillshire Road. Somehow they must have figured out how we got away."

"Shoot," Anne said.

"What if you leave me at the neighbor's house and I go through the woods?"

"How well do you know this neighbor?"

"Not very well."

"Nope," Keira said. "Bad idea. Remember Minnie Greer."

"Who is Minnie Greer?" Derrick asked.

"She was the neighbor of one of our clients who is a famous opera singer," Anne explained. "Long story, but the opera singer had a PR issue a few years ago that involved some plastic surgery that went awry. For obvious reasons, she didn't want anyone to see her. She insisted she could trust her sweet neighbor, Minnie. Minnie was like a second mother, she assured us. Turned out, Minnie was a traitor who sold her photos to one of those online gossip sites."

"That is horrible. Minnie should have gone to prison. How is the opera singer now?"

"I agree, she should have. The diva's doing very well. She used the incident as a platform to warn others about the risks of cosmetic surgery."

"Thanks to Anne," Keira said. "She's a hero to women everywhere. Anne scored her the interview of a lifetime with Oprah, and she is now performing in New York City. You can imagine the blowback on Minnie. Last we heard, *she* hasn't taken another photo since."

"Well, good for her, I suppose," Derrick said.

"Agreed," Anne said. "Loyalty means everything. It's so hard to trust people. But the point is, Keira is right. It's too risky."

"Should I stay at a hotel?"

"Absolutely not!" Keira insisted. "People are always looking for celebrities at hotels. I don't even follow baseball, and *I* know who you are. You'll have to stay at Anne's."

# CHAPTER TWELVE

STAY AT ANNE'S?

Derrick tried not to show his reaction to these happily unfortunate circumstances. When Anne pulled her vehicle into the parking garage before dropping Keira anywhere, he thought she must be staying over, as well. Not ideal, but it could work to his advantage. He liked Keira and could tell she returned the sentiment. Maybe he could quiz her about Todd.

In order to foster the reconnection between himself and Anne, he needed her to focus on them, rather than her and Todd. He had no intention of resorting to nefarious means, but he'd take all the ammunition he could gather.

But when they got inside the elevator, Keira pushed the ninth-floor button and then the tenth. "You two live in the same building." He said it like the revelation it was.

Anne looked at him with a confused

frown. "Yes, what did you think? We were all three having a sleepover?"

"Not that we don't occasionally do that," Keira informed him cheerfully. "I mean, me and Anne. After a late night of Netflix and ice cream, I have been known to crash on Anne's delightful sofa." The elevator dinged, and she stepped out, tossing a wave over her shoulder. "Nighty night, you two.

"That reminds me," she said, stopping abruptly and pivoting to face them. "Derrick, feel free to eat the carton of Monster Mash-Up in Anne's freezer if you guys decide to do some bingeing. If you eat Anne's chocolate-fudge brownie, she'll—"

"Good night, Keira," Anne called with a little finger wave as the elevator doors closed.

Derrick asked, "How long have you both lived here?"

"Going on seven years."

"Who moved in first?"

"Funny story. We moved in at the same time, which is how we met. Both of us moving in our stuff on the exact same weekend, sharing the elevator full of furniture and boxes, et cetera."

"So she didn't work with you then?"

"No, that came a few months later. She didn't like her job at the time. I offered her a position at McGrath, she accepted and she's been with me ever since."

"That's very cool." The elevator dinged again on Anne's floor.

"I know," she agreed and led the way down the hall. "Instant friendship. I've never experienced anything like it. It's extra fun for me because I don't have very many friends. I work all the time, so it's hard to schedule things and to keep commitments. And the time I do take off I like to spend with my family. But Keira and I, we manage to squeeze stuff in—often while we're working at the same time."

"Like this weekend," he said. "I'm sorry you had to dedicate your off time to us."

"I'm not," she said and unlocked the door to her apartment. They went inside, and Anne turned on the lights. "It makes what I do worth it when I can help someone like Easton. Especially Easton, if I'm being honest. It's funny how all my old feelings for him have come rushing back."

Derrick was thrilled by those words. The sentiment was precisely what he'd hoped for.

Now, if she would only have the same revelation about him, or, even better, admit that
she'd already had it.

He looked around her apartment and felt
a new kind of warmth spread through him.
Followed quickly by the thought that staying
here might not be a great idea, because he had
the feeling he wasn't going to want to leave.
The space was roomy and replete with decor
yet neat and tidy. The colors were rich and
vibrant, and the furniture looked every bit as
inviting as Keira had inferred. There were
throws and pillows, and he could see why
Keira would crash on the big cushy-looking
velvet sofa. Just looking at it had him thinking about kicking back with a good book.

The walls held a variety of art that reflected her interests; a vintage print of Willie Mays, a pencil sketch of Fenway Park, a
framed photo of the old lighthouse he recognized as the one at Rhys and Camile's. There
was also a watercolor of a beach that looked
like Pacific Cove.

Bookshelves lined one entire wall and were
stuffed with books, reminding him of all the
evenings they'd opted to stay in and read together instead of going out. He couldn't wait

to inspect the titles and discover if she'd kept the one that had helped forge their initial connection.

Baseball curios and souvenirs were arranged here and there, and included signed baseballs, ticket stubs, trading cards and figurines. One entire shelf contained a collection of baseball-player bobblehead dolls.

"These are fantastic!" he exclaimed, moving to admire the assortment. "Al-l-tho-o-ugh…" He drawled out the word. "There is one prominent former player from the Knights who is conspicuously absent. He's an all-star catcher, so it can be tough to find, but I'll see if I can hook you up."

Anne laughed but appeared self-conscious when she explained, "I know it sort of looks like I'm still in college. It's a bit embarrassing. One of these days, I'll hire a decorator, but…"

"Hire a decorator? What for? It looks like you. Who could not love that?"

He meant every word; his senses were reeling. The place even smelled like her, hints of vanilla and lavender teasing his senses and making him remember… Everything. How could his feelings for her be this strong so quickly? Because they'd never really waned, he silently answered, and this was further proof. Anne was watching him with an expression he couldn't identify—one he didn't like.

"Anne, what's wrong? Did I say something wrong?"

"Not at all. It was a very sweet thing to say." She pivoted quickly and headed into the kitchen.

"Wait!" Derrick said. "It's Todd, isn't it? He doesn't like your style. Let me guess—he wants you to fill the place with tan-and-white furniture, leather-bound books that you're not supposed to touch and weird artsy statues of things no one can identify."

Anne ignored the question and continued walking. "Do you want some ice cream? I don't know about you, but I'm exhausted."

"I'm right, aren't I?" He followed her into the kitchen, where gleaming stainless-steel appliances and a marble countertop greeted him. Even here were traces of who she was. A Panther Project calendar hung on the wall, and her cookie jar was a baseball cradled inside a mitt.

"Fine," she conceded, taking two cartons

from the freezer. She placed them on the counter and crossed the room. "Yes, okay, you're right. Todd doesn't like it. Particularly, my bobblehead collection, which he says is cheesy and juvenile."

"Please, tell me that's why you keep them so prominently displayed."

"Maybe," she conceded, her mouth fighting a grin.

After opening a drawer, she then removed two spoons and pointed one at him like a sword. "Keira wasn't joking, by the way. If you eat my ice cream, I will use this to remove your tongue."

"Duly noted," he said with a satisfied grin. Any man who couldn't appreciate this apartment as a reflection of who Anne was, was not in love with her. That was the bottom line. Then he opened his container and scooped out a bite.

ANNE WENT TO bed that night with the fear she'd lie awake tossing and turning with Derrick only feet away in the guest room. The opposite happened, and she didn't even stir until sunlight peeked through the one permanently kinked slat in her bedroom window blinds.

This morning, she wouldn't make the mistake of assuming Derrick would still be sleeping. She also admitted, in opposition to the previous morning, that she was looking forward to seeing him. And, indeed, upon opening her bedroom door, she could smell the coffee brewing.

She discovered him sitting at her dining-room table with his back to her. His head was down, reading a book she assumed, and she found herself hoping it was one she'd also read so they could discuss. Another image flashed before her; what would it be like to feel this anticipation every morning? To look forward to seeing his quick smile and the teasing glint in his eye?

It was so easy to make him happy. Unlike Todd, who was great, yes, but she had to work so much harder around him. Not to please him, necessarily, but to keep up with his exacting standards. Why hadn't she seen this before? Todd didn't understand her baseball preoccupation, and she barely tolerated his sailing obsession. Just the thought of Todd right now, comparing the two men, made her feel guilty. And also glad she hadn't kissed Derrick.

Or rather, it was Derrick who'd cared enough about her not to kiss her. What man would do that? A fresh surge of affection flowed through her, and this time she let it. She wasn't used to that kind of consideration. The thought prompted her forward. But as she closed the distance, she realized it wasn't a book but a laptop that was open before him.

"Good morning," she said when she was only a few feet away.

His body jolted in surprise. "Jeez!" he exclaimed and then let out a chuckle. "Sneaky much?"

"Paybacks are so much fun," she said and laughed. "It was almost too easy, though. You are intent on something, aren't you? Please, don't tell me you're reading gossip about Easton." She'd advised him against looking at anything, assuring him that Keira was keeping on top of it. And with Jack monitoring Twitter, there was no reason for Derrick to read comments and get upset.

"Nope. But that probably would have been more productive than what I am doing."

"That doesn't sound good."

"Yeah, I don't even want to admit to you how much money I've lost in the last two hours."

"Derrick, what are you doing? You're not gambling, are you?"

"Sort of," he said. "This makes about as much sense to me as gambling does. No matter how much I study, it all feels so random. The one time I went to Vegas, I did better at playing blackjack than I'm doing here. Hey, that's it, maybe I should be a professional gambler."

"What are you talking about?"

"Okay, so a retired baseball buddy of mine makes a nice living from playing the stock market. So I thought I'd give it a try."

Startled, Anne stopped in her tracks. "You mean like day trading? They make it look easy on TV, but there's a lot that goes into that."

"Tell me about it. I've been doing it for a while now."

She recalled a story Rhys had told her about a guy he knew who'd lost everything he owned and most of what his mother had, too. Almost like an addiction. Her body went cold.

"Derrick, how much have you lost? You don't have to give me a number but—"

"Let's see..." he drawled, squinting at the screen. "In total, I'm currently down eighteen-point-two—no, make that three... Eighteen-point-three million dollars. But it'll be okay."

Anne gasped, slapping one palm hard against her chest. "Derrick! Eighteen *million* dollars." She knew he'd made a lot playing baseball, but regardless, this was too much for him to be throwing away. He was still a young man with a lot of years ahead of him. "You can't just—"

"Because I'm not using real money." He winked. "Gotcha, didn't I? What was that you said about paybacks?"

"That wasn't funny, though." Anne loosened her fingers where her hand was gripping her shirt. "I'm having palpitations." She chuckled, because it was a little funny. "You're such a brat—you know that?"

"I'm sorry," he said, but his grin told a different story.

"What are you doing, really?"

"Before I ventured into the real-life market, I decided I'd learn first, see if I had a knack for it. I downloaded an app where you can enter your trades and monitor your progress. I think it's safe to say I have no knack. I am officially knackless."

"Well," she said, continuing into the kitchen to get a cup of coffee, "I, for one, am glad. I don't think it's your thing, sitting in front of a laptop from morning 'til night."

He sighed. "I'm beginning to think there are no profession-related things for me."

"Of course, there are." Anne finished her trek to the kitchen, where she poured a coffee and then returned to the dining room to sit across from him. "You alluded to this yesterday, too, when we were talking about construction. Before we discuss this, can I ask you a personal question?"

"Anne, you know you can ask me anything."

"Do you need to work?"

"No, but it's not about the money. I want to work. It's about my self-worth. You know how I am—I have to do something. I have to be *good at something*. Preferably the best, but what are the chances of that happening again?" He winked at her.

"I understand." And she did. She couldn't

imagine ever not working, either, or at least not living without a purpose or a passion. Like the Peace Corps or motherhood. Motherhood? Where had that come from? "What else have you tried?"

"Let's see... Of the things that I thought might interest me, I've ruled out restaurant owner, real-estate agent and sportscaster."

Anne recalled how he'd majored in exercise science in college, with a plan to go on to physical-therapy school if baseball didn't work out.

Before she could mention it, he said, "My leg precludes almost anything physical at this point, and I don't want to go back to school. I didn't like it that much the first time around. I tolerated it for baseball's sake."

"What happened to the construction idea?"

"I'm not good enough."

Anne scoffed. "How do you know that?"

"Anne, I stranded myself on the roof," he joked.

"An easy mistake to make."

"I know. But after seeing what your brother does, I've accepted that I don't really have the brain for it, much less the skills."

"Don't compare yourself to Rhys! No one

is as good at stuff like that as he is. But that's because he's spent his whole life practicing and studying and…crafting things."

"I'm not comparing," he said. "Don't think this is me having a pity party. It's more that it doesn't feel right. It's interesting, and I could learn if I wanted to dedicate myself to it, but I don't. I'm going to hire someone to fix my chimney. Grandma is right—I am…impatient. Plus, the whole time I was on the roof, I kept thinking, what if I fall off and break something worse than my leg?"

"Well, that's okay then. Besides, Rhys isn't nearly as good at other things like you are."

"Like what?"

"Like…" Anne thought while Derrick looked at her pointedly, his expression conveying enough that he didn't need to say the words: *See what I mean?*

"Baseball, obviously," she said.

"Besides baseball," he said. "We've already established my greatness where that is concerned. That's the problem, though. All my greatness went into one skill." He brought up an index finger to emphasize his point. "One skill, Anne," he repeated firmly. "And now that's gone, and I'm…" He flipped his hands, so they landed palms-up on the table.

"You're what?" she whispered, because so much emotion had gathered in her throat. She should have realized how much this bothered him. How much had she contributed to these feelings with that long-ago email?

"Adrift," he said. "And terrified. What if I never have that feeling about anything again?"

Anne reached over and took his hand. "Derrick, I'm so sorry."

"Don't be. I know how lucky I am that I got to do what I love for so long. The only thing that would have made it better is if the woman I loved had been with me."

Anne didn't even bother to chastise him for such a personal comment. What was the point? He wasn't going to stop. Did she even want him to? The answer filled her with an uncomfortable mix of feelings. Guilt, obviously, because enjoying Derrick's attention felt like betraying Todd. Regret that she'd been so foolish and presumptuous all those years ago.

But the bottom line was that she liked how he made her feel so unconditionally *liked*.

She didn't have to try to be anyone but herself with him. Even though they hadn't been together in years, it was like he knew her. Still. And he liked her. And her longing for more trumped all her doubts.

She was going to have to break up with Todd. And that was scary, too. What if she ended things and it didn't work out with Derrick? That she was even asking that question gave her the answer she sought. It wasn't fair to Todd to keep him on the back burner "in case."

She was ready to announce all of this when Derrick said, "I'm going to be late if I don't get going."

Disappointment flared inside of her before she could stop it. She wanted to ask him to stay a while longer. But she and Keira needed to get to the office and see what Oliver had discovered about the photo. And that was telling, too, because she couldn't remember the last time she hadn't been anxious to get to work.

She asked, "What are you up to today?"

"I've got my first batting lesson from the auction. Kellan is letting me use the facilities at NPU, so I don't have to worry about the press or privacy. Then I need to run a couple of errands."

"I hope we can talk about this again," she said. "Because, Derrick, I think you could do anything you want." *And I want to tell you how I feel*, she added silently. Because first, she needed to talk to Todd.

"Thank you," he said. "I'd like to talk some more. I value your opinion."

Anne stood and went into the kitchen, where she retrieved a key from the drawer next to the stove. Back in the dining room, she handed it to him. "Here you go. Just make yourself at home. I don't know what my day is going to look like or when I'll be back."

He stared at the key in his open palm for a long beat. Slowly, he looked up, his fingers curling around the metal. His gaze caught hers while his mouth curled up at the corners. Anne found herself smiling in anticipation of whatever he was about to say.

"If Todd doesn't like your decorating, imagine what he's going to say about your new roommate?"

# CHAPTER THIRTEEN

THE WEIRD PART, Derrick would later realize, was how he hadn't intended to spy. This fortunate happenstance was a byproduct of his attempt to do the right thing. What he'd told Anne was true; he did have his first batting lesson later. What he hadn't mentioned was the intended detour to Todd's office.

He felt it was only fair to have a conversation with the guy and be straight with him. Derrick was in love with Anne, and he intended to win her back. Fair warning.

Anne had been warned, too, which is why she wouldn't be surprised when she received her first bit of "fluff" today at work.

At the offices of Barnes, Gideon & Jarvik, Derrick revealed himself as a "friend" and learned from Todd's assistant, Trina, that Todd was "down at the marina." She was very accommodating in providing Derrick with the directions, all the way to the wharf and including the slip number where Todd kept his sailboat, *Whirlwind*.

The exclusive Riverscape Marina was located in downtown Portland on the banks of the Willamette River. Since it was only a few blocks and a beautiful day, and because his physical therapist recommended a walk on a flat surface five days a week, he headed there on foot.

What he hadn't anticipated, and Trina hadn't prepared him for, was the security gate located at the end of the walkway blocking public access to the pier. She probably assumed Derrick would just text Todd and let him know when he'd arrived. But Derrick didn't have his number, and asking for it would surely give away the little white lie he'd told regarding their friendship.

From a distance, he watched a woman tap on the keypad and enter. The gate closed with a click and a buzz behind her. He was ready to turn around and formulate a new plan when three men, overloaded with gear—lifejackets, ropes, bags and other assorted seafaring gadgets Derrick couldn't identify—stepped into view.

One guy was carrying an ice chest, which

he nearly dropped before lowering it to the ground. He was adjusting his burden, including an ice chest, a huge jug of water and what looked like a battery charger, when Derrick approached.

"Hey, can I give you a hand?" Derrick asked, stopping before him and pointing at the ice chest.

The man paused for a second, his expression uncertain, like maybe he wanted to decline. After looking Derrick over, he smiled and said, "You know what? That would be great. I aggravated my tennis elbow yesterday, and I was thinking about leaving this here and coming back for it."

"No problem," Derrick said, stepping forward and lifting the chest.

"You a boat owner?" one of the other men asked. He had what looked a mile of coiled rope slung over one shoulder and draped across his body. That was one of several things Derrick never liked about boating— all the paraphernalia.

"Nope," Derrick said. "I've spent a fair amount of time on them, though. Lived in Florida for eleven years, gulf side."

Truthfully, being a boat owner had never

appealed to him at all. Tons of his friends had boats. It seemed as if they were always buying parts and fixing things and fiddling with this or that. Aside from his tendency to have motion sickness, boats seemed like more trouble than they were worth.

"I love Florida!" the third man chimed in. "I'm hoping to retire there."

That did it. They set off, with Derrick carting the ice chest. A lively conversation was in full swing about boating in the Keys by the time they reached the gate.

Rope Man paused and eyed Derrick warily. "You, uh, coming inside? That's why I asked if you had a boat. Sorry, buddy, but security is tight. We're not supposed to let people in who don't have a reason to be here."

"Oh, yeah, of course," Derrick said. "I'm meeting my friend, Todd Marino. He has a boat moored here, *Whirlwind*, in slip twenty-one."

"Oh, heck yeah! We know Todd! Great guy! That'll get you in the door. *Whirlwind* is a beauty, too, and boy, can he sail her!"

"Isn't that the truth?" Derrick answered obliquely, a scratch of conscience niggling at him.

Was it fair for him to pursue Anne when she already had this "great guy" who adored her? But Derrick loved her, too. More, he reasoned, than Todd did. It wasn't as if she and Todd were married or even engaged. Plus, these were unique circumstances. He and Anne should still be together.

The reason he was here was to discuss this with Todd, level the playing field. If Todd turned out to be the one for Anne after all, then so be it. In the meantime, Derrick was going to make his intentions known.

Luckily, the men weren't going far, so Derrick wasn't prompted to answer questions about how he knew Todd. After depositing the gear on the dock beside the boat, which he learned belonged to Rope Man, he said his goodbyes and continued along his way.

Near the end of the pier, as per Trina's instructions, he made a right turn. He calculated he was halfway to *Whirlwind*'s assigned slip when he noticed the couple standing on the bow of a boat without realizing who, or what, he was seeing. From a distance, looking over the tops of multiple vessels, it was impossible to tell which boat they were on. As he got closer, the couple embraced, and still, the possibility didn't dawn on him. Probably because he could see more of the woman, and she had her back to Derrick, shielding the figure of her partner.

Or, more likely, it was because he would never have anticipated what then played out before him. The pair began to kiss so passionately Derrick felt as if he was intruding on a moment. He started to turn around when he noted the name scrawled in elegant black font across the stern—*Whirlwind*. He froze. No, it couldn't be… And yet, the height, the build, the blond, gel-coiffed hair was all consistent with his recollection of Todd.

He had to know.

The man and woman parted, and with their hands entwined, turned toward the dock, giving Derrick the confirmation he sought. The woman smiled at him. Todd, however, overlooked Derrick because he was too busy gawking at the woman.

Cheating. Betraying Anne with this woman, Derrick acknowledged as a fiery ball of anger ignited inside of him.

"Derrick?" Todd said when he finally noticed him, presumably prompted by the woman whose focus was now on Derrick.

She wore a curious expression while Todd's previously smitten countenance morphed into surprise. That's when Derrick realized the woman was the same one he'd seen Todd with at the auction. How right his instincts were.

"Hey, Todd," Derrick greeted him coolly.

"Uh, what brings you here? You have a boat?"

"I was looking for you, but it seems like you're pretty busy, huh?"

"Oh," the "other woman" said, now looking somber but not quite as panicked as Todd. "I was just leaving." She stepped onto the dock, and Derrick realized she looked familiar beyond the coziness he'd witnessed at the auction.

He stuck out a hand for the sole reason that he wanted to know who she was. "Hi, how are you? I'm Derrick Bright."

"I know," she said with a warm smile. "I recognize you. I'm Bailey."

First name only, Derrick noted. A clear indication, in his experience, of dodging. Meaning she likely knew about Todd and Anne.

"Have we met?" he asked.

"I don't think so."

"Hmm. You look familiar." He raised a finger and bounced it toward her thoughtfully. "Weren't you at the auction last Friday?"

She glanced helplessly at Todd as if asking him how to proceed. Derrick was satisfied when Todd was at least man enough not to lie.

"Yes, she was." He sighed and then explained, "Bailey is a meteorologist at Global Weather. You've probably seen her on TV."

"That's it," Derrick said with a finger snap. "I used to live in Florida, so I've seen my fair share of *Hurricane Watch*. It was my go-to during storm season." He smiled, but inwardly his temper was flaring. How long had this been going on? How could he do this to Anne? No matter where things stood between Derrick and Anne, he would not stand for anyone treating her this way.

"Thanks," Bailey said. "Nice to meet you, Derrick." Then she glanced at her wrist, pretending to check the time. "I have to run."

"I'll call you later," Todd said with a beseeching look.

Silently, the two men watched her traverse the dock.

Once safely out of earshot, Todd asked him, "Would you like to come aboard?"

"I'd planned to," Derrick said. "Before I caught you cheating on Anne. Now, you're going to be lucky if I don't throw you overboard."

"Here it is," Oliver declared, clicking the mouse beneath his hand. "This is the original photo."

Anne, Keira and Oliver were gathered in the conference room so Oliver could show them what he'd discovered on the big screen, now lit up before them. Anne studied the scene, which appeared to have unfolded as Easton had described. Cropped from the original image, an older woman stood off to one side, Dr. Lenox, she presumed, watching the student nurse administer the injection.

"She's even wearing a lab coat," Keira said, referring to Dr. Lenox. "Couldn't be better."

Anne asked, "Do you have any idea where it originated?"

"Yep, from a university's site for nursing students. They have a separate website, and this pic was posted as part of a project by a student whose name is..." Oliver shuffled some papers.

"Brita Penticoff?" Keira said, finishing for him.

"That's her," he confirmed. "It gets better. See this?" Using a pencil, he pointed at the doctor's hand. "You can barely see it, but she's holding a small vial. The post contained a link to a photo-sharing site, where I grabbed the original higher-resolution image. I was able to enlarge that one so you can see this." Another photo appeared onscreen. Among the words on the vial that could be easily discerned were... "Vitamin B-12."

"Yes!" Anne said. "Brilliant, Oliver. You are the best."

"I know," he said. "I'm happy this kid is being vindicated. This foul deed represents everything I despise about the internet I love."

Anne said, "Easton already texted a screenshot of the prescription. He also called Dr. Lenox, explained the situation and asked if he could give me her number. She agreed and said she'd be willing to go on record confirming Easton's anemia condition, too, if we need it."

"Excellent," Keira said. "After you call her, we'll put the package together and get it out on social media ASAP."

"Jack is standing by to tweet whatever we need, and I'll forward all of this to Easton's attorney in case the police need confirmation." Anne couldn't wait to tell Derrick about how neatly this was all coming together.

"Still no word from the cops?" Oliver asked.

"Nope," Keira answered. "We're keeping up with one athlete. Imagine how busy they are trying to sift through all the rumors about multiple ones, including the daughter of the university's president. Hopefully, this will help keep Easton off their radar."

"Now, if we can only figure out who keeps trying to put him on there." Anne didn't need to add that until they accomplished that feat, Easton would still be vulnerable.

"We will," Keira said confidently, standing and gathering her laptop and notes.

Oliver and Keira stayed put so they could work on a few other details while Anne headed to her office.

On her way past reception, Monique, their receptionist, said, "Delivery for you, Anne."

Assuming it was a package she ordered,

she was about to tell Monique to stash it in the employee lounge when she noticed that it was a cellophane-wrapped basket, not a cardboard box. Personal, not business, and she had a good idea who it was from. She veered toward the front desk and scooped it from Monique's desk.

Once inside her office, she unwrapped the bundle. Inside was a package of peanuts, some Cracker Jacks and a Derrick Bright bobblehead doll. The note read:

All I need is just one (more) chance.

With tears in her eyes and laughter in her heart, Anne picked up her phone and texted Todd.

ANNE HURRIED ALONG the waterfront, where a waiting Todd was standing very still staring out at the river. He looked pensive and a bit melancholy, and the idea that she'd done that to him made her feel terrible.

"Todd, hi! I'm so sorry I'm late."

"Hey," he said and smiled gently before leaning in to kiss her cheek. "No problem. We're actually early for our reservation." He gestured at the restaurant behind them, where he'd secured their favorite table. "How are you? Did you have a good time at the beach? How's your family?"

Anne felt a fresh niggle poke her conscience. Todd. He was always so thoughtful and solicitous and forgiving of her lack of attention. Once again, she took solace in the fact that she hadn't kissed Derrick. Technically, she didn't have anything to feel guilty about, right?

"Good. Everything is fine with me."

"I know you're swamped with the Easton Bright thing, so thank you for carving out some time for me."

And just like that, she knew she was doing the right thing. She shouldn't have to carve out time for him. Her relationship with Todd was so easy and comfortable, like a nap on a really comfy sofa. A treat to indulge in when time permitted. Spending time with Derrick, on the other hand, was like a thrill ride. An adrenaline rush of excitement and adventure and unpredictability. More like a passion she couldn't deny. She'd never made Todd a priority like she should have. And that was the problem in a nutshell. Who made napping a priority?

Derrick was right when he'd pointed out how it used to be between them. How when they were apart, she would count the minutes until they could be together again. Over the years, she'd written that off to first-love sickness, immaturity and a failure to prioritize. Now she knew unequivocally that was not the case. It had been difficult to leave him at her apartment and come here to meet with Todd tonight.

Especially after everything Derrick had done. Besides the gift basket, there'd been a gorgeous potted plant to "enjoy with tea on your patio." Next had come the collection of assorted teas, along with a jar of Easton's honey and three mugs—an extra one for Keira. He'd saved the best for last; two books, duplicate titles, and an official invitation to start their own private book club.

She'd gotten home before him and found herself waiting anxiously for his return. Pure delight had sparked inside of her at the sound of his key in the door. *His* key. Todd didn't even have a key! Then she'd thrown herself into his arms and smothered him with a hug for all of his thoughtfulness. And, yes, the embrace had nearly gotten away from her again. Again, Derrick had been the one to exercise restraint.

But not before she'd experienced a variation of her old fantasy. This time it was she and Derrick at the farm with Grandma May and Easton. Christmas decorations filled the house. Keira was there, along with Rhys, Camile and Willow, who were visiting for the holidays. Stockings hung around that fireplace he wanted, including a tiny sock she'd knitted herself in pink-and-blue marbled yarn. She didn't even know how to knit. A point that finally managed to propel her back to reality.

"Todd, I'm sorry I've been so busy lately."

"That's okay! I'm glad you're helping him out. It's funny, though, right, how I made a joke about Derrick Bright stealing you away, and then you went away with him for the weekend?"

"Nothing happened," she blurted.

"Anne, what? No! I didn't… I know that!" He laughed, but it was a stiff, forced sort of guffaw. Did he sense something? Was he jealous? He went on, "I know how loyal you are and how much integrity you have. I've always loved that about you. That, and a lot of other things. Which is why I—"

*Love. Oh, jeez.* "Todd, wait, I—"

"I have to break up with you."

"You…" She did the rapid eye blink, trying to process. "Excuse me, what?"

"I'm so sorry, Anne. I think you are so incredible. Literally, you are one of the coolest people I've ever known." He paused, gathering his thoughts. "But I feel as if we're more like…"

"Friends," she suggested. "Or maybe even cousins? That sounds kind of weird, though, doesn't it?" She rushed to add, "But I know what you mean. I feel the same way."

"No, it's not weird. I was going to say family."

"That's funny."

They exchanged smiles before Todd turned serious again. "Anne, I'm seeing someone else."

A jolt went through her, and she took a moment to analyze what it meant. Surprise mostly, she realized with relief.

"Anyone I know?"

He blushed, his eyes lighting with a certain special sparkle. In the year they'd been together, Anne had only seen that look one time. She let out a gasp. "It's Bailey, isn't it?"

"Wait... How did you know?"

"You look like you did the day I introduced you to her."

"Do I? That's embarrassing. Yes, it's Bailey. But it *just* happened. Like this last weekend. We saw each other at the auction. She likes to sail and is thinking about getting a boat. I told her she could ask me any questions she had. She texted on Saturday with questions. I offered to give her a tour of *Whirlwind*. Then we spent the rest of the weekend texting and talking."

"Oh."

His next statement came out in a rush. "Then we met again this morning, and I kissed her. I'm so sorry."

"I see."

"That was not right, I know. Bailey and I agreed that you and I needed to resolve things first before we went any further."

"That's commendable."

"She thinks very highly of you, too, and this is eating her up inside."

Anne stared at him, thinking. The kiss stung a little. But there wasn't a lot she could say, was there? If Derrick hadn't stopped, she would have done the same. Even without being in love with Todd, his admission hurt. She was even more glad she had nothing to confess.

"Anne, say something."

"I am happy for you." She meant that, too. "Please, tell Bailey you have my blessing."

"Wow."

"What?"

"Well, it's just that this went a little easier than I anticipated. I mean, if you were doing this to me last week, I probably wouldn't have taken it quite as well as you are."

The mix of happiness and relief emanating from him was compelling. But it was the glow she noted. Did she look like that, too? she wondered. Because Todd wasn't the only one who wanted to pursue a promise of more. She couldn't wait to tell Derrick, to finally follow through with that kiss. Clearly, she was reverting to those lovesick days, but she didn't even care.

"Why, Todd Marino, are you having an ego moment?"

"Maybe, just a little." He shrugged. "But I would never want to hurt you, Anne. I'm so sorry if I have."

"You are a great guy—do you know that? Bailey is lucky to have you."

"Thank you. That means a lot coming from you."

"I can't believe she likes to sail. You'll never have to worry about the weather forecast again."

He chuckled. "Or about my girlfriend knocking herself cold when she runs into the boom."

"Hey," she retorted, "I never lost consciousness."

They laughed together before Todd said, "At the risk of sounding like a major cliché, I hope you find someone special, too, Anne. A man who deserves you. Maybe even one who likes baseball."

"Well." Anne felt her cheeks go warm.

"So, funnily enough, your instincts about Derrick Bright weren't that far off."

Todd eyed her sharply. "What do you mean?"

"He was the love of my life."

Todd lifted his eyebrows in question. "Was?"

"Yes, and now he's back. Nothing has happened, though." Aside from Derrick declaring his intentions, but that wasn't relevant to this anymore, was it?

Todd snuffled out a sound of part amusement, part disbelief. "Well, that explains a lot."

"About what?"

Todd went wide-eyed. "Oh, shoot, he's going to drown me."

"He's going to what? Did he say something to you?"

He scrubbed a hand over his jaw. "I can't say. I promised I wouldn't tell you."

"Todd! Tell me. What did Derrick do?"

"He, um, uh, he may have paid me a visit. He saw Bailey and me… And he, uh, insisted that I break up with you. To be fair, Anne, I was already thinking it."

"He. You. I…" she wheezed, puffing out

words like some sort of over-the-top Lamaze student. "He did what?"

When Todd finished telling her about the encounter, he offered weakly, "He's got your back, Anne. At least you can feel good about that, right?"

# CHAPTER FOURTEEN

WHERE IN THE world was she? Derrick checked the time again. Anne should have been back hours ago. Freaking cheating Todd! How long could it possibly take to break up with a person? Surely, not more than two hours and eleven minutes!

Anne had gotten home after work, given him the best hug ever. Confirming for him that she wasn't quite as far above the romantic fluff as she'd claimed. He'd been ready to announce his plans for a romantic evening when, in a mad rush, she'd informed him she was meeting Todd at a restaurant "right around the corner."

Before she'd left, she'd added, "Derrick, I'm going to talk to him," which had Derrick believing she was in a breaking-up frame of mind herself. Between her statement and knowing Todd's intentions, he'd anticipated her return in, like, twenty minutes—an hour at the most.

He'd even ordered extra Chinese food in case they opted to skip dinner and she was hungry when she returned. Then he'd had a quick shower and put on fresh clothes. Because breakups could be hard, even ones that were for the best, and what if he needed to console her? He hoped he wouldn't need to console her too much, but regardless, he didn't want to smell like sweat and dirt after spending the afternoon attempting to teach a ten-year-old how to hit a baseball.

Thinking about today's lesson made him smile, despite his current Anne angst. Albert was a great kid. Smart, funny and mature beyond his years, he'd made Derrick laugh. Albert's uncle had won the lessons for him as a birthday gift, but he'd seemed undaunted, almost skeptical about Derrick's credentials, so intent was he on learning to be a better hitter. Who cared about the major leagues? He had a Little League game next week!

Albert was unskilled but determined, and Derrick immediately spotted his potential. By the time the lesson was over, he'd shown marked improvement. Derrick had felt good about it, and apparently, he'd passed Albert's test, because the boy had then informed Derrick that he'd go ahead and show up for the next lesson. Derrick had thanked him and managed not to laugh. He couldn't wait to tell Anne all about it.

If she ever got back from her date with Todd, that is. After stashing the Chinese food in the fridge, he tried to read his copy of the matching mystery novels he'd bought for himself and Anne. When he'd reread the same page approximately eleven times, he gave up and turned on the TV, only to click aimlessly through the channels.

Not in the mood for his usual home-improvement shows, he settled for a travel channel, which placated him until a show about Iceland came on. It was a place he and Anne used to dream about visiting. He changed the channel. The cooking network seemed safe. And would have been if Anne hadn't been out to dinner with Todd. Frustrated, he finally shut it off.

A check of his email proved fruitless; too distracted. He called Grandma May, but the conversation was brief as she informed him that she was "right as rain" and sounded preoccupied. He was typing out a text to Easton when he finally heard Anne's key in the lock. In an effort to conceal his worry, he grabbed his book and kicked his feet up on the ottoman.

"Hey," he called out in a casual tone. "How was dinner? How's Todd?" He managed to mask his trepidation with a friendly smile.

Anne came around and sat on the opposite end of the sofa. She puffed out a loud sigh—a contented-sounding one.

"Honestly? Derrick, it was incredible! I don't know how to tell you this. I was going to talk to Todd and, you know, tell him about you and me and how I'd like to explore whatever this is." She motioned between them. "But then, something happened tonight. Todd was…" Her face transformed, and she had a dreamy look, while her focus drifted away for a few long seconds. "He really stepped it up."

"Huh." Derrick tensed, barely managed to swallow around his snarky reply. He should have listened to his instincts and tossed the guy off the dock.

"We started with dinner at my favorite restaurant, where he ordered oysters and champagne."

Despite his best attempt, Derrick felt a scowl forming. "Since when do you eat oysters?" In the past, he'd urged her to try them. She'd always refused, calling them "slime on the half shell." It had been a running joke between them.

"Since tonight," she gushed. "Why didn't you ever tell me they were so delicious? Not as good as the lobster, however."

"Lobster," he repeated blandly. Her favorite. "I bet."

"Delicious. I've never had it so sweet. So then we took a carriage ride through the city to the marina."

"The marina?" Derrick felt his blood pressure spike. How dare he take her to the scene of the crime?

"Mmm-hmm," she said. "For an evening sail. While we were out on the water, this boat came zipping up to us, and guess who was on it? No," she said, waving off any response. "You'll never guess, so I'll just tell you—this local singer, Carmen Petrillo, who I adore. And she was accompanied by an entire orchestra. It was so..." She trailed off, searching for a word, then finally said, "Ro-mantic."

That two-timing snake was trying to win her back! Everything Todd had told Derrick had been a lie. Well, Derrick had warned him. If he didn't tell her the truth, then he would.

"Anne—"

"And *then*," she drawled, "we went swimming with the dolphins in the moonlight. It was like a fairy tale."

Okay. Uh-oh. Todd had come clean, all right. Too clean, apparently. Derrick had explicitly told the cheater not to mention his visit.

"Kind of like the fairy tale you're telling me right now?"

"Pretty much," she answered, meeting his gaze head-on, the wistful expression now firmly replaced with a challenging, annoyed glare.

"That was cruel."

"You deserved it! You *ordered* Todd to break up with me? How dare you?"

"Ordered? I don't know that I'd characterize it quite that dramatically. I encouraged him to do the right thing and then—"

"Did you or did you not tell him you would take him out into the Pacific Ocean and leave him there with a life raft, a coat hanger and a pillowcase to sail his way home if he didn't confess all?"

"Okay," he conceded. "Yes, but did he tell you why?"

"Yes, Derrick, he did. He told me all about Bailey, about the kiss. The issue here is not Todd. The problem is you manipulating your way into my life. Again."

"Anne, I'm sorry. But when I saw Todd and Bailey together, and I thought about what happened with us—what you thought you saw. The idea of you going through that again just… I lost it a little."

"A little?"

"I still think he deserved it. He deserves worse when you really stop and consider it. Besides, I didn't *do* anything to him."

"Derrick, promise me, you won't do anything like this again. If we're going to give this—us—a serious effort, I have to be able to trust you. No more string-pulling and back-room deals. You can't manipulate circumstances—or people—to get what you want."

Now would be the time to tell her he was

Sally's anonymous source. *Except.* Should he tell her now when they were so close to the "us"? Because that's all that mattered right now. What good would it do to confess and apologize and make her upset? He could silently promise not to do anything like it in the future without revealing what he'd done in the past, right?

Right, he told himself. "I promise," he said. "I won't do it again."

"Well." She sat back and grinned like a happy cat. "I think you've learned a lesson here. And I hope you were miserable sitting around and waiting for me."

"I wasn't *really* worried," he said with exaggerated emphasis.

"Is that so?" she asked, her mouth twitching with a smile.

"Yeah, I was just kicking back and relaxing. Doing some reading. I sort of forgot you were even gone." He gave the sofa cushion beside him an affectionate pat. "Keira is right. This thing is a little slice of heaven."

"Get some reading done, did ya?" She got up and moved to sit closer.

"Sure did."

Her hand darted out to pluck the book from

his hands and then she flipped it over. "When exactly did you start reading upside down?"

"Fine," he said and chuckled. "I was out of my mind with jealousy. There, are you happy? Where have you been, anyway?"

"I am very happy," she confessed and then answered, "I was downstairs at Keira's, dreaming up this tale."

He grinned. "Should have known."

"The dolphins were her idea."

"It was a nice touch, very creative."

She chuckled. "I do have good news, though."

"Yeah?"

"Todd and I did break up. Just so you know, I was already going to break up with him. Before he broke up with me first."

"Honest?" Derrick felt his soul take flight.

"Yes." She scooted closer, so close that her thigh pressed against his. Derrick's pulse jumped, then began tapping a wild rhythm. "So you know what that means?"

Shifting to look at her, he found her gaze focused on his mouth. They remained that way for a long moment. Derrick waited. It was excruciating, but finally, she leaned toward him. He followed her lead until their lips met in a deliberate and perfect kiss.

For so long, he'd dreamed about this moment. And now he eagerly absorbed every sensation; the velvety softness of her lips, the silky texture of her hair, the perfect curve of her neck, the warmth of her skin as he cupped her cheek. He breathed in the subtle, sweet vanilla scent that was Anne.

She moaned softly, and the sound, the feel of her hands on him, too, made him aware that this was no dream. And he was struck with the realization that it had been eleven long years since his world had felt so right.

ANNE KISSED DERRICK, and she remembered, she knew, she understood, why she'd never been able to give her heart to anyone else. All these years, she'd believed the reason was that Derrick had broken it so severely that it was too fragile to withstand another go-around. But the truth was he'd had it all along.

Pulling away enough to catch her breath, she whispered, "Derrick."

"Anne." He tipped his forehead to rest against hers for a few seconds. Then he shifted to look at her, and she could see the love shimmering in his deep brown eyes. Derrick *loved* her. She knew it because she'd seen it already, hadn't she? Felt it in nearly every move he made toward her. Even the protectiveness he'd exhibited where Todd's misdeed was concerned, as intrusive as it was, spoke to his feelings.

Maybe Derrick was right. Maybe it really was as simple as picking up where they left off.

"CHECK THIS OUT," Anne said later, setting aside the container of dumplings to hand Derrick her phone, where the latest tweet from @JackDerryPop was blowing up on Twitter. "I think this will dispel any lingering suspicion about Easton."

Know the facts before you speak! True Panthers don't cheat! #EastonBright is a Panther. You want to share some truth? Spread this one around: Bonus Baby Bright is sound & MLB bound. Like and retweet to receive a #FREE bag of #DerryPopPopcorn #PantherPride #BonusBabyBright

Anne picked up the dumpling box again. Thoughtful how Derrick had asked Keira which Chinese restaurant was her favorite. Even better how he'd made sure to discover which dishes she preferred.

"You probably won't be surprised to hear that 'Bonus Baby Bright' is trending." Bonus baby was a baseball term used to describe a particularly young player who received a substantial contract. Jack's tweet included the original photo of Easton with Dr. Lenox and Brita. There was also a link to an article detailing the truth and another about how to get your free popcorn.

"Does he realize this is going to cost him a fortune?" Derrick asked, touched and incredulous that the man would go to such lengths for Easton.

"Trust me, he knows. Jack is the most generous person I've ever met."

"Has Easton seen this?"

"I just texted a screenshot to his new number."

Derrick's phone began to buzz with an incoming call. He frowned at the display. "I don't recognize the number."

Anne did. "It's Easton."

Derrick smiled. "Things are looking up."

"Things are definitely looking up," Anne repeated as Derrick answered the call.

"ANNE!" KEIRA HOLLERED as she burst through the door of Anne's apartment early the next morning.

"Out here!" Anne called from the patio, where she and Derrick were eating breakfast before leaving for the farm. The reporters were gone, and Camile was dropping off Easton there later, too.

"You're not going to believe this. Good morning, Derrick," she said, tossing him a quick smile.

"Hi, Keira. Your hair is wet. Have you been swimming with the dolphins this morning?"

She busted out a laugh. "You are a keeper, Derrick Bright." Hitching a thumb toward Anne, she asked, "She is going to keep you, right?"

"Working on it," Derrick answered before exhaling a loud sigh. "I gotta tell you, Keira, I'm giving this tryout everything I've got. Last night, I got a first kiss and secured a firm commitment for a date. So, that's something. Really hoping I make the cut."

Keira nodded with mock solemnity. "Well, Derrick, I can tell you that's the kind of enthusiasm you need if you intend to join Team McGrath. You need to dig deep, Bright. If it helps at all, I can report that you're doing well in the all-important impress-the-best-friend category."

"That's a relief because sometimes best friends can throw all their loyalty points to the old boyfriend."

"Nope, not happening. Don't get me wrong. I like Todd. A lot. He's charming and sweet, almost too much, though. Not nearly enough flash and sass for the likes of this one." She nudged her chin in Anne's direction. "Know what I'm saying? He's not a starting player. He's more like mascot material. And Anne needs—"

"Hey!" Anne said, lifting a hand and pointing at herself. "Anne is right here. I'm the head coach. I have all the say in who makes the cut on my team. And…" She paused to look from Keira to Derrick and back again. "This is a weird metaphor, even for me."

"Whatever you say, Coach," Keira said while she and Derrick laughed together like old friends. Then Keira asked her, "Can you delay your departure for an hour or so?"

"Probably. Why?"

"Jennifer Katzen wants a meeting with us!"

"No way."

"Yes way! Anne, she called just now while I was in the show…err, *river* with the dolphins." She winked at Derrick. "Her voice mail said if it was at all possible that she'd like to meet this morning because she's leaving for India tonight."

"Yes!" Anne said, popping up from the sofa. "Let's go. Call her back. Wait!" She turned to look at Derrick. "Derrick, is it okay with you if we postpone your return home for a bit?"

"Of course, yes—go do your thing. Kellan texted to see if I wanted to meet today, anyway. We were going to have dinner tonight, but I'll see if he can squeeze me in this morning."

"GOOD NEWS FOR the baseball team," Kellan informed Derrick later, tenting his fingers on the tabletop. They were at a coffee shop near Kellan's house in northwest Portland, where they'd scored a table outside in the courtyard under the shade of a giant old oak tree. A wrought-iron fence separated them from a bike path, where riders were pedaling past.

Derrick sipped his cappuccino while Kellan explained, "So far, anyway. Two guys from the football team and one member of the swim team have been arrested and charged with dealing. We'll see if they name anyone else once the attorney general's office starts offering plea deals. I don't know how many athletes will ultimately be suspended. The ones who test positive, obviously, but you know how that goes. Testing is so tricky."

Derrick shook his head. "I gotta say, I'm relieved that Gavin wasn't involved. Poor guy, all that happening at his parents' house. I can't imagine how terrible he feels."

"Me, too. He's a good kid. There's a reason he and Easton are friends, and they're both leaders on the team. The other players look up to them. Like I said, things are okay for our guys, but you know, I'm not holding my breath until this thing shakes out."

"That is probably wise. Nothing about Hailey?" Derrick asked.

"Nothing but rumors. Like Easton, I think

she's a target because of her well-known mother. There's been talk of Celia Greenwich getting pressured to resign. She's a smart cookie, though. She hasn't said a word, and neither has Hailey. Of course, they have attorneys and experience with the blood-doping accusation. A double-edged sword there, right? They are being awfully harsh on her on social media, worse than Easton now that nothing has panned out about him."

"Easton hasn't talked to her or Gavin. I don't even think he knows all of this."

"So far, Easton is the only athlete who looks like he might come out of this thing looking better than he did before."

"Yeah, thanks to McGrath PR. And she's not done yet. Anne knows David Beyer, and he's agreed to do a story on Easton. He's coming out to the farm next weekend with a photographer."

"Awesome," Kellan said. "A photo of Easton cuddling one of those chickens of his will have people half in love before they ever see him play."

Derrick chuckled. "That's what Anne says, too. We are so lucky. She is incredible, and her colleague, Keira, really likes Easton, too. And they've got this guy who can find out pretty much anything from a photo. He solved the mystery of the B-12 injection in about thirty seconds."

"I almost cried when I saw that photo," Kellan said.

"Tell me about it! If it weren't for Anne, I would have handled it much worse than I did. Which was not great to begin with." That was an understatement. Her level head and calming influence had kept him from reacting worse than he had.

"How did you manage it, by the way? Getting her to agree, I mean, beyond the auction package you won."

"Oh. Uh, Anne and I knew each other years ago. She had a soft spot for Easton way back then, and once she realized that Easton was innocent, she agreed to keep working with him."

Kellan paused, eyeing him speculatively. "You knew each other, huh?"

"Yep." Derrick tried not to smile but could feel it creeping through. How could talk of Anne not make him smile at this point?

Kellan barked out a laugh. "Mmm-hmm,

and now you're getting to know each other again?"

"We are."

"That's sweet. Maybe you guys could come over for dinner next week? Sarah and I are having a party, inviting the other coaches and staff, a few of our neighbors, and some people Sarah has met at work." Kellan's wife, Sarah, was a doctor who'd landed the job of her dreams at a local teaching hospital. "I'm grilling."

"Sounds fun. I'll ask Anne."

Kellan nudged his chin toward Derrick. "How's the leg?"

"Pretty good."

"Have you decided what's next for you yet?"

"Still working on that."

"Well, I've got a proposition for you."

"What kind of proposition?"

"A coaching one." Kellan plunged ahead before Derrick could respond. "I know you're considering something outside of the game, but I promised Tommy I'd run it by you."

"Tommy? Tommy Sipley?"

Kellan grinned. "Yep, the owner of the

Colorado Sharks asked me to talk to you and find out if I thought you might be interested in the head coaching job."

# CHAPTER FIFTEEN

*THWACK!*

The unfamiliar sound reverberated through the air as Derrick opened the passenger door of Anne's SUV. He paused, but didn't hear it again, so he wrote it off as insignificant. Noise sometimes carried differently out here in the country.

Derrick was looking forward to seeing Easton and catching him up on the latest. He was thrilled with how things had worked out for his brother so far, even though it meant moving out of Anne's apartment. He knew she wasn't yet in the same place he was relationship-wise, so some distance might be good. His deepest hope was she'd miss him enough to get there with him quicker.

Her meeting with the client whom he'd accidentally thwarted at the auction had gone well. He and Anne were both in high spirits, and he felt a stirring of love for her so strong he could barely contain it.

Patience was not his strongest suit. How long did he need to wait before moving forward? Before making things official and permanent? Would she want to move here to the farm with him? Her apartment was fantastic, too, and convenient for her work. It was close to Kellan's, and if she and Sarah hit it off, it would be fun to be near them. Maybe they could keep both places.

He opened the back door to retrieve his bag and heard it again. *Thwack.* Unmistakable this time when another *thwack* followed.

He shut the door and looked at Anne. "Did you hear that?" It was obvious she had because she was peering curiously in the direction of the house.

"What was that?" she asked.

"I have no idea."

*Thwack, thwack.*

This time, it was accompanied by a shriek and a "Woo-hoo!" and then a booming, masculine laugh.

"Grandma," Derrick said.

"Jack," Anne said at the same time.

Together, they headed around the side of

the house, stopping in their tracks once they arrived. At some point during the weekend, a stall of sorts had been constructed in the backyard. The back wall consisted of smooth thick wooden planks. A large bull's-eye covered one half of the surface. Another identical bull's-eye covered the other half.

Grandma stood nearby holding an ax. Her best friend, Grace, was next to her. They were both grinning. Derrick recognized the look; they'd just finished cracking up laughing about something. Both had axes casually draped over their shoulders like two gray-haired lumber-jills out for a wood-cutting jaunt through the forest. Except, she wasn't a logger, she was his grandmother, and this looked...dangerous.

"Hey, kids!" Grandma called, noticing them where they were still standing by the house, taking it all in. "Look what Jack and I built."

"This is a hoot!" Grace exclaimed. "You kids have gotta try it." Grace was the closest thing to an aunt Derrick and Easton had ever had. Technically, they had two on their mom's side, but they both lived back east, and they'd only seen them a few times grow-ing up.

Jack and Easton were there, too. Jack was also holding an ax and beaming proudly. Easton sat in one of two chairs positioned be-hind a clearly defined line in the grass, where a bright, pink ribbon was stretched across the ground and held in place with wooden stakes. He gave Derrick a wave along with a look that suggested he knew what he was thinking.

"Wow!" Anne exclaimed.

"I know!" Grandma said. "When I men-tioned to Jack what the gamers had planned this week, I learned how he's in to ax-throwing. He volunteered to teach me, and, well, one thing led to another, and here we are. It's a blast!"

"I bet!" Derrick called loudly and then lowered his voice so only Anne could hear, "One thing led to another? What does that mean? I don't even know what to say."

Derrick lowered his duffel bag to the ground. Anne reached over and took his hand. She whispered, "It'll be okay."

"My grandmother is throwing axes in the backyard. How is that okay?"

"That's the way Jack rolls. There's no later, or tomorrow, or someday. After losing his wife, he's very life-is-short, and let's-do-it-now."

Derrick groaned softly. "A perfect match for Grandma."

"Yep," Anne agreed and then urged him into a walk toward Easton.

"'Bury the hatchet,'" Derrick said to Easton. "this is what you were trying to tell me the other day about Grandma and the gamers expanding their horizons."

Easton grimaced. "'Fraid so."

"Is it dangerous? Because it looks like the modern-day equivalent of lawn darts."

"Not when you do it like this. Jack is very safety-conscious. Grandma's original plan was a piece of plywood nailed to that stump by the orchard. She asked me to set it up for her, but I hadn't gotten to it yet before everything happened. He did us a favor."

"Oh, good grief!" Derrick said with a groan. "No wonder you didn't tell me."

"Yeah, there's been a lot going on. I thought it best to wait until you got here."

They all watched as Grandma chucked her ax at the target and hit inside the circle, far to the left of the bull's-eye. Jack let out a whoop and tucked her in close to his side. She slipped her arm around him. Their heads dipped close together, and then Grandma emitted a high-pitched noise.

"Is she giggling?" Derrick asked.

"I do believe that was a giggle," Easton confirmed with a snicker of his own.

"Since when does Grandma giggle?" Never, in his entire life, had he heard such a sound come from May Bright.

"I am as dumbfounded as you are." Easton shrugged a helpless shoulder.

"What is happening?" Derrick asked.

Easton slid him a smile, which then traveled to Anne and down to their still-joined hands before landing on him again. With a deliberate eyebrow raise, he said, "Clearly, *a lot* happened this weekend while we all went our separate ways, huh?"

Derrick sighed. "There have been some exciting developments," he confirmed, squeezing Anne's hand.

KELLAN AND SARAH NICHOLS lived in a trendy, historic part of the city. The neighborhood consisted mainly of older well-kept Victorian-style homes. The backyard was spacious and enclosed with a wooden fence. Perfect for entertaining, there was a large expanse of lush, green grass with a line of tall shade trees off to one side. A beanbag toss was set up near the fence line, where four players were battling it out.

The grill was already smoking, and Derrick and Anne joined the mix of people swarming around two picnic tables. Anne was surprised by how many people she recognized, mainly fellow Panther Project supporters. Derrick seemed to know most everyone and seamlessly performed introductions.

When the crowd had thinned around the host and hostess, they approached the couple. Anne was a little nervous about meeting Coach Nichols in person, especially after she'd turned down his job offer only to accept Derrick's. But he was gracious and funny and made her feel at ease.

His wife, Sarah, was just as kind, although Anne felt a curious degree of intensity emanating from the woman as they made small talk. Possibly it was a personality trait or a byproduct of her demanding profession.

Sarah, she'd learned, was a pediatric surgeon, and thrilled to be here in Portland, as she'd grown up in a small town a couple of hours away near Oregon's capital of Salem.

The four of them chatted about the Northwest, the tricky housing market and baseball. Soon, plates were overflowing with burgers and chicken and other assorted picnic foods. Laughter and cheerful conversation filled the air. Anne appreciated the laid-back crowd and especially enjoyed watching Derrick interact with his friends.

He was outgoing and funny, and obviously well-liked. But he was also constantly in tune with where she was and if she was having a good time. He kept casting her sweet, heat-filled glances that made her stomach flip. Getting reacquainted this way was more fun than she could have imagined.

When everyone finished eating, Sarah said, "Kellan, I'm going to run inside and grab the desserts and make coffee."

"Can I help?" Anne offered.

"That would be wonderful," Sarah said.

"Your home is just lovely," Anne said once they were inside. Truly, it looked like something from a magazine. Despite the age of the house, the furnishings appeared bright and new. The kitchen was outfitted with an assortment of gourmet gadgets and state-of-the-art appliances.

"Thank you," Sarah said. "I'd love to take the credit, but my sister did the decorating. Left to my own devices, the walls would be covered with anatomy charts, a periodic table and posters of Kellan in his baseball uniform."

Anne laughed before confessing, "You should see my place. It's basically a larger version of my college apartment. The only thing missing is a beanbag chair and a lava lamp."

Sarah laughed. "I'm so happy you and Derrick have found each other again. Kellan told me you two used to be a couple a long time ago?"

"That's true." While Sarah got the coffee going, Anne gave her an abbreviated version of the events, calling their breakup a misunderstanding on her part.

"You know, Kellan and Derrick played together for seven years."

"I did know that, oddly enough. I'm a bit

of a baseball fanatic. One of the best catcher to second-base combinations I've ever seen."

"Right?" she gushed. "Derrick was Kellan's best friend on the team. They're still best friends. There's a group of us who hung out together a lot. Six players, two of them married, one with a long-time girlfriend, all of whom I'm still close with."

Anne nodded, unsure of where she was going with this and hoping she wasn't about to get the you-better-not-hurt-him or else speech.

"Then we had two serial daters, as we called them, who went through girlfriends faster than we could keep track of their names."

Anne managed not to cringe, but something must have shown on her face because Sarah's hand shot out. "Not Derrick!" she clarified. "He wasn't one of those. My point is, in all the years I've known him, we *never* met a woman he was seeing."

"Really? Why?"

"Kellan did a couple of times, but only by accident. Like he'd run in to a random woman at Derrick's house or something. But on birthdays, celebrations, team functions, or dinners, Derrick always showed up single. It was like a thing people talked about, speculated about. We all tried setting him up, but he always made it clear he wasn't interested in anything serious."

"Oh," Anne breathed as her soul took flight.

"Well, imagine my surprise when Kellan came home and said Derrick was coming today with a date."

"I can't even…"

Sarah grimaced. "So now it's confession time. I texted my little wives club to tell them Derrick was bringing you. They were literally beside themselves. I'm pretty sure Zale would have flown all the way from Florida today to meet you if she wasn't eight months pregnant."

Anne flipped a thumb toward the backyard. "So that photo you took of Derrick and me when we got here?"

"Yep, sent it straight to them."

Anne tried to absorb this information. Even after the way she'd broken up with Derrick, the things she'd said, he'd still been in love with her. Like her, he'd hung on to his feelings for a long, *long* time. Like him, her feelings were still there. She was positive of that now. So what was she waiting for? It almost felt cruel at this point to keep the truth from him.

"So they're all anticipating your report?"

"Not anymore," she confessed with a sheepish grin. "I already texted everyone how awesome you are."

"Oh. Wow. Thank you."

"We all want Derrick to be happy. I've always thought—" Sarah broke off the sentence there.

"Thought what?"

"I always thought he'd had his heart broken and never quite recovered."

Yep, that sealed it. Anne was through waiting. Laughter bubbled up inside of her, because all of a sudden, she realized she was guilty of the very thing Derrick had reminded her that they used to do. As wonderful as Kellan and Sarah were and as much fun as she was having, she couldn't wait to get out of there and be alone with Derrick.

A SHORT WHILE LATER, Anne had the sense Derrick was feeling the same way. He found her outside, where she'd been chatting with some of Sarah's work friends.

He slid an arm around her shoulders, leaned close and then whispered in her ear, "You wanna go back to your place and eat ice cream and read?"

"Yes, I do," she answered without hesitation. Less than an hour after that, they were snuggled on the sofa.

"So…" Anne nervously cleared her throat. "Derrick, I have something I need to tell you."

"Okay," he said, eyeing her curiously.

"For a long time after we broke up, for the whole time, really, I was so glad I'd never told you I loved you. I repeated that exact phrase to myself so many times—'at least I never said I love you.' But I think that might have been a mistake. Maybe if I'd told you then, and you'd told me, I wouldn't have had the insecurity when I saw the man who wasn't you kissing another woman. Maybe I would have been more secure in the notion you would never cheat."

"Anne, no, that's not fair. I'm the one who screwed up. I got scared, and—"

"Shh," she breathed and then leaned in to

silence him with a quick brush of her lips to his. "What I'm trying to say is I don't want to make that mistake again. I'm not waiting for you to say it first this time—I love you, Derrick."

"I love you, too, Anne," he said and then kissed her. "Although," he continued when he pulled away, "I already said it. So technically, I did say it first."

"No, you didn't."

"Yes, I did. When we were at the beach, and I pointed out how we should still be together."

"That doesn't count."

"How does that not count?"

"You admitted that you *had* been in love with me, not that you are. You said you still had feelings."

"Same difference."

"No, actually it's not."

He frowned. "Technicality. The intent was there, making it a clear I love you."

"No, it wasn't," she returned adamantly. "There was no declaration. I can't believe we're arguing about this. Does everything have to be a competition with you?"

"No," he said, shrugging a shoulder. "Not

everything. Just the important things. Like baseball and love, apparently. Anne, I love you."

She grinned. "Thank you, Derrick. I love you, too."

"I love you," he repeated.

"I love—"

"I love you," he interrupted. "I love you. I love you."

"Wait…"

"I love you."

"No, you are *not*—"

"Claiming the title of Most 'I Love You's' Stated in the Relationship?" he said, finishing her sentence. "Yes. That's exactly what I'm doing, and I win."

"You…" She slapped a palm on her forehead. "I give up."

"Good." He grinned. "Because this title is important to me. Now, what do you think is more important? Who says it first, or who has said it the *most*? Because I think most wins out every time. Like in baseball, you don't get recognized for the first home run of the season. It's the most that make you special."

"Impossible. You are impossible."

"I know," he agreed and then sighed dramatically. "I am. I guess it's a good thing you love me, huh? Because I sure do love you…"

## CHAPTER SIXTEEN

"STANCE," DERRICK DIRECTED his young charge.

He and Albert were inside a batting cage at the NPU practice fields getting ready to hit some balls.

Bending at the knees, Albert hefted the bat into position just as Derrick had shown him.

"Nice," he said. "You've been practicing."

"Yeah, well, homework is kind of my thing," Albert commented dryly. "In case you haven't figured that out yet."

"I may have caught on to that detail," Derrick said, matching his tone. "Elbow up, just a little higher."

Albert's face twisted with an uncertain grimace.

Derrick said, "I know it feels strange but trust me."

"I'm trying. How is this?"

"Perfect. Now, let me see your swing."

Albert swung the bat. Beautifully.

"Albert! That follow-through brought tears to my eyes. Now, remember, you're going to watch the ball hit your bat."

Derrick still couldn't believe no one had ever explained to the kid how the goal was to see the ball connect with the bat. When'd he'd explained this to Albert, he'd scoffed and informed Derrick that he was pretty sure the laws of physics made such an action impossible.

Dumbfounded, Derrick had asked him if he'd ever heard the expression "Keep your eye on the ball"?

"Sure," Albert had answered. "My coach shouts it at us all the time."

When Derrick asked him what he thought it meant, he'd shrugged and said, "You have to watch the ball coming at you, so you don't get hit with it."

Derrick had agreed, explained how there was a little more to it and then shown him how he could make magic happen.

Now Albert said, "I'm still not sure how I can do that when it's moving so fast."

"We've already discussed the physics of it, and you agreed it was possible." Derrick motioned at him. "Keep swinging."

He did. "I know. It just seems improbable."

"You have eyes, don't you?"

"Mr. Bright," Albert intoned, lowering the bat once more. "Where are you going with this?"

This kid. Derrick tried not to smile. "Where I'm going with this, Albert, is that you have the same eyes as I do and that Bobby Taylor does, right?"

At their first lesson, Albert had informed him how Bobby Taylor was the best hitter on their team. Albert's aspirations weren't to be better than Bobby; he just wanted to be a "solid hitter," so Bobby would quit calling him the strikeout king. He was fast, he'd informed Derrick, and if he could just get on base, he could "steal home all day long."

"And by the same..." Derrick qualified, "I mean we all have working human eyes." Albert was prone to debating science, his favorite subject in school.

"Yes." Albert lowered the bat, intrigued.

"Well, you already told me Bobby wasn't the sharpest pencil in the desk. Your brain works quicker than his. Wouldn't it follow that your eyes do, too? Or at least, just as fast as his."

"Maybe," he conceded. "But Bobby is also a beast. I think he's shaving already. Not even kidding, Mr. Bright, his voice is deeper than yours."

Derrick chuckled. "People often make the mistake of thinking that hitting is all about muscles and power. And don't get me wrong, those are helpful, too. Especially after you learn the fundamentals. But hitting is more about reaction time and balance." And confidence, he added silently. Confidence was key and what Albert needed most right now.

At its core, baseball was about belief.

There were plenty of other elements involved in successful hitting, too. But they would cover those later if there was time. This was the fourth of their five lessons, and Derrick already wished they had more time. How much fun would it be to watch Albert's progress over the course of years instead of weeks? The beauty of teaching a kid like Albert was that he was too young to have developed any truly bad habits.

Albert tapped his cleat with the bat and resumed his stance. "All right, enough stalling. Let's do this. I'm gonna crack this bat."

"Yeah, you are," Derrick encouraged, then headed to the pitcher's mound.

IT HAD BEEN a very long time since Anne felt like skipping anywhere. Like maybe in third or fourth grade. But Jennifer Katzen of All I Wear had officially signed on with McGrath PR, Easton's interview was scheduled for the following day, and since they'd quashed the photo gossip there'd been nothing new connecting him to the ongoing PED chaos. The combination of her good news and the lush green grass of the NPU practice fields beneath her feet made her want to skip. Maybe even do a cartwheel.

Possibly, she could credit her and Derrick's evolving relationship status for the impulse to cartwheel.

She spotted Derrick inside the batting cage with a kid she assumed was Albert. Derrick had his back to Anne, and was pitching balls to him. Anne approached slowly and remained silent so she could watch.

*Crack!* Ball and bat made perfect contact and reverberated through the air. Anne loved that sound, and she extra loved that Albert had been the cause of it. Derrick had been

keeping her apprised of both the boy's progress and his funny commentary.

"Nice shot!" Derrick shouted, clapping his
mitt against his thigh. "That one just landed
in right field, kiddo."

Albert grinned. "I am so stoked for my
game on Friday. I'm going to get a hit."

"You swing the bat like you have been
today, and you will get a hit, Albert."

Albert noticed they had an audience.
Holding up a hand in greeting toward Anne,
he said to Derrick, "Hey, is that your lady
friend?"

Derrick turned. His expression shifted
to eager surprise, and Anne felt her stomach flutter. She was early for the sole reason
that she couldn't wait to see him. Funny how
she'd suddenly developed the ability to duck
out of work at a decent hour.

"Yes, that's Anne, my girlfriend. Hi, Anne."

"Hey, guys." Anne lifted a hand in greeting and stepped a little closer.

"Anne, I'd like you to meet Albert. Albert,
Anne."

"It's wonderful to meet you, Albert. I've
heard great things about you."

Albert lit up. "Same."

"You've got a nice solid swing."

"Thanks to my batting coach. I'm hoping to get a hit at my game this week. Bobby's head is going to explode. My uncle is going to record it so I can show Mr. Bright."

"That sounds like a plan," Anne said. "Don't let me interrupt."

"Unfortunately, we're about finished," Derrick said, looking beyond Anne and then back to Albert. "Here comes your uncle."

"Too bad," Albert agreed.

Albert introduced her to his uncle Graham, and then Anne listened while the three of them discussed the details of Albert's final lesson. They exchanged goodbyes and then uncle and nephew headed off. Anne offered to help Derrick gather the baseballs scattered about the cage.

Derrick thanked her, and she pushed the wheeled cart inside. He told her about Albert's progress and how much he enjoyed teaching him. Anne shared her news about All I Wear.

Derrick swept her into a hug. "So am I officially forgiven for winning your consultation in the auction?"

"You were forgiven for that as soon as I realized Easton was innocent."

They decided to celebrate by inviting Keira up for pizza.

"I'm sorry we can't go out in public yet," Anne told him after she'd texted Keira. They'd agreed that Derrick and Easton should keep low profiles until the gossip had died down a bit more.

"I don't care," Derrick responded with an easy shrug. "Though I'll admit, I wouldn't mind seeing Bobby's head explode when he gets a hit," he added with a grin.

"I don't care much, either, to be honest." She tossed a ball into the cart. "That's a regular occurrence for me—dodging reporters and wannabe social-media personalities. But you know what?"

"What?"

"Depending on what happens the next couple of days, I think we could chance it and go to Albert's game."

"Really? Anne, are you sure?" His grin was hope-filled and irresistible.

"I'm sure," she said. Funny, how making Derrick happy now seemed an integral part of her own joy.

ALBERT'S TEAM, THE TIGERS, were warming up. It wasn't difficult to pick Bobby out among the players. Derrick laughed out loud at how Albert's description so aptly matched up with the kid's appearance. A full head taller and several decibels louder, he was the kind of player Derrick had always disliked intensely. And enjoyed tagging out at home.

The coach was hitting fly balls and then calling out at which base to make the play. Albert was in center field. Derrick found himself holding a breath when the coach knocked one over his head. But not to worry—he made an impressive running catch and, at the coach's command, made a commendable attempt at throwing it to home plate. Accurate but a bit shy of the distance. The kid would have an arm once he grew a bit more.

They were standing just behind the fence and Bobby's position was first base, so Derrick and Anne heard him loud and clear when he called, "Wimp can't throw for beans." And then he snickered.

Derrick felt his blood pressure spike.

Anne gasped. "Did that big lug just call Albert a wimp?"

Derrick glanced around, waiting for someone to call out the bully on his remark. "I have to do something. Should I talk to the coach?"

Anne's expression twisted thoughtfully. "Is that what you would have wanted at that age?"

"No, I'd want to punch him. But instead, I would have waited until he was trying to steal home and wiped him out at the plate."

Anne grinned. "You know, in my vast experience, bullies are insecure cowards. Something that might get to Bully Bobby is if you made your presence known to Albert. Maybe poke your head into the dugout, wish him luck, give him a fist bump, or whatever it is you cool baseball players are doing nowadays."

Derrick grinned. The plan had been for him to show up without Albert—or anyone else—knowing he was there until the end of the game.

"Are you sure? People might recognize me."

"I'm sure they will. We'll deal with the consequences," Anne assured him. "Nothing has happened in the last few days as far as Easton goes, anyway. We're probably in the clear where he's concerned."

Things did seem to be finally dying down on the scandal front. Derrick agreed, and waited until the team headed into the dugout before speaking with the coach. He introduced himself, then asked if it would be okay if Derrick said hello to Albert.

The coach enthusiastically consented, and Derrick went over to the metal fencing that enclosed the dugout.

"Hey, Marquez!" he shouted. "Look alive!"

Heads turned. "Mr. Bright!" a beaming Albert cried, popping to his feet and running toward him.

"Hey, that's Derrick Bright!" one of his teammates yelled. Excited chatter erupted.

"Come in so I can introduce you to my friends." Albert opened the gate and let him inside. Soon the kids were all gathered around. Albert introduced them all, even Bobby. Ten years old, Derrick thought, and already a class act. One kid asked Derrick to sign his mitt, another his cleat, then a gum wrapper, and on it went. The team manager, the mother of the shortstop, produced a Sharpie. Derrick signed everything.

Their coach was still in conference with the other team's coach, so Derrick took the opportunity to give the boys a quick pep talk about working together and how the team was like a family, and everyone should support one another.

He wasn't presumptuous enough to think it would change Bobby's behavior, but he believed the words himself, so he spoke them aloud. "At the end of the day," he explained, "your relationship with your teammates makes a difference in both how you perform as a unit and as an individual." The kids listened, and he could feel the buzz of enthusiasm when he finished. The coach entered the dugout, and Derrick exited to join Anne, where she'd found them a spot in the bleachers.

The Tigers took the field. Their opponent, the Vandals, started strong with two walks and two hits. They scored three runs before the pitcher then struck out two batters in a row. The Tigers answered with a base hit, and then Bobby knocked a double that allowed the runner to score. But that was all they could manage. Top of the third, they played stronger in the field, and, after a walk and a strikeout, Albert caught a fly ball and threw it to second base for a double play to end the inning.

With the Tigers at bat, Albert came up with two outs and a runner on third. Derrick felt that familiar butterfly twitch of nerves when the boy stepped into the batter's box.

The first pitch was a ball, and Albert let it fly right on by. Derrick exhaled a small sigh of relief. His biggest fear was that Albert would swing and miss once and then psych himself out.

That didn't happen.

As the pitcher wound up, Derrick's years of catching experience told him a fastball was coming. The perfect pitch for Albert because he had a tight, quick swing. And if he could only connect...

*Crack!*

He stood. Beside him, Anne also jumped to her feet. The ball flew up, up and up some more, sailing over and between the shortstop and third baseman. Landing with a bounce, it skipped past the left fielder and then kept on rolling...

All the way to the fence!

Meanwhile, Albert rounded second and slid into third. The third-base coach instructed him to stop. Derrick would have waved him around—the kid truly was that fast. Albert listened, holding up at third. A triple! Derrick was elated. Albert's gaze found his, and the grateful grin on his face landed hard on Derrick's heart. He answered with a victory punch.

In the stands, the crowd was going wild. The dugout was even louder as Albert's teammates shouted with joy. Even Bobby stood against the chain-link fence jumping up and down and cheering.

The spectators quieted as the next batter came up. Two pitches later, just as Albert predicted, he stole his way home.

WHEN THE GAME ENDED, Albert had racked up a walk and two additional hits, a single and a double—a ground ball to third, and a beautiful line drive. He scored two more runs and chalked up the most stolen bases. The Tigers won the game nine to four.

Anne and Derrick took a few minutes to congratulate Albert and the team. Albert's uncle, Graham, introduced them to more family, including Albert's parents, grandma, aunt, another uncle, two little sisters and a brother.

As ecstatic as Anne was about Albert's performance, she couldn't imagine how Derrick was feeling. He hadn't stopped smiling since Albert's triple. How tragic it would have been for him to miss this experience. It was absolutely the best decision she could have made to bring him here. No, the *best* decision was to give this relationship another try. That was literally what she was thinking as they headed into the parking lot.

So, she was caught off guard when someone called to them, "Derrick! Anne?"

They both turned at the sound of their names. Sally Cabot popped out from behind a silver van. Anne's good mood crashed.

"Sally, hi," she chirped too brightly. "How are you?" She expected a question about Easton or an invitation to comment on the scandal and was ready with a polite refusal.

"Great! Thanks for asking, Anne. How are you?"

"Not bad. Sorry to waste your time, but we can't comment on the NPU PED situation at this time. Maybe after—"

"Actually, I wanted to ask *Derrick* a question," she interrupted in a syrupy-sweet tone that set Anne's teeth on edge. "Unrelated to the NPU situation."

"Oh." She shrugged as if to say "go ahead and ask, but he's not answering."

Sally looked at him. "You're not answering my calls, Derrick."

*Why does she have your number?* Anne wanted to ask, but knew better than to give away her surprise.

"I haven't answered any reporter's calls or questions," Derrick returned diplomatically.

"Hmm. Well." Sally's eyebrows arched high. "I thought we had an understanding."

"I don't know what you mean," he returned. But Anne could tell by the look on his face, the tension in his body, that something was off.

Sally narrowed her gaze at him. "Fine," she said. "If that's how you want to play it. Derrick, do you have any response to this morning's comment from Tommy Sipley?"

Anne thought fast but couldn't land on why Sally would be asking Derrick about the owner of the Colorado Sharks. If they were hoping to get Easton on their roster, they were sadly misinformed. They were Triple A, and Easton was bound for the major leagues.

"What are you talking about?" Derrick asked. "What comment?"

"Derrick," Anne said, "let's not engage. We don't want to speculate on where Easton will be playing. He still has another season at NPU."

"His comment wasn't about Easton," Sally returned coolly. Watching Derrick closely, she said, "Tommy Sipley implied in an interview today with David Beyer that you are going to be the new head coach for the Colorado Sharks."

"Did he?" Derrick said and then chuckled.

"Yes, he did. When asked about who might be filling the position next season, he said, and I quote, 'Well, David, my short list currently includes one name, and that name is Derrick Bright.'"

Derrick blinked and gave his head a little shake. "Anne is right. I am not going to comment on that or anything else right now."

Anne felt her stomach drop because that blink had lasted just long enough to tell her there was substance behind the statement. But it was Sally's subsequent comment that made Anne realize what a complete and utter fool she'd been.

"Not even anonymously?" Sally asked. And then, as if Anne needed further confirmation about what he'd done, the reporter winked and added, "After all, that's kind of your thing, huh?"

# CHAPTER SEVENTEEN

WHY HAD HE ever believed he could keep this from her? Derrick climbed into the passenger's seat of Anne's SUV. Why hadn't he just told her what he'd done, explained how he'd contacted Sally out of the same desperation that had compelled him to bid on her consultation, and then apologized?

Anne appeared calm and serene as she stowed her bag behind the seat and buckled her seat belt. Derrick knew better. He could see the tension in her jaw as she started the vehicle, in her fingers as they gripped the steering wheel, in her shoulders as she turned her head to back out of the parking space. Slowly, silently, she navigated the SUV along the gravel lot and then pulled onto the road.

"Anne, I can explain. I—"

"Please, don't," she interrupted smoothly. "Don't say one word, Derrick. I don't even want to hear you breathing right now."

Derrick had left his car at Anne's apartment building in the underground garage. Once they arrived, she parked in her assigned space, turned off the engine and remained in the driver's seat, staring straight ahead at the concrete wall. The silence dragged on painfully, tension thickening the air between them.

Finally, she spoke. "I need you to get out."

"No, Anne, please, you have to listen. You have to let me explain."

"No, I don't," she answered sharply. She inhaled a deep breath before continuing. "I don't *have to* do anything you want me to do anymore, Derrick. We are finished. I cannot believe I didn't figure this out sooner. There aren't any sources close to the Bright family who also know me. As if forcing my hand with the auction bid wasn't bad enough, you talked to Sally *anonymously*? And you lied."

"No, I didn't. Technically, you were already representing Easton. The auction ensured that much, even if it only lasted for as long as your consultation."

"Really?" She scoffed. Ice-blue eyes stared hard at him for a few seconds. "That's the best you can do? That's how you justify treating me like your little puppet? I cannot believe I allowed you to play me like that!"

"I had to! It was for Easton. I had to make sure—"

"You got your way?" she interrupted, completing his thought. "That's what you were doing. No matter what excuse you give me right now, your goal was to get me to do this for you. It's like a game. You're always thinking about what move you can make, what tactic you can employ, so that the other players will react how you want them to."

She went on before he could respond. "Is that how life with you would be? Me, worrying about the tiniest minutiae of every single thing I say or do? Wondering how you might twist and exploit it for your own purposes? I say no, while you find a way to turn it into a yes?"

"Anne, no." But how could he dispute what she was saying? Hearing the truth was like a punch to the gut. "It wasn't like that. I—"

"It was exactly like that."

"I talked to Sally before you met with Easton. And, yes, I probably jumped the gun a little, but remember this all happened before we worked everything out between us."

"That doesn't matter to me. In fact, it makes it worse that you didn't tell me the truth. Especially after what happened with Todd. You promised you wouldn't do it again."

Derrick stayed silent on that technicality because she was right; he should have told her then.

"The greater point here is that it shows your character that you tried to control me in the first place."

"I wasn't trying to control you—I was trying to control the situation."

"Is there a difference? The auction, talking to Sally, my breakup with Todd, even the circumstances with Easton where you wanted to take over. Can't you see the pattern?"

He could.

"And what about later? Like when I told you I loved you, and we talked about our future? You should have at least told me then. Is that how you wanted to start our life together?"

"No, but I didn't see the point in going backward. I want to move forward with you, Anne."

"To Colorado? When were you going to tell

me about your new job? After you tricked me into moving there with you?"

"Anne—"

"Never mind, it doesn't matter."

"It does matter. I—"

"I'm glad you're taking a job in Colorado. You'll be an excellent coach. I'm sure you'll figure out a way to manipulate your players into winning every game."

With that, she grabbed her bag and climbed out of the vehicle. "Lock the doors when you leave."

A potent combination of fear and panic flooded through Derrick as he watched Anne stride away. He froze briefly before his hand then flew to the door handle, where it froze again. He didn't know what to do. He'd never seen her quite like this. Angry, irritated, frustrated, exasperated—yes, he'd produced all of those reactions in her at some point in the past. Not fun, but they always dealt with it, got past it. And he'd take any one of them right now over the expression he'd just seen. As long as he lived, he would never forget the look of sheer hopelessness on her face.

He'd messed up; he could see that so clearly now. Grandma was right. He didn't always think things through like he should. But he already knew that and, yes, occasionally, he paid for his impulsiveness. He didn't mind that, though, because the truth was it usually worked. He had good instincts. He'd always credited the trait with giving him an edge as a baseball player, especially a catcher.

On the rare occasion when this strategy didn't pan out, he would just try a new angle or pick up the pieces and move on. Knowing he'd tried was always more important to him than the inconvenience of dealing with the mistake. This time, he realized, as fear reached inside his chest and gripped his heart with a tight fist, he might have gone too far.

What if he'd finally made an error he couldn't fix?

"ANNE?" KEIRA SAID, sitting on the end of the sofa, where Anne was lying cocooned inside a fleece blanket. The same blanket she'd been wrapped in for the last two and half days.

"Annie? Hey, are you okay? I've been texting. You must have your phone off. You're not getting sick, are you?" Keira reached forward and flattened the palm of one hand to Anne's forehead.

"No, I'm not sick. Phone is off, yes." Anne shimmied her way up into a sitting position. "I take that back," she said, pushing one frowsy lock of hair from her eyes. "I am sick of thinking about him."

"I know," Keira said, sympathy infusing her tone. She'd stayed late at Anne's apartment the last two nights. Not even Netflix and ice cream and a good amount of crying had taken the edge off her misery. "I'm so sorry. Have you slept?"

"Not much," she admitted. Bleary-eyed, she glanced around at nothing before focusing on her friend again. "Keira, why can't I shake this? It's not like we were together for ten years or something. And look at Todd and I. We dated almost a year, and then he cheated on me, and I was basically fine."

"I don't think time necessarily corresponds to our level of attachment and the resultant degree of heartbreak. You weren't in love with Todd, were you? I think that smoothed the way to an amicable breakup."

Anne winced at the word. *Love.* Everything she'd done to avoid this pain from happening again, and yet here she was. And she hadn't just fallen in love again; she'd fallen in love with the same guy twice.

"Why him?"

Keira tsked and shook her head. "We could get so rich if we figured out the answer to that question."

"You always hear that old saying about how there is plenty of fish in the sea." Anne gestured around the room with a helpless shrug. "Where are they?"

"Excellent question."

"I've been thinking about it, and I'm pretty sure I have a bad sea."

"A bad sea?" Keira repeated in that interested, enthusiastic way that a super awesome friend does when they don't know quite what you're talking about, but they know you need to vent. Maybe you didn't even know what you were talking about, but they pretended you did. Keira was the best.

"Yeah. It's defective. In my sea, there is exactly one fish. And he's the wrong fish. That makes my sea faulty."

"I see." One hand shot out. "No pun intended."

"Wait! You know what's even more likely? He's controlling all of the other fish. Like a conductor. Derrick is a fish conductor. He's a...maritime maestro."

"Hmm." Keira cocked her head like she was pondering the possibility. "I think you might be giving him a little too much credit, but there is some merit to your overall theory. It is horrible how you've had your heart broken by the same fish two times. Even though the first time was mostly the result of a case of mistaken fish-*dentity*."

"That's funny." Anne almost managed a smile. "Thank you for listening to my ramblings."

"It's the least I can do. Are you coming in to work today?"

"I don't know. Is he still calling?" She'd blocked Derrick's number from her phone, so he'd started ringing the office. In a fit of frustration, she'd deleted him from her contacts.

"Yes, and he sent another gift basket. Don't worry—we refused delivery. Everything is good at the office, by the way. We are handling things just fine."

Anne curled her fingers around the arm of the sofa, gripping it so tightly it caused pain to shoot through her hand. That's when she realized an important point. After letting go, she shook out her hand. "That makes me mad."

Keira grinned. "You're angry that the company you built is running okay without you? I'm sure it's only temporary." She reached out and patted Anne's leg. "Don't worry. Undoubtedly, a crisis will occur soon that only you can fix."

"No! I'm happy about that part. What makes me angry is that he's done this to me, made me miss work. Work has always been my happy place, the place where I feel safe and where I know what to do. He's not only broken me—he's destroyed my sanctuary. I can't let him do that. I need to go..." She shifted as if to stand, noticed the smudge of last night's ice cream on her pajamas and whispered, "I think I need to shower first."

"No, you cannot," Keira agreed. "And, yes, you do. But first, I have a plan to get you feeling like yourself again—or at least closer to yourself."

"Donuts?"

"No," Keira said with a chuckle. "First, you need to sleep." She reached into her bag and removed her tablet. "I have a meditation app on here. I'm going to get your earbuds and then fire up a guided-sleep session. You are going to listen, get Derrick off your mind and take a nap. This afternoon, we'll go to yoga class and then have a healthy dinner. And then tomorrow, we will spend the morning at my sanctuary and then head to yours."

DERRICK CLICKED OFF the call with Tommy Sipley and tried to analyze how he felt. Despondent, he decided. And helpless. Leaning forward in the patio chair, he placed his forearms atop his thighs and tried to think.

There had been a time in his life when he would have happily moved to Colorado. But he couldn't leave Grandma, and Easton needed the farm to come home to, where the people he loved would always be available. And he liked the Northwest. It had always felt like home. Although with Anne by his side, he'd be willing to settle anywhere. Without her, it didn't matter. Nothing mattered.

He knew he needed to shake off this despair, but it seemed impossible. Helpless was not a good feeling for him. Doing something would be better than sitting still, and yet there wasn't one thing he wanted to do. Except be with Anne, who no longer wanted anything to do with him. This was even worse than her long-ago email because now he had nothing to turn to, no baseball to distract him, no future whatsoever.

He'd tried everything from texts and phone calls to flowers and gift baskets, asking her to listen. She was now refusing delivery. And the truth was, even if she agreed to talk to him, he wouldn't know what to say. He knew Anne, and a simple apology was not going to cut it.

He couldn't help wondering if Sally hadn't known about the job offer, then she never would have sought him out, and Anne wouldn't have discovered the truth. Not that this would have changed the fact that he'd given Sally the anonymous tip in the first place. He was beginning to accept that Anne would have found out eventually. Bottom line, he should have confessed. And yet, Easton had needed his help.

Easton emerged from the back door and took a seat in the chair next to him. "I got a draft of the article from David Beyer. It's pretty great. He says some nice things about you, too. He asked me a few questions about you, you know?"

"Oh, yeah? Like what?"

"Like if I felt any pressure following in your footsteps."

"That's not very original."

"I didn't think so, either. How can I feel pressure when you're like a hundred years older than me?"

"You're hilarious," Derrick returned flatly.

"Hey, you're almost smiling, aren't you? This is the happiest I've seen you in a while. Don't worry. I didn't say that *old* part to him. I saw you on the phone, was it—?"

"Nope," Derrick replied, cutting him off. "She's still not speaking to me. It was Tommy Sipley."

"He offer you the job?"

"Yep."

"What did you say?"

Derrick sighed. "He didn't press me for an answer. He asked me to think about it."

"You should think about it."

"You want me to move to Colorado?"

"No, of course not. But… I know you wanted to move back here to be with Grandma and me, and I love that. But I'll only be here for another year. And you do realize that Grandma is going to marry Jack, right?"

"What? Did she say something to you?"

"No. But it's obvious they're soul mates. Like you and Anne. And Jack isn't the kind of guy who is going to wait." Easton grinned. "He doesn't waste time, in case you haven't noticed."

Derrick admired the trait, and he had to agree with Easton; Jack and Grandma were a good match. If Jack asked her, he hoped she'd say yes. Thoughts of marriage caused a yearning so intense it stole his breath. Easton was right; Anne was his soul mate. He wished he was the one proposing.

"Speaking of soul mates, how did it go with Hailey?"

Easton shook his head. "Not great. We broke up. Not that we were even officially together, but we agreed it wasn't going to work out between us. More like we didn't think it was worth it to try."

"I understand. I'm sorry."

"Thanks, but it's fine. Honestly, it's a relief." He shrugged a shoulder. "I think it's for the best."

Derrick thought so, too.

Easton added, "I feel bad. She's kind of a mess."

"What do you mean?"

"This thing has messed her up. She is super angry."

Derrick frowned. "At you?"

"I don't know. Maybe. It's hard to tell because she seems pretty ticked off at the entire world right now. She thinks everyone believes she's guilty because of the blood-doping allegation, which she also claims she didn't do. But because of how it was handled with high-powered attorneys and secret meetings, they assume she did. People are saying she's getting away with something again because of her mom. She's afraid she'll lose her shot at running on the national team, and she's worried about her mom."

"Do you think she's guilty?"

"I honestly don't know…" Easton shook his head. "Before this happened, I would have said no. But now I've seen a different side to her. Not all that surprising because I didn't know her that well to begin with. I'm not sure. But I also know how I felt when I was unfairly accused. It's one of the worst feelings in the world."

"It is," Derrick agreed.

"One more thing. I doubt it matters, but she asked me about Anne. For some reason, I feel like I should tell her."

"What did she ask about Anne?"

"Hailey said she wants to fight back, but her mom wants to hide behind their attorneys. She wanted to know if I thought McGrath PR would help her."

"Hmm." Derrick doubted Anne would want anything more to do with this situation. He said so, and Easton agreed.

"Do you think I should tell Anne?"

"Yeah, I do. A heads-up would be nice. I have no idea what she'll say. I know it won't be easy for her to turn down the president of the university."

"I'll do it. In the meantime, you should legitimately think about coaching. You keep saying you don't want to do baseball anymore, but I don't get why."

Derrick had been thinking about that, too.

Not surprising, Easton seemed to sense this. "You are an amazing coach, Derrick. And not every good player is. Graham can't stop talking about what you've done for Albert. *That's* what I told David. I told him about how you always had time for me when I was little. How you taught me everything I know and spent hours practicing with me.

"If it weren't for you, I would never have been a switch hitter. I told him about how you used to have Grandma record my batting practices, and then you'd call me up, and we'd go over them."

Derrick smiled, and for the first time in nearly a week, his heart smiled, too. Good memories. Sometimes he'd be dead tired from his own workouts or from being on the road, but he'd review the footage, anyway. How could he not when he knew his little brother was waiting?

"You're my brother. That's what family does."

"No," Easton said firmly. "That's what *you* do. And that's what you do for baseball."

For so long, he'd wanted to prove to himself that he could be something besides a ballplayer. But now, he realized most of this obsession was due to his dad and Anne. Anne was right; he'd put too much stock in both his dad's words and in her email. His dad was only trying to motivate him while Anne was dealing with her own broken heart.

Baseball was a part of him—a part he didn't want to let go of. And why should he? He was half-joking when he said it to Anne, but he really was great at it. Why did he have to be good at something else when he loved the thing he was already great at? Baseball had given him so much. Why not stop this obsession at mastering something else and give back to the game he loved? Something shifted inside of him.

Easton went on, "You would do anything for someone you care about. I also told David about how you and Grandma saved me after Dad died. If it wasn't for you two, I don't know where I'd be right now. And then you did it again with this whole PED thing. Somehow you convinced Anne to help me. Without her and Keira, I don't know what would have happened."

Derrick swallowed around the emotion gathering in his throat. "I'm so proud of you, kiddo. I know it hasn't been easy. But it's all going to pay off for you after this season. I promise."

"Thanks, Derrick. I hope so. But stop trying to change the subject."

"I don't want to move to Colorado. You

said you'd only be here for one more year, but to me, that's twelve long months I get to spend with you."

"Good." Easton smiled. "And you don't have to move away to coach. Lots of coaching jobs around."

"True."

"In fact, I just heard about one."

"Is that so?"

"Did you know Albert's coach quit?"

"What?"

"Yep, Graham told me he had a bicycle accident and broke his leg. He's going to be fine, but he's looking for someone to take over for the rest of the season."

The thought alone lit a spark inside of him. Coaching Albert was the only job he'd tried since retiring, which brought him any sense of satisfaction. He'd enjoyed the heck out of watching his game, too. It had taken all his self-control not to offer advice to all the kids.

"Derrick, you told me yourself how much you loved working with Albert," Easton said, echoing his thoughts. "It's only a few weeks. A month if they make the playoffs."

"Honestly, Easton, it's tempting. But I'm not feeling very motivated."

"I know," he said, sympathy softening his enthusiastic tone. But not, he realized, squelching it. "But you will—that's the point. Derrick, you need to get out of this house and quit moping around. Once you get on the field and start working with those kids, you'll feel better."

"Let me think about it."

"Well, you'd better think fast. I already told them you'd do it."

## CHAPTER EIGHTEEN

NEBULA SPA & RESORT was a short but scenic drive from the city, winding up a narrow, two-lane, tree-lined road into the mountains. Anne and Keira departed bright and early and spent the entire morning undergoing one delightful treatment after another. Following a pedicure, a reflexology session, a Swedish massage and a facial, Anne did feel better. Keira's sleep app had done the trick, and a good night's sleep had helped, too.

"The Sanctuary" included a full-sized swimming pool and a series of smaller, warmer ones, all filled with natural hot-spring water and set in a beautifully landscaped courtyard. The spa included complimentary use of towels, lounge chairs, shaded tables and lemon-and-cucumber mineral water with any treatment. Most customers opted to spend an hour or two soaking or sunning there after completing their spa services.

At the moment, Anne and Keira had an entire pond all to themselves. Bordered by tall fir trees, the breeze was refreshingly cool and smelled fresh and piney. The sound of rippling water mingled pleasingly with birdsong and squirrel chatter. Anne couldn't imagine a more peaceful way to spend the day.

From the corner of her eye, she saw two women exit the doors onto the grounds. They paused to look around, as if deciding on which inviting nook to visit first. Something familiar kept her attention, and as she watched the pair, recognition slowly dawned.

"Are you kidding me?" she whispered.

"What?" Keira asked drowsily from where she was reclining on the underwater bench. Eyes closed, her friend had her head tipped back against the stone. "Is that bird trying to fly off with my bag again?" Earlier, a curious Canada jay had been peeking inside her duffel. "Just give it whatever it wants. I'm not moving."

"I think that's Celia and Hailey Greenwich."

"No way!" Keira's head came forward, her eyelids popping open and reforming into a squint. "What are the chances?"

"I'm going to say one hundred percent," Anne answered. "And they are walking in our direction."

Easton had called the evening before to let her know about his meeting with Hailey. He'd recalled the conversation rather casually, but when she'd pressed him for details, she'd gotten the impression Hailey may not have been on the same page as him regarding their breakup. He'd also relayed how Hailey had asked about Anne and hiring McGrath PR.

She braced herself for a conceivably awkward exchange. Keira shifted her position, sitting upright on the bench.

"Anne McGrath?" Celia said, stopping before them. At Anne's confirmation, she went on. "Celia Greenwich. I won't pretend like you don't know who I am." She introduced the younger woman beside her. "My daughter, Hailey."

"Nice to meet you both," Anne said. "This is Keira Chkalov, my friend and colleague."

"I've heard about you, too, Keira," Celia said with an easy smile. "All good things."

"How nice," Keira replied.

By silent mutual consent, Anne and Keira were allowing the woman to lead the conversation. There was still a chance, however slight, that this meeting was a coincidence.

Hailey slipped off her sandals then sat on the edge of the pool, dangling her feet in the water. Celia did the same and looked at Anne. "I tried to call you at your office yesterday, but they said you were out and couldn't be reached."

"Yes," Anne confirmed, "I took a few days off."

"You don't check your messages? I told your assistant it was urgent."

"My assistant is under instructions not to bother me unless it's an emergency. Your call should have been forwarded to another agent."

"Oh, she offered. But I don't want another agent."

"I understand," Anne said, seeing no point in pretending otherwise. "It's been rough, huh? I know this ordeal has been really hard on Easton."

"Rough?" Hailey, who had been silently glowering up until this point, interjected sharply. "I've had death threats. Mom might lose her job. Easton has no idea what rough is."

"Death threats?" Keira repeated. "Have you contacted the police?" Anne studied the young woman.

"Yes, but the police don't care." Hailey used a foot to splash at the water. "They only want me to admit to something I didn't do. The prosecutor offered me a deal. My attorney wants me to take it, which means saying I took some steroid drugs when I didn't. No one will listen to me!"

Celia sighed. "We did report the calls, but unsurprisingly, they were both anonymous calls from disposable phones. As for the gossip and vitriol on social media, the police say they can't do anything about it. Meanwhile, our attorney is advising us not to speak to anyone, including the police."

"That's usually best from a legal standpoint," Anne said.

Hailey snorted. "Yeah, keeping it legal has worked *real* well for me, hasn't it?"

"Hailey, please," Celia said before looking pointedly between Anne and Keira. "I admire the way your firm handled the situation for Easton Bright."

"Thank you," Anne replied. "But Easton made our job pretty easy. He's an exceptional young man."

"He certainly is," Celia agreed. "I am here to ask you to do the same for Hailey."

"I'm sorry, we can't. We don't typically work with athletes."

"But you helped Easton," Hailey argued.

"That was an exception."

"Because his brother is your boyfriend?" she asked in a tone bordering on snide.

Anne looked at her, struck by the surge of sympathy she felt. Despite Hailey's bravado, the poor girl was only nineteen. And an immature nineteen at that. If she was telling the truth, she'd been targeted, too. Which was appalling and a perfect example of the unfair and unexpected consequences of wealth and privilege, not to mention the darker side of social media.

"No," Anne responded carefully. "Because Derrick Bright won a consultation with McGrath PR at a charity auction. I already knew the family, and once I realized Easton was innocent, I agreed to help…as a friend."

"I'm innocent, too!" Hailey cried and then huffed. "But what does that matter these days, right? Social media can ruin anyone. Evidence doesn't matter, only perceptions and opinions."

Sad but true, Anne silently agreed.

"It matters to me, Hailey," Celia assured her. "That's why we're here."

"Nothing sticks to him, though, and I don't understand it. It's so unfair."

"So," Celia went on, ignoring Hailey's comment to focus again on Anne and Keira, "I went to some pretty extreme lengths to track you down and ask for help, but I can see that you're declining our request."

"Unfortunately, we are," Anne said. "I can recommend Mitchell West. They have experience with athletes, and Beverly Frankel is excellent with the type of problem you're facing."

"Well," Hailey intoned, jumping in again as she flipped her long blond hair over one shoulder, "then I guess I have no choice."

Anne felt her scalp prickle as she acknowledged that while Hailey's youth and lack of maturity might excuse a lot, they were features that might also make her more dangerous.

Keira asked, "No choice about what?"

"Easton told me how you guys figured out about the photograph. Your guy isn't the only person who is good with computers." Hailey's smug expression set off as many warning bells as the statement she made.

"I'm sure he's not," Anne said. "Is there something specific you're referring to with that statement?"

Hailey crossed her arms like a defensive schoolgirl. "I know Derrick Bright has a gambling problem."

"Excuse me?" Anne blurted.

"Yeah, you might be interested to know your boyfriend has lost *millions* of dollars, and soon the whole world is going to know, too. I'm going public. I have proof. I also have it on *very good* authority he's going to be hired as the new coach of the Colorado Sharks. If word gets out that he's betting on baseball, his coaching career will be over before it even starts."

"Hailey!" a wide-eyed Celia cried, horrified by her daughter's threat. "What in the world are you talking about?"

"What, Mom? It's not fair! It wasn't fair the last time I was accused, and it's even worse this time."

Hailey's previous statement flashed in Anne's consciousness like a neon sign. *Nothing sticks to him.* Subsequent thoughts followed; Easton's positive social-media attention, his comments about Hailey's angst, the flattering article about him. And suddenly, Anne figured it all out.

"It was you," Keira said, echoing Anne's revelation. "You're the one who kept Easton's name in the scandal."

"You cropped the photo, too," Anne stated. "The one of him getting a B-12 injection. And then you sent it to the newspaper."

Hailey confirmed it all. "I found it right after Easton and I first met at this barbecue for student-athletes. I went home, and I was checking him out. You know, trying to get a feel for what he was all about and decide if he was someone I even wanted to date. Not easy when the guy posts almost nothing on social media.

"I searched the university's site for like baseball stories and stuff. But everything was all accolades—Easton being the best baseball player, setting some new record, volunteering with old people and winning the scholar-athlete award. I didn't find anything even questionable. It was sort of annoying how perfect he was. Like too good to be true.

"Anyway, my roommate is in the nursing program, and they have their own website. She was looking something up, so just kidding around, I reached over and typed his name in, and that photo popped up. I didn't think anything of it at the time. Just another example of Easton being a good guy. But then the party happened, and, *of course*, Easton left before it got busted." Hailey rolled her eyes. "Every hint of bad stuff passes right on by him."

Anne wanted to point out how he took great pains to avoid these "hints of bad stuff" Hailey referred to, but didn't want to derail her confession.

"Meanwhile, my life and my chances of making the national track-and-field team are basically over. Then Easton goes dark—won't even return a text. I get questioned by the police. Then *he* gets a glowing story in the national news. Next thing I know, Easton breaks up with me. He's going to head off to play pro and make a million dollars while I *won't* be running on the national team. He doesn't even have to finish college."

"Hailey," a now-pale Celia asked, "what did you do?"

The girl shrugged one cocky shoulder and said, "I leveled the playing field."

DERRICK PLACED A bag of groceries and a stack of mail on the countertop. Grandma and Easton were outside picking fruit for the day's applesauce project. They'd sent Derrick to the market for supplies, a gesture he knew was intended to keep him occupied and distracted from all things Anne.

Easton had been right about the coaching, though. After only one Little League practice, he knew he'd made the right decision. It hadn't made up for losing Anne, but for a couple of hours in the evenings, at least it wasn't all he thought about it.

Flipping through the mail, he discovered an envelope with his name scrawled across the front: no address, no postmark, just "Derrick Bright" in bold, black printed letters. Hope bloomed inside of him. He didn't recognize it as Anne's handwriting, but he couldn't help but wish it was a note from her just the same. Maybe she'd finally decided to answer one of his pleas.

With trembling fingers, he tore open the envelope and removed the single sheet of paper. But as he read the typed message, the optimistic beat of his heart turned to a cold hard thud inside his chest.

When Grandma and Easton came through the back door a few minutes later loaded down with bins of apples, he was still staring at the note and the series of screenshots. It would be funny, except it wasn't. He'd been so worried about Easton's actions that he hadn't stopped to consider his own. He should have been more careful with his privacy. How much damage could this do?

"Derrick, what's wrong?" Grandma asked.

He looked up and sighed. "I think someone is trying to blackmail me."

"What?" Easton lowered his load of apples to the floor and jogged toward him. Derrick stepped sideways. Easton read it and then slid the paper across the counter to Grandma, who'd joined them.

"What's it say?" Grandma asked without looking down. "What do they want?"

"That part isn't clear. They said they'd be in touch. Mostly, it's screenshots showing how I lost two million dollars betting on baseball, but—"

"You need to call the police," Grandma stated firmly.

"I'm not sure it's a police matter, is it? They haven't asked for anything yet."

Easton said, "I'm not sure, either, because you didn't technically do anything *wrong.* Well, except embarrass yourself. Seriously, Derrick? You bet on the Vikings over the Titans? How could you do that with the Titans' pitching lineup."

"Franklin and Benno were both injured!"

"They still had Wiest and Shackle," Easton countered, shaking his head in disbelief before studying the pages again. "I don't think whoever sent this understands what it really is…"

"Me, either," Derrick agreed. "But I still don't want people to see it."

"I wouldn't, either. You suck at gambling. You should definitely call Anne. She'll know what to do."

Derrick blew out a sigh and shook his head. "The last thing Anne wants to do is help me, Easton. She blocked my number, remember?"

"I'll call her," he offered.

"No," Derrick said, even though he desperately wanted to agree. "I need to figure this out myself."

"What are you going to do?"

Not listen to his instincts, which were telling him to be proactive. It would be difficult, but if there was one thing he'd learned from Anne, it was patience. "For now, I'll wait. Let's see what they want."

THE SPA HAD a no-phone rule, and Anne and Keira had happily left theirs secured in a locker. But now that Celia and Hailey had departed and they'd struck a deal of sorts with Hailey, Anne needed to speak to Derrick ASAP. And Easton. She could only hope Derrick wouldn't do, or say, anything rash before she could get to him. Her hope was that he wouldn't say anything at all. But knowing Derrick, that was unlikely.

A surge of nervous energy shot through her. "Keira, did we do the right thing?"

"Yes, absolutely," Keira assured her, fingers tapping out the code on the locker door.

"Almost certainly," she amended and added firmly, "Hopefully. I doubt he's even gotten the letter yet. I mean, he would have called you by now."

"I blocked him, remember?" Anne said.

"Oh, shoot, that's right." Keira swung open the door and began removing their belongings.

Anne found her bag and fished her phone from an inside pocket. A flush of guilt went through her as she tapped out the code to unlock it. What immediately followed was genuine panic as she stared at the display.

"I did more than block him," she confessed aloud. "I deleted his contact. I have no idea what his number is. Do you have it?"

"No…" Keira thought for a second. "But Derrick would have Easton call and tell you about this, right?"

"Maybe. If Derrick even told him about it. It would be just like Derrick to try and handle this himself."

"Call Easton," Keira advised. "You can always make up some reason for the call if he doesn't sound distressed."

Anne agreed, tapped on Easton's contact and waited for him to pick up. The call went straight to voice mail. She hung up. "Let's go," she said. "With any luck, we'll get there before Derrick opens that letter."

"But what if he already has?" Keira asked.

"Then I hope he and Easton and May understand what we've done and why we did it."


"It's ANNE AND KEIRA!" Easton exclaimed, peering at the security system's screen.

Derrick watched his brother touch the button to open the gate and tried to decide what this meant. Was it a good or bad thing? Had Anne heard about this already? Had his "blackmailer" already posted this falsehood about him?

Minutes later, he had his answer when the women came through the door.

"Derrick," Anne asked, "did you get some sort of letter in the mail today?"

"I did. How did you know?"

"Have you done anything about it?"

"Not yet," he answered. "I don't even know who it's from or what they really want."

"Good," she said and exhaled a sigh of relief. "I already took care of it."

"How could you...? That means you know

who sent it. Did they contact you with a demand?"

With a sympathetic look at Easton, she revealed, "It was Hailey."

"Hailey?" Derrick repeated. "What is she? Some sort of computer hacker?"

"Not exactly. Apparently, she was here at the house one day and saw a folder on your computer desktop labeled 'gambling.' She opened it up, saw the images and snapped some photos."

"Why would she do that?" Derrick asked.

"I'm not sure. You know how kids are these days—they take photos of everything. At first, I think she thought it was funny. Maybe later, she thought she could sell them to a gossip site."

"Wow."

"Did you call the police?" Easton asked.

"No…" Anne grimaced. "Um, what we did do was agree to take her on as a client. On the condition that she delete the photos and not post anything about it online. She signed a contract."

"Anne, you didn't have to do that. None of it is true. You know me, I've never gambled in my life outside of Goody's bachelor party in Vegas. This was from a practice app, like the stock thing."

"Yeah, we know. It didn't take Keira long to figure it out. She was suspicious as soon as she looked at the images. She sent a couple to Oliver, who confirmed where they'd come from."

"Which reminds me," Keira said, frowning at Derrick. "Derrick, you used your real name on this gambling site?"

"Uh, yeah," he confessed with a sheepish shrug. "A couple of my friends were doing it, too. And it's not real gambling. It's like a game."

"Doesn't matter," Anne insisted. "It looks real. And if she would have posted the images, we would have had to straighten it all out. You know how this works—there would forever be people who thought you'd lost millions of dollars gambling. On baseball, no less."

"I see your point," he conceded.

Keira told him, "We are going to arrange a computer-security lesson for you from Oliver. We need to know where else you are vulnerable and fix it."

Anne said, "Easton, I'm so sorry to tell you

this, but Hailey was also the one who posted the photo of you getting the B-12 injection. I think that gave her the idea for this scheme."

Easton scowled. His voice was fruaght with frustration as he asked, "But why?"

"Jealousy, and she was angry with you. Hailey has been falsely accused twice now, while you, on the other hand, escaped this unscathed and according to Hailey, you appear to have everything. She tried to take you down with her, and when that didn't work, she went after Derrick. Hoping that might tarnish you, too. She knows how close you and Derrick are. In Hailey's mind, it was like payback for how the online mob went after her and her mom."

Easton took a moment to process this news. He was a sharp cookie; it didn't take long for him to comprehend Hailey's twisted reasoning.

"I'm not all that surprised after some of the stuff she said to me. But why would you all help her after everything she's done? Going public with a false accusation against someone like Derrick would make everything worse for her, wouldn't it? Why not let her do it and look like a fool. You know, make her face the logical consequences?"

Anne started to explain. "Yes, but—"

"Let me guess," Grandma May chimed in. "At the end of the day, she's just a scared kid, and you ladies couldn't stand the thought of her ruining her own life over this."

"That was a big part of it," Anne confirmed, quickly catching Derrick's gaze before smiling at Grandma. "But as I mentioned earlier, there would have been plenty of bad publicity for Derrick in the meantime. Prevention is always a better cure. But you're right, May, Hailey was a victim, too. A terrified and angry young woman trying to right an injustice. Granted, not in an appropriate or effective manner, but in her misguided way, she was trying to fight back."

"She seemed contrite when we left her," Keira assured them all. "We hope she'll learn a lesson. She's committed to doing some volunteer work, which will give her a new perspective and boost her image at the same time."

"I like that a lot," Derrick declared. "She needs to see the world without herself as the center. That was always Grandma's approach where we were concerned."

"I agree," Easton said. "None of this was fair for Hailey, either. It's horrible to be wrongly accused. I don't want her to suffer anymore. I never wanted anything bad for her or her mom. Thank you so much for bailing her out."

Keira smiled. "You are a remarkable young man—do you know that?" She stepped forward to hug Easton. "And you," she said to Grandma, embracing her next. "I can see why these boys are so incredibly fabulous with you as their role model."

Hope and relief blossomed inside of Derrick, partly because of how Anne and Keira had so generously dealt with Hailey. But primarily because of what this meant for him.

Anne had just admitted that Hailey's well-being wasn't the only motive. She'd done it for his benefit, too. Thwarting Hailey helped him as much, maybe more, than it did Hailey. He was the one in the public eye. His reputation was the one on the line.

Anne obviously still cared about him. Would she admit it?

"Well, then," May said. "That takes care of that. Easton and I did some baking this morning. Who wants apple pie?"

# CHAPTER NINETEEN

"So-o-o-o..." Derrick drew out the word as he settled into the seat next to Anne on the patio. "What was the rest of it?"

Anne was watching the latest ax-throwing lesson. Jack had arrived, and an enthusiastic Keira had volunteered to learn. Grandma and Easton were offering advice and cheering her on.

"The rest of what?" Anne asked, scooping up a bite of pie.

"Earlier, you said saving Hailey from herself was a big part of the reason you took care of this situation. The word *part* implies there was more to your motivation."

"Oh." *Shoot.* She thought while she slowly chewed and swallowed. Stalling. The truth was she hadn't thought past saving Derrick from a mess of gossip and preventing herself from having to untangle it.

And then, she'd been worried he might

not understand why she'd thwarted Hailey by helping her. The notion that Derrick might question her deeper motivation hadn't occurred to her. Honestly, there'd been no time for her to question it, either. But now, confronted with the realization, and Derrick's kind and sympathetic reaction, she acknowledged what was right there in front of her. She still loved him. Did she want to confess that, though? Because it didn't change anything.

Derrick's stare was intense. Her face heated while she struggled for a believable excuse. "Um… I couldn't let you lose your coaching job?" Why had she stated it like a question?

"But if you knew the gambling wasn't *real*, then you knew I wouldn't lose a coaching job over some silly app."

"Well, true. But it would be humiliating to have people see how terrible you were at it. Derrick, you finished dead last in the pool you were in."

Derrick grinned. "That's it? That's all you've got?"

"What else is there?" she asked, attempting

to sound defensive and confident and failing miserably.

"Anne, I know you. You wouldn't have done this if you didn't believe in what you were doing—in *who* you were doing it for. That's how you've always worked. It's how you've structured your entire business. I think you still love me. And I love you, too."

"Derrick—"

"And I know," he interrupted softly, "what you're going to say. That it doesn't change anything." She couldn't keep eye contact for fear he'd see the truth. He went on, "But it does. It changes everything. It makes *us* worth fighting for, at least to me. So here's my final at bat.

"Anne, I am so sorry that I tricked you into helping us—me. You were right about that— I only wanted *you*. I can be manipulative and a little controlling when I want something. It can be effective, although it's not a positive quality. Heaven knows Grandma has told me that enough times. I acknowledge that truth. But I promise to try and never do either where you're concerned ever again.

"I acknowledge that I am far from perfect and that I'll mess up. Probably on a regular basis. That's a part of my big personality, most of which I know you like."

She couldn't help but chuckle at that, and she certainly wasn't going to deny the truth of it.

"Just know that when I do mess up, it won't be on purpose. I also know that I'm not good enough for you. But I believe that what we are together is rare and precious and perfect. And if you give me another chance, I promise I will not waste it."

Anne brought one hand up to cover her aching heart. It was a good ache, though, wrought from tenderness and love. Because that was the thing about Derrick—he gave everything he attempted his all. And she knew that his love for her would be no exception. Tears clouded her eyes, emotion tightened her throat and she didn't trust herself to speak.

And he knew, too. Derrick *knew*. Of course, he did, because no one had ever known her so well. He reached out, took the dish from her trembling hands and placed it on the end table beside his chair.

Then he turned toward her and whispered,

"I love you, Anne. All you have to say is that you love me, too. That's all I need right now."

Anne stared into his eyes. "I love you, too, Derrick," she told him before stifling a joy-filled sob. There was so much more she wanted to say. She had plenty of her own apologies and revelations and declarations to make.

But he didn't need to hear any of it. And in the end, Anne loved him even more when he responded with a simple vow. "Then we will be okay."

"We will," she agreed and then leaned toward him and sealed it with a kiss.

THREE WEEKS AS a coach, and Derrick was delighted with all things Little League. Okay, most things. A few of the parents could benefit from some encouraging words about teamwork and camaraderie and kindness. But they'd figure out soon enough that he couldn't be bullied, bribed or cajoled to play their kid at whatever position they "knew" best suited their future all-star. That was Derrick's job. More than that, it was his job to teach these kids to love the game.

Derrick was old-school that way. Kids had

to earn their positions, sure, but he also knew it was vital for them to play more than one. They needed to explore their abilities and find the best fit. Which was why Albert was standing beside him and wearing catcher's gear while Derrick hit balls to the team.

"Is Anne coming to the championship game?" Albert asked, catching the ball thrown to him and then tossing it to Derrick.

Derrick chuckled. "We haven't even made it to the championship yet. We still have two more games to win."

"We'll win," Albert said with a newfound confidence that overflowed Derrick's cup of pride. "If we play even half as well as we have the last three games, we're in. Wouldn't you like for Anne to see that—your first championship win as a coach?"

He would indeed. He tossed the ball into the air, swung the bat and aimed for center field.

"Nice catch, Jerome!" he yelled after the center fielder executed an impressive running catch. "If we make it, she'll be there." Now it was his own confidence that had him smiling. It felt so incredible to have Anne in his corner again. He might never look into the stands as a player and see her there, but he certainly would as a coach.

"You know what would be really awesome?" Albert asked. "If you asked her to marry you at the game."

"Wow," Derrick intoned. "How did we go from her coming to the game to my proposing at the game? We've only been back together a few weeks."

Hands down, they had been the best weeks of his life. The truth was Derrick couldn't wait to take it to the next level. He'd wanted to propose to her since... Well, forever.

"You want to marry her, though, right?" Albert asked, somehow sensing his thoughts.

Derrick chuckled. "Yes," he admitted.

"Imagine winning your first championship as a coach and getting engaged on the same day. How amazing would that be?"

"I can't argue with you there."

"So what's the holdup? Are you worried she'll say no?"

"Not exactly." He wasn't. Not really. She'd dropped a few hints about their future together.

What had him stalled was the fear that he'd botch the delivery. When he did ask her, he wanted it to be perfect and memorable. Just like their wedding; too big and Anne would balk, too small and they'd both be disappointed. For the first time in his life, he was the one lacking confidence.

"Okay. So if you want to lock that in, what you need is a grand gesture."

"A grand gesture?" Derrick repeated skeptically. "You mean like asking her on the Jumbotron?" he joked.

Albert scooped up another catch and then tossed it to Derrick. Like a pro. Just as he'd hoped, as Albert's confidence grew in the batter's box, so went his infield skills. He was now their starting catcher and backup second baseman.

"That could work," Albert confirmed, purposely bypassing Derrick's attempt to deflect. "But we don't have a Jumbotron at the ball field. I suppose you could use the scoreboard, but how about something more original? Like taping a ring to a ball and hitting it to her during warm-ups? Or you could use the announcer's microphone after the national anthem and sing a romantic ballad and then ask her."

"Can't sing a note," Derrick said, trying not to laugh.

"Okay… Rusty pipes might kill the mood. I know! How about we make some signs, and us players could hold them up?" Albert snagged another ball out of the air before acting out this suggestion. Throwing both his arms up with each word, he said, "Anne. Will. You. Marry. Me?"

"That's only five words," Derrick cheerfully pointed out, even as the thought occurred to him that the kid might be on to something. "There are nine players on the field."

Albert rolled his eyes before suggesting, "Then how about this. Dear. Anne. I. Love. You. Please. Marry. Me? And then a big red heart."

"I don't know…" Derrick surprised himself with the answer. No, what surprised him was that he was considering this suggestion. Was this how desperate he'd become, taking proposal advice from a ten-year-old? Yes, he immediately answered. It had to be better than what he'd come up with. "I like it, but do you think it might be overkill?"

"Maybe," Albert agreed thoughtfully before tossing him another ball. "I see what you're saying. Anne doesn't strike me as a spotlight seeker."

Derrick was constantly amazed at this kid's insight.

"But you know, a grand gesture doesn't necessarily have to be a public one."

Also true. And those words, *dear Anne*, were like a spark. And just like that, an idea coalesced in Derrick's mind.

"Albert, has anyone ever told you how brilliant you are?"

"Coach, you know they call me Einstein at school, right?"

"THANK YOU AGAIN for doing this," Anne told Keira as they found seats in the bleachers.

"My pleasure," Keira said, settling beside her on one of the seat cushions Anne had brought along. Reaching into her bag, Keira produced bags of sunflower seeds, peanuts, pretzels and a long, skinny box of red licorice. "Do I look like a real fan?"

"Yes, you most certainly do," Anne said, raising her eyebrows in surprise and taking a strip of the offered candy. "I am impressed."

"Thank you. I Googled baseball snacks.

Because now that McGrath PR is officially accepting athletic clientele, I need to learn all the sports stuff, right? Now, tell me about this infield-fly rule everyone is always yakking about."

Anne laughed. Best thing she could have done was invite Keira to the game. Her friend was the perfect distraction and one she desperately needed. Anne was on edge.

Things were going great with her and Derrick. With one paradoxically tiny-huge exception, every time she brought up the future, he changed the subject.

At first, she'd thought maybe she was imagining this little quirk as they'd had issues to discuss and the past to resolve. Important topics, both. Immediately following their reconciliation, there'd been a lot going on and much to celebrate when May and Jack announced their engagement. The following weekend, they'd all flown to a resort in Idaho to attend their wedding.

The entire trip, Anne had half expected him to propose. Especially when he'd suggested the two of them leave a few days early for their own romantic getaway. She'd happily obliged, and they'd spent two nearly perfect days mountain biking, hiking and swimming. Evenings they'd indulged in gourmet meals and ice cream and hours reading.

The whole time, she'd suspected it was a buildup. Since it was totally Derrick's style to propose where his family could share in the event, she'd anticipated "the question" at the reception. She was ready to say yes and only hoped he wouldn't upstage the newly-weds with something overly grand.

Instead, he'd delivered the sweetest speech, thanked his grandmother for making him and Easton the people they were, toasted the happy couple and danced with Anne until late into the evening.

It had been a fabulous and joy-filled occasion. So she hadn't been disappointed…just surprised. Okay, maybe there was a smidge of disappointment. But only because before their "second breakup," Derrick had been adamant about how they belonged together. He didn't want to waste another second of their time together being apart. She felt the same.

In every other way, things were wonderful. Derrick had even acknowledged that just because he couldn't play baseball didn't mean baseball was no longer his life. Coaching was his future.

And it wasn't until the ninth inning of the game that would mark his first championship as a coach that a new notion occurred to Anne. The Tigers were ahead seven to three with only one out to go when Derrick called a time-out. One that was completely unnecessary because the game was essentially won.

That's when Albert looked up from the huddle and waved at her. The expression on his face was priceless—pure joy and…something else she couldn't identify. Curiosity, maybe? Derrick, she realized, was watching her, too.

"The Tigers' coach is staring at you," Keira said in a teasing tone.

"He is, isn't he?" Anne agreed, staring right back at him.

"He looks *really* happy."

"He does, doesn't he? Keira, I think—"

Keira gasped. "Oh, my gosh. He's going to propose right after they win this game, isn't he? It's perfect. The moment he's been waiting for."

"You read my mind."

"Now I'm happy, too!" Keira clapped her hands while the players resumed their positions. "I get to be here to witness the most romantic moment of my best friend's life."

The huddle loosened. The players hustled back onto the field. Derrick resumed his spot while Albert headed behind the plate, his swagger reminding her of a tiny Derrick.

And then, the very next pitch, the batter knocked a line drive—*smack*!—right into the third baseman's glove. Game over! Tigers for the win.

BEHIND DERRICK, THE crowd went wild. The kids were shouting. He was ecstatic as the team mobbed him. He said a few words, keeping it short but issuing a quick congratulations and letting them know he was proud of their effort, the grit they'd displayed and their sportsmanship. The boys cheered for the other team and jogged over to line up for a round of high fives.

One of the boys' parents had arranged for a celebratory pizza party. Derrick searched the crowd for Anne, zeroed in on her smiling face and hurried in her direction. Nervous tension tightened inside of him. Was he doing the right thing? All he wanted to do was get down on one knee, shout out the question and give her the ring. He reined in his instinct and stuck with the plan.

"Congratulations, Coach," she said when they met on the edge of the field. She slipped her arms around him and gave him a tight hug. "I'm so happy for you, and for Albert, and all the boys. So much improvement in just a few weeks."

"Thank you," he said when she pulled back enough to smile up at him. "What an awesome day. I feel like I've won fifteen times, once for every player on my team."

"That is sweet," Anne said. "So does this confirm that coaching is officially your thing?"

"Nope," he said with a teasing glint in his eye. "You, Anne McGrath, are my thing. Coaching is my *other* thing."

Derrick reached into his pocket and Anne felt a hitch in her chest. *Here it comes.* She froze with anticipation. Even her lungs seized up, stealing her breath.

He withdrew his hand to reveal…

Anne squinted down at the offering in his hand. A pack of breath mints? Seriously?

"Anne?" he asked, popping a mint in his mouth.

"Yes, Derrick," she answered, taking a candy because maybe this meant he didn't want to ruin the postproposal kiss with bad breath.

"Will you…?" Her heart crashed against her rib cage. The question fizzled out as he paused to glance over her shoulder.

"Will I?" she repeated, willing him to stay on track.

Frowning a little, he focused on her again. "Uh, yeah, sorry. I need to get back to the team. Will you do me a favor?"

"Oh," she said, her lungs deflating with a disappointed exhale. "A favor. Sure."

"Can you check your email and see if there's a message from a guy?"

"What guy? Derrick, what are you talking about?"

"It has some important information you need to read."

"About what?"

"You'll see. Let me know as soon as you

get it, okay?" When she paused, he added urgently, "Please?"

"Of course," she said. "If it's important to you, then yes."

"It is. Extremely. Thank you, Anne. I'll see you at your place later after the pizza party?" At her nod, he leaned in and kissed her cheek. "Until then, remember how much I love you." And with those parting words, he jogged away into the crowd.

"Where did he go?" Keira asked, joining her. "What happened?"

"To a pizza party, and what happened is he asked me for a favor."

"Oh, boy, me and my big mouth. It was just... I'm sorry. I really thought this was it."

"Please, Keira, don't apologize. I thought so, too." Anne was surprised by the weight of the disappointment settling inside of her. How could she have misread his feelings so drastically? Unless...

Reaching out a hand, she grabbed Keira's arm. "Keira, be honest—do you think he's having second thoughts? You know how worried I've been that he would discover I'm not the same woman he fell in love with. Eleven years is a long time. What if that happened and he doesn't know how to say it? What if—"

"Anne, calm down," Keira interrupted. "That is not what's happening. I've never seen two people more in love than you and Derrick." She tipped her head and amended, "With the possible exception of May and Jack." Then she grinned. "You've said yourself things are going great. In fact, you've said it multiple times a day for many, many days now."

"Okay." Anne inhaled deeply before nodding. "Yes. You're right. Ugh. What is wrong with me? How did I go from the woman who never wanted to marry to the one who suddenly can't wait? How pathetic is that? I am not the desperate, needy girlfriend type." She shook her head as if clearing the cobwebs. "What happened?"

"Love happened." A chuckling Keira draped an arm around her shoulder and steered her toward the parking lot. "How urgent is this favor, anyway? I'm not sure I'm cut out to be a true baseball fan." She patted her tummy. "I think those pretzels and licorice are burning a hole in my stomach. I need sustenance. Do we have time for food before favors?"

Anne dredged up a smile for her friend. "Fortunately, this is the type of favor where I can do both."

# CHAPTER TWENTY

KEIRA DECLARED ITALIAN food the remedy for what she deemed "baseball stomach." They headed to their favorite bistro, where the owner, who had a crush on Keira, found them a table in short order. Upon hearing the specials, they both ordered the sausage-and-three-mushroom ravioli.

While waiting for their wine, Keira excused herself to use the restroom. Anne had made a promise to Derrick, so she took out her phone and pulled up her personal email account. Scrolling through the junk and ads, she had a suspicion the message had something to do with Derrick's chimney-reclamation project. He'd been showing her ideas he found on Pinterest, but truthfully, she didn't care what kind of mantel he decided to…

Her eyes landed on a familiar subject line: Our Relationship.

What…? Her body felt frozen in place, and yet heat flooded her bloodstream while her brain attempted to process what she was seeing. It was a response to the email she'd sent to him eleven years ago. Fingers trembling, she tapped to open the message and read:

Dear Anne,

I hope you'll forgive my delayed response. It's taken me a while to find the right words. Even now, I'm struggling to get them right. But I finally decided that what I want to say is more important than how I say it. I hope you agree. So here goes.

These last few weeks have been the best of my life. Even better than our first go-round, and I didn't think that was possible. Thank you for this second chance.

More importantly, thank you for showing me how "me" is enough. As we've previously discussed, a big part of who I am is going after what I want. And using any means available. This is no exception. I've been struggling to find a way to ask you a question. As referenced above, I'm inclined to use gifts and flowers (and even orchestras and dolphins) to persuade you. (Albert suggested the Jumbo-tron, and I'll admit I was tempted.)

The point here is that I so badly wanted to use anything and everything at my disposal to persuade you. At the same time, I don't want to have to persuade you. So I'm resisting the urge to use anything but "me" to accomplish my goal of you agreeing to be my wife. (Hoping this is proof that I've grown and not just grown cowardly, ha!)

Eleven years ago, I found myself because of you. And then an email broke us apart. I was never the same again. Since I found my way back to you, I am finding myself again. Now, I'm hoping to put us back together forever. So here I am, finally answering your email in the way I should have all those years ago. By asking you to be my wife and trusting that I, just me, am enough to be your husband.

Anne, will you marry me?

Love,

Derrick

Anne didn't even realize she was crying until she heard a concerned Keira asking, "Anne, what is it? Why are you crying? What happened?"

Looking up at Keira, she answered, "Derrick finally emailed me back."

"Surely, you don't mean…?"

"Yep, he kept my breakup email for *eleven years*."

"No." Keira's face went pale.

"No! Don't worry. Here," Anne said, handing over her phone.

When Keira finished reading, her eyes were sparkling, too. "Oh, my baseball-playing goodness! This has got to be the most romantic proposal ever."

"I know! An email proposal to counter my breakup email. It's so perfect. He got it so *right*, and I can't stop reading it. He wants a big wedding, I bet, and I don't. Will you be my maid of honor? I hope we can—"

"Stop!" Keira interrupted with a chopping motion. "You mean you haven't answered him?"

"Not yet. Too busy daydreaming."

"Okay," Keira said, and then rapidly ticked off the following responses, "I'd be honored to be your maid of honor. I understand, but I hope you don't go too small, wedding-wise because I've never been a best person anything before. And I promise I will be the best."

"I know and—"

"Anne, you need to respond, now! My guess is he's staring at his inbox, waiting for your answer."

"You're right! I do!" And so, she did.

Dear Derrick,

I think your response is remarkably timely and perfect in every way. I hope you will forgive my delay. I'm only now checking my email. You were right—the message contained herein is of extreme import. (Although you should have mentioned it was urgent, too! ;)

Yes, I will marry YOU! I cannot wait to marry you!

(Seriously, I'd like to do so very, very soon. I know you want a big wedding, but please don't make me wait too long. xo)

Yours forever,

Anne

PS: Keira says the wedding can't be too small as she's never done the best-maid thing before and is greatly looking forward to it.

# EPILOGUE

"Um, is it a good idea, do you think, to have the maiden voyage of fires on Christmas Eve?" Easton asked while Derrick stacked kindling on top of the shredded paper.

"I guess we'll see, huh?"

"Good thing we put those brand-new batteries in the smoke alarms," Grandma quipped, strolling into the room with a steaming mug cradled in her hands. "This cocoa is delicious."

"I appreciate your faith in me, Grammy," Derrick said, striking a match and lighting the bundle. "And thank you, I think I've finally hit on just the right chocolate-and-malt ratio."

They were teasing, of course, but regardless, it didn't matter. Derrick had done his research. They were in for a treat. He'd hired the best expert he could find to fix the chimney and restore the fireplace. Of course, the guy had already built a test fire, but Derrick had made sure he'd done it when no one else was around. There was also a fire extinguisher tucked inside a nearby cabinet.

They all stood back and watched the flames roar to life. Derrick added a seasoned log, and soon the flames were steadily flickering. A soft crackling sound accompanied a wave of heat.

"Hey, this is cozy," Jack said, coming in from the kitchen, where he and Grandma were cooking dinner.

"Thank you, Jack," Derrick said. "It's nice to see that someone appreciates my efforts."

The sound of the back door opening and Anne calling out made his heart go fluttery inside his chest. She and Keira had been out running some last-minute Christmas errands.

He and Anne had been married for four months now, and he wondered if that feeling of anticipation, followed by unabashed happiness at the sight of her, would ever go away. So far, it hadn't faded at all. If anything, he grew to love her more each day.

"Merry Christmas!" she called, entering the room.

"Look at that fire!" Keira exclaimed, coming in behind her with a frosted sugar cookie in hand. "It's *so* beautiful. Bravo, Coach Bright. And look at that mantel all decorated."

"Thank you, Keira."

Anne said, "Whatever is cooking smells delicious, and I cannot wait."

Derrick was pretty excited about it, too. Cooking was another thing Grandma and Jack had in common. Meals served from their kitchen were always a treat. And because they split their time between the farm and Jack's house on the lake, this pleasure was a regular occurrence. Combined with Easton's baking, Derrick and Anne felt spoiled. Just last week, Anne had complained about how she was putting on weight. If she had, he couldn't tell. To him, everything about his wife was perfect.

Frowning, Anne walked closer and put her hands on her hips. "This mantel does look nice, but we're missing a stocking."

Derrick studied the mantel. Each oversized stocking had a name embroidered on the cuff—Grandma May, Jack, Easton, Keira, Anne, Derrick. "No, we're not. Easton and I hung them ourselves."

"Maybe I can help…"

Derrick watched as Anne rummaged inside her bag and then withdrew a tiny, knitted sock. Derrick felt his heart go light, and then he went light-headed as she stepped closer and hung it right between theirs.

Embroidered on the cuff were the words *Bonus Baby II.*

She turned and met his gaze, and he hoped she could see all the love shining in his eyes because he couldn't seem to form any words.

Jack was the first to respond. "Annie!" he shouted and gathered her in for a hug. "Congratulations! I'm going to be a grandpa?"

Laughing through tears, she confirmed, "You're going to be a grandpa. Grandpa Jack, we're going to have to get you a new stocking."

"I want one that says Uncle Easton!" Easton swooped her up for a hug. "Congratulations! You're going to be an amazing mom."

"Oh, I am so thrilled!" Grandma cried, elbowing her way in to embrace Anne. "I cannot wait to have a baby to spoil again."

When Anne got to him, Derrick held her tight and whispered an "I love you" in her ear before releasing her. He asked, "How far along?"

"Three months."

Easton said, "It'll be born during baseball season. Does that mean we can name it Willie? Or Babe? No, not Willie, it's too close to Willow."

"I've got it!" Jack declared. "Jackie! For Jackie Robinson, that'll work for a boy or a girl."

"It sure would," Derrick said diplomatically. "We'll put it on the list." Jack, Jackie, Will, whatever. Right now, he didn't really care what they named their baby.

A potent mix of joy and gratitude filled him from the inside out. Anne must have felt it, too. Her hand slipped into his, her fingers warm on his skin. She squeezed tightly and Derrick thought he could feel the pressure right in the center of his heart.

Looking around, he took a moment to savor it all; the fireplace, the decorated house, the tree lit up in the corner, his family. His wife. Their friends. The farm.

"Merry Christmas, Coach," she said, reminding him how thankful he was for that, too. For baseball.

*A baby.*

Life.

Simple things all made perfect because of the woman standing next to him. "I love you, Anne."

Blue eyes twinkling in the firelight, her smile seemed to reflect his thoughts as she told him, "I love *you*, Derrick."

\* \* \* \* \*

*For more romances from acclaimed author Carol Ross and Harlequin Heartwarming, visit www.Harlequin.com today!*

# Get 4 FREE REWARDS!

### We'll send you 2 FREE Books
### <u>plus</u> 2 FREE Mystery Gifts.

**Love Inspired Suspense** books showcase how courage and optimism unite in stories of faith and love in the face of danger.

FREE Value Over $20

---

# HARLEQUIN SELECTS COLLECTION

**From Robyn Carr to RaeAnne Thayne to Linda Lael Miller and Sherryl Woods we promise (actually, GUARANTEE!) each author in the Harlequin Selects collection has seen their name on the *New York Times* or *USA TODAY* bestseller lists!**

---

COMING NEXT MONTH FROM

# ⟨H⟩ HARLEQUIN
## HEARTWARMING

## #403 THE WRONG COWBOY
*The Cowboys of Garrison, Texas*
by Sasha Summers

Everyone knows Crawleys and Briscoes don't get along.
When horse whisperer Mabel Briscoe helps Jensen Crawley's
daughter overcome her fear of animals, Mabel and Jensen
are the talk of the town. What happens when they fall for each
other unexpectedly?

## #404 WORTH THE RISK
*Butterfly Harbor Stories* • by Anna J. Stewart

Cautious Alethea Costas is still grieving the loss of her best
friend when a wrong turn throws her into the arms of
Declan Cartwright—a daredevil race car driver who could
possibly help her embrace life.

## #405 A RANCHER'S PROMISE
*Bachelor Cowboys* • by Lisa Childs

Rancher Jake Haven has always done the responsible thing.
Now that means raising his orphaned nephews. When his ex
Katie O'Brien-Morris returns home with her young son, can he
let past wants distract him from family needs?

## #406 A NEW YEAR'S EVE PROPOSAL
*Cupid's Crossing* • by Kim Findlay

Architect Trevor Emerson doesn't trust anyone after an
accident at his last job site...which makes it tough to renovate
a local mill with Andie Kozak! As a woman, the contractor has
been questioned too often. Can working together change them
both?

---

YOU CAN FIND MORE INFORMATION ON UPCOMING HARLEQUIN TITLES,
FREE EXCERPTS AND MORE AT HARLEQUIN.COM.

HWCNM1221